And It Arose From the Deepest Black

A John Black Novel

Keith Soares

Bufflegoat Books

© Copyright 2016 Keith Soares. All rights reserved.
First print edition 1.0, July 9, 2016
ISBN 978-0-9977707-1-1
Original publication date July 9 2016

Edited by Christopher Durso

Special thanks to Yasmin, who begged to be the first reader of this novel.
As you wish.

Σ

Prologue

A grizzled, sea-weathered man named Mac — I've never heard him called anything else, or even learned his last name — was the first human ever to lay eyes on an alien from outer space.

Well, unless you count me.

It was possible, even likely, that the thorns inside my body were alien, although I had no way to really prove it. But that's not my point.

I saw them first. Me and Holly. We just had no idea what we were looking at.

But Mac, he knew. I mean, how could he not? What he saw was definitely not from Earth. I never met Mac, but I saw him countless times on TV, recounting his story, usually standing on a dock somewhere, often wearing black all-weather gear. He was a squat, greying man, not old, but definitely not young. He had a thickness to his body that spoke of a hard life on the water, and skin that looked boiled and tough as leather. As his story went, he was alone, fishing the deep and frigid waters off the northwest coast, when a thick layer of fog rolled in to surround him. Like most people in that part of the world, he seemed to accept the possibility of his gruesome death in stride. If he was socked in — that's what they call it when the fog is so thick you can't see a thing in any direction — he'd be lucky to find his way back. Even if he located the shore and hugged it as he headed home, hitting an errant rock could mean the end. And it wasn't like he could swim to shore in water that hovered just below freezing. Yes, that's actually possible; I looked it up. It's called supercooling, and I can tell you, if I thought I might freeze to death in water like that, I would find it neither *super* nor *cool*.

Anyway, like I said, Mac didn't seem to care. Every time I saw him tell his story, he skimmed over that part, like it was all in a normal day. Yet, I found his whole lifestyle to be so strange. An experience so alien to me that I thought maybe we really didn't need to go to outer space to find something out of this world. And so, of course, we truly didn't.

The water in that area ran cold, dark, and deep, and with the fog enclosing him, Mac said, it seemed like the setting sun itself had been blacked out. Like night came early and blindness set in. He couldn't see more than 50 feet in any direction. He was alone, in 300 feet of ice water, with near-zero visibility, and night was coming.

Still, none of that worried him.

It was the *swell*.

Mac had been fishing those waters for decades, had bumped into pretty much anything there was to bump into, sometimes literally. Nothing surprised him. Except this.

He heard a deep, low sound, seeming to come from everywhere at once. I remember him saying it didn't sound natural, and that was why it got his attention. Surrounded by so much nature, I guess you don't expect to find something unnatural. Then the ocean itself heaved upward. Not a wave, not the tide. Just the area around his boat. Like an immense bubble rising. His boat was carried upward.

Mac was, reasonably, surprised. He looked into the rising water and saw two lights. He described their color as nearly orange, but sometimes seeming to waver between deep red and amber. At first, he told reporters, he thought a ship had gone down. Maybe the swelling water was a belch of gas escaping the hold, the lights indicating the last flicker of a dead vessel. He knew there wouldn't be any hope of survival. Any human under that water was dead, for sure. He stared at the lights, and he said it made him sad, thinking of the sailors who were probably down there. The ones who had met their doom.

But the swell kept rising, and strangely, it seemed like the lights were coming up as well. *This is bad*, Mac thought. Finally, right? I mean, I would have thought that in the very beginning, possibly as soon as I boarded the boat, before anything at all happened. But Mac said he only thought that when he noticed the lights were rising toward him. He assumed a sunken boat was bubbling to the surface for one last hurrah, and his concern was that he was in the way. If his boat got tangled with the other one, he might soon meet his own watery grave.

Mac rushed to the wheelhouse and twisted the key to start his inboard engine. He never really described his boat in anything I'd heard. Maybe to him, it was so commonplace that it'd be like describing his own face. Maybe it simply was. Nevertheless, TV news shows can't help but make graphics and 3D visualizations. So I kinda feel like I was there that day, given how I saw it from every angle.

His boat was maybe 30 feet long, metal-hulled, with a smallish wheelhouse toward the middle. To one side of the wheelhouse, there was an entry to the hold below, where he could store his catch. I don't know if the hold was empty or not on this particular day. I guess it doesn't matter. Mac got the engine running and dropped it into gear. He said he started to putter forward, which made him feel better by diminishing his chances of being hit by the rising boat, but also gave him a new concern: He was moving off the center of the swell, which was like sliding downhill. His boat picked up speed fast, and he lost control. For a time, he stopped watching the rising lights and held on for dear life as his boat slipped off the swell and splashed down into calmer, flatter waters. He bobbed and swayed, not knowing if he would be flung overboard to his death. Again, he didn't seem all that concerned when telling this part of the story. Mac was a strange fellow.

The slide also spun his boat around, so suddenly Mac's engine was pushing him back toward the swell, which wasn't ideal. He dropped to neutral, then to reverse, trying to back away, his eyes once again locked on the rising lights.

Until they stopped moving.

Mac described the lights as enormous, separated by maybe 20 feet. Each light was the size of a car. The two lights floated just under the surface of the water, and Mac tried to make sense of what they were, what part of a boat had lights like that. No, he tried to figure out what *kind* of boat had lights like that. Then the water fell away. The swell remained, but the water slipped off it, and the complete *strangeness* of what he was seeing finally broke through. Mac said he simply couldn't put the dots together to understand what he was seeing. It made no sense to him at all.

Unable to comprehend what his eyes were showing him, Mac decided to talk it through to himself. *What am I looking at?*

Here, almost all of the interviews sound the same, with Mac reciting some internal monologue.

A mountain in the water. Curved. Bigger than the boat. It's bumpy, rough. Are those rocks? No, I don't think so. Not rocks, just bumps. A low sound, deep and weird. I can't tell where it's coming from. The boat is vibrating. The mountain is black, so dark it's hard to make out anything. But the lights. Big and round, glowing. Like they're alive. Like they're looking at me.

Mac's lead-in varies a little bit from interview to interview, but the ending is always the same. After he says the lights seemed to be looking at him, Mac always pauses, straightens his back, opens his eyes wide, and says the same thing.

Jesus, Mary, and Joseph. It's a head.

1

"Johnny!"

I closed the door, trying to blot out the flashing lights and shouting voices before it was too late. I went to my sister, pressing my forehead against hers for a moment. "Hi, Holly."

"Johnny," she said again, but her smile drooped. She shivered. In the weeks that had passed since our time in the desert, life with Holly was *different*.

She didn't have the full-blown seizures that literally shook the earth. She just faded out for a bit.

The problem was, so did other people around her. I turned and saw my mother, eyes closing like she might be dozing off, although she was standing. I saw a droplet of blood slide from one of her nostrils.

"Holly? It's okay, Holly," I said. Then I reached out to her with my mind. *I closed the door. You don't have to see all the people yelling and the bright lights.*

Slowly, her eyes regained focus. She came back. So did Mom, who shook her head and walked into the kitchen.

It wasn't just Holly that had changed. Life in general was different. We were celebrities, of a sort. Perhaps infamous was the better way to put it. Mom had driven us out of the desert and unwittingly into the living room of every home in the country.

Mom Saves Children From Kidnappers! read some of the headlines.

The others were less kind.

Did Family Stage Kidnapping for Fame?

Family Seeks Reality TV Deal

Should Andrea Black Face Prison Time?

That's why the flashing lights were always outside our door. TV cameras. Reporters. Paparazzi. For us. It was insane. They yelled questions at us any time we went outside. I don't even think they much cared about our answers, just wanted us to turn their way for a photo, or maybe get a rise out of us. I thought often about giving them the one-finger salute, but that'd just get my picture on the front pages all over again.

And the craziest part was that they had no idea what I could do, or what Holly could do. The sandstorm, earthquakes, even tsunamis out at sea — they didn't link that to us at all. What did a couple of kidnapped kids have to do with crazy weather? Instead, they focused on my mom. They thought she must be manipulating us for profit. Some of the bastards even claimed she sabotaged Dad's car, causing his fatal crash.

I'll be honest. If I really were Superman, I'd have punched this bunch of Lois Lanes and Jimmy Olsens in the mouth.

So, yes, Holly had changed, but not as much as we'd hoped, Mom and I. When she spoke to me, I thought, *She's back!* And in some ways she was, but not in every way. She was more, I don't know, *present* than before, but language and mobility were still big issues. She said "Johnny" and "Mommy" just fine. Other words were hit or miss. Mom signed her up for physical rehab, to see if she could walk again. So far, it had been a struggle. That meant Holly remained in her chair, the same one she and I had ridden so high, out of the atmosphere. Knowing that really happened was surreal. Thankfully, Holly seemed to have better control of her mental powers. Or maybe, because she wasn't as trapped, she had controlled her anger. I hoped.

And the seizures — the ones that created earthquakes and a dust storm that could rend flesh — they had diminished to just these strange *fades*. Usually initiated by some jerk's camera flash going off as he shouted our names.

Another thing was slowly changing. I could communicate with Holly. I could tell Mom what she was saying, or technically, what she was thinking. We could link minds and she could talk to me. It was awkward, because I had to remember no one else could hear her, not even Mom. But it worked. For some reason, Holly couldn't contact me first. Only I could start a conversation. At least in the beginning.

I reached out. *You good, Hol?*

Yes, Johnny. But hungry.

Okay, Hol, I'll tell Mom. Grilled cheese?

She didn't reply in words. Instead I just got a feeling back, a bright, warm type of feeling that I knew meant *Yes*. "Mom?"

"Yes, John?" she called from the kitchen.

"Holly's hungry," I said.

* * *

Bobby was a weird case. Given all the publicity we got coming back from the desert, everyone wanted a happy ending. They wanted Mom, and me, and Holly, back in our own house. And they wanted Bobby back at his parents' house. I could tell Bobby hated the idea, but he had nowhere else to go, and I wasn't about to ask Mom if he could stay with us. Could you imagine the press? *Kidnapped Boy Shuns Parents for Questionable Mom!* Our lives would devolve into a teaser headline. Plus, that would just keep us in the public eye longer. We tried to maintain as boring a life as possible, so the photographers would give up and go away. Maybe it was working, because it seemed like the numbers were diminishing. But it was hard to tell. The prospect of selling a photo of my mom doing something nefarious was too great. *Someone* was always willing to sit in a car across the street from our house all day and night, waiting. God forbid Mom should sneeze somewhere outside. The image of her face contorted would be sold as *Andrea Black in Public Rage*.

Sometimes, just before bed, I'd look out my window at the dark of our street and see a strange car parked there, the orange glow of a cigarette lighting up the face of whoever was behind the wheel. I hated that glow. I wanted nothing more than to walk across the street and tell them everything. Tell them about Sol, Jose do Branco. *Look up the name!* I still felt Sol was a mystery. Who was he, really? And why did he do what he did? Maybe I could kill two birds with one stone — get the photographers off our back and learn more about Sol at the same time. It was a nice dream. But I knew they really didn't care about the truth. They just wanted to take an easy photo and get paid.

Sol was dead, but he haunted me. Sure, he'd disappeared into a billion tiny bits, but somehow that was less, I don't know, *final* than seeing him lying dead on the ground. I knew in my head that Sol had been ripped apart, killed, but my heart wanted something permanent. A grave to visit, to be sure he was still there. Or to spit on, perhaps.

I had to be careful. We had so many people around, I never knew when someone might be watching. I had to assume the answer was *always*. So every moment of every day was like a prison. Don't do anything strange. Don't draw their attention.

Bobby shunned the awkwardness of being back at home with his parents, so he still came over a lot. The paparazzi didn't ignore him, but he was less of a focus for them, as was I, and even Holly, despite what their attention did to her. They really just wanted to catch my mom doing something they could sell. So photos of Bobby at his house or walking to mine weren't important enough to bother with. Sometimes I thought Bobby was lucky that way.

Although we'd hang out, there were no trips to Mount Trashmore, or anywhere else. Just school and back. Otherwise, we stayed inside, curtains drawn, and played video games. It was really, really boring after a while.

We had to get out. Go somewhere they wouldn't see. We had to. And of course, it didn't take long for Bobby to start harping on the issue.

"Come on, Johnny! We can do it, trick a bunch of lazy adults, half asleep, sitting in their cars all night!" Bobby said. "It'll be too easy."

Of course I agreed. I was getting bored to tears at home. So we made a plan to sneak out one Friday night. Bobby would slip out of his house around midnight, somehow get to my house, and tap on the window by our back door. All I had to do was wait until I heard the sound, then walk out the door. Bobby was already going to check that the coast was clear. If he got caught, or someone was watching, there simply would be no tap and I'd go back to sleep. Easy.

Mom and Holly went to bed as usual. I pretended to do the same, waited an hour or so, then snuck out to the living room and hovered by the back door.

I checked my crappy digital watch three times: 11:47 p.m., 11:58 p.m., and finally, 12:03 a.m.

Tap tap tap.

2

I opened the door and saw Bobby crouched beside it like a spy in a movie. "Get down, you idiot!" he hissed. I dropped down next to him, pulling the door closed behind me with a light *click*.

For a second, I panicked. "Oh my God, I think I just locked myself out!" I started patting my pockets, looking for a key that wasn't there. *Crap.*

Bobby didn't flinch. He just reached up and turned the knob. The door clicked again and opened. Bobby looked down his nose at me, and despite the darkness, I'm pretty sure he could see me turn red.

"Oops. Sorry," I said, giving a nervous little laugh.

"Can we go now?" Bobby said. I nodded.

* * *

Turns out that sneaking away from my house was the easy part. I mean, we hadn't done it before, so the guys in cars out front had no reason whatsoever to be on the lookout. Once we were a few houses away, we looked back, giddy. There were four paparazzi cars on our street. In two of them, the drivers were asleep. In the third, a woman was on her phone, the bright glow lighting up her face and ensuring she would never see us sneaking around in the dark. The last car was empty. Maybe somebody had to pee.

Bobby and I slipped behind houses, and I remember being surprised at how dark it was. Dense clouds filled the sky and blotted out any possible moonlight or starlight. Turning left and right down random streets reminded me a little of the day things began, when Bobby had chased me through town. Only then I had been worried about being killed and this time I was laughing.

Still, we stayed quiet. Stalked by paparazzi or not, laughing kids running through back streets at midnight would be noticed. At first, I don't think we actually had a place to go. It was just fun to be out. Not worrying about who was watching us. But finally, running around aimlessly lost its charm, and Bobby started to wordlessly guide us.

Running behind him, I watched as he took certain turns. Were we headed to Mount Trashmore? Definitely not. We hadn't been there since Walter Ivory died, anyway. The warehouse bay? At first, I thought so, but no. I would have objected if Bobby had steered us there. No, he was heading toward the middle of town. Some place central.

Bobby guided me to the row of brick shops, the place where he had once tried to launch his bike from roof to roof.

It was after midnight, and the shops were deserted. As expected. I mean, not a lot of people need greeting cards at midnight. Once I realized his goal, I happily followed. I mean, sure, Bobby and I had our history at the place. Like the time I thought I'd killed him. But, you know. We were 15 and didn't get bent out of shape about those sorts of things.

We went around to the parking lot behind the buildings, to the same spot where Bobby had once used the fire escape to lug his bike up to the roof. Assuming the roof was once again his goal, I stood below the fire escape, waiting for him to come help me pull down the ladder. When he didn't appear, I turned around. And Bobby was gone.

Son of a...

"This is awesome!" Bobby said from somewhere above me. Behind the row of stores, in the long and grimy parking lot, a series of tall lights illuminated pockets of space in yellow hues like old teeth. Twenty feet or so away, off the ground by maybe the height of your average adult, the curved edge of the nearest light showed me only a pair of jeans hovering in mid-air, ending in colorful low-top sneakers.

I blinked. And I realized Bobby was all there, in the dark above the legs, half in the light, half out.

He was flying.

Well, hold on. Not flying. That might make you think of someone zooming through the air, one fist forward, ready to take on the bad guy or spin the Earth's rotation backward or whatever. Bobby wasn't doing *that*.

He was flying without moving. Hovering is probably a better word.

It was clear the process was new to him. Bobby's body was arranged in a weird kind of sitting position, like the way you see astronauts or even unborn babies. Maybe that pose was the body's default floating position. Anyway, Bobby looked like he was both perfectly at ease and yet supremely uncomfortable.

"How the heck are you doing that?" I asked, staring up at him.

Bobby grinned. "*You* told me about it, remember? Sol floating off the cliff and down to you, like he was flying. So I've been trying it at home, in my room. I've been able to get a few feet off the ground like this, but you know, in my room, I run out of space." Bobby looked at the wide open sky above him. "Not here, though." He started to float upward.

"But how are you doing it?"

"It's like when you move something with your mind," he said, clearly distracted by the fun he was having.

I tried to rationalize how to do it, simplify it. I knew that if I thought too hard or stressed too much, it probably wouldn't work. I tried to follow him, make my body float off the ground. "So you just move an object, but that object is you?"

"Uh-huh!"

Imagine trying to use your muscles to lift yourself off the ground, but the leverage you need *is* the ground. How could I both push off the ground while not touching it? Impossible. That's how it felt.

Meanwhile, Bobby was getting higher. In the dark, he was a dim shadow against the clouds overhead. Even knowing where he was, I could barely see him. "It's harder than that, Johnny," he said. "You gotta sort of trick yourself into not believing you're moving your own body. It's weird."

I tried again, without success. No movement at all. Above me, Bobby paused to look down.

"Try this: Look at your shoes. Don't think of them as *your* shoes on *your* feet. Just think of them as shoes. Shoes that you could easily toss around with your mind, right? Just try to slowly pick those shoes up." Then he turned and continued to climb.

Pick up my shoes. No, wait. Pick up shoes that are not mine. Don't think about them being mine, on my feet.

This is impossible, too.

Bobby was nearly to the top of the building next to us, the same one we'd climbed with our bikes. The one where he'd tried to jump his bike off a ramp, only to crash down to the pavement just feet from where I stood. Leaving me thinking he'd killed himself.

I tried what he suggested, working to calm myself and concentrate. A minute or two passed. "It isn't working, Bobby."

"Come on, man, just try it," Bobby called out from the darkness above. "You can do it."

"What're you two doing?" a voice said from right behind me. Spinning around, I came face to face with a tall, gangly guy, maybe 18 or 20 years old. From one corner of his mouth, an orange-glowing cigarette hung at an angle. He wore a white, button-up shirt and dark pants, with a dark apron wrapped around his waist. On his left chest pocket was pinned a little rectangle that read Stuart.

"*Shit*," I said.

Stuart chuckled at me, taking a drag on his cigarette. "Busted. Ha ha. You guys are so loud, we heard you from inside."

"In— inside, where?"

"Inside the restaurant." Stuart jerked a thumb over his shoulder, pointing to a partially open door at the back of one of the buildings. A thin blade of light slashed from the doorway, showing another person standing beside it, also smoking. "Me and Joey worked till close, then had to clean up. So we were making noise, washing dishes and all, but *still* heard your voices out here. I just came to see what's going on."

I thought about Bobby, magically floating in space above our heads. Thankfully, he'd had the sense to be quiet ever since Stuart spoke. But all they had to do was see Bobby and... And what? How would we explain it?

"Holy crap, you're that John Black kid. The one who was kidnapped. I've seen you on TV!" Stuart said, taking another puff of his cigarette. Then he fumbled through his apron, producing a scrap of paper and a pen. "Can I get your autograph?" He smiled at me.

I was truly living in bizarro world.

My friend was flying above me in the night sky, while back on Earth, a stranger thought I was famous enough to get my autograph. Weird, right?

"Seriously. Can I?"

"Uh, sure? I guess." I scribbled my name on the paper, and Stuart looked at it with a big grin.

"Very cool. Thanks." Stuart turned to head back to the restaurant, and I thought somehow we'd gotten away with it, that he hadn't noticed Bobby flying above after all. Until Stuart called back over his shoulder as he walked away. "Oh, and tell your buddy on the fire escape to be careful. I don't want to have to call an ambulance if he falls and cracks his head open on the pavement." Stuart gave a wave, dropped his cigarette to the ground, and put it out with a twist of his shoe. Then he was gone, along with the other guy, Joey. The restaurant door clicked shut behind them.

Above me, dark against the night sky, I saw Bobby shaking. I'm pretty sure he was laughing.

3

We managed to sneak back without being seen again, despite Bobby being so thrilled with himself that I thought he was going to erupt in giggles at any moment. We were so focused on slipping in the back way that I didn't pay much attention to who was out front. I got inside, gave Bobby a quick salute, shut the door, and headed to bed.

It was the next morning that everything seemed different.

I woke up like any other day, maybe a bit late due to my nighttime adventures. Mom was none the wiser, and even Holly seemed to have no sense that anything had changed. I walked into the kitchen wiping my eyes.

"Morning, John," Mom said. "Eggs?"

Holly brightened to see me, so I went to her and we tapped our foreheads together. *Sup, Hol?*

Sup? Supper? Breakfast time, Johnny.

Sorry, Hol. I meant What's up? *When you say it fast, it sounds like* Sup.

Holly furrowed her brow. She didn't much like it when she wasn't up to speed on things. But she got over it quickly.

Sup, Johnny! She smiled and went back to eating her cereal.

I went to the fridge, grabbed the milk, and poured myself a glass, then sat at the table next to my sister. Mom was cooking eggs and sausage. The whole kitchen smelled like heaven. It was Saturday morning, and I had nothing to do but relax. I suspect that if I were a normal kid I wouldn't have appreciated it as much. But I had survived on the road, faced Sol, then lived in a paparazzi-induced prison. A day to do nothing was amazing.

Mom shuffled back and forth across the kitchen floor, tending to the cooking, rinsing utensils she was finished with, fetching things from the fridge. I wasn't really paying attention to what she was doing. Until she went silent.

I looked up and saw her staring out the small window by the sink. She didn't move for a long time, and, based on the smell, I think the food on the stove started to burn. "Mom?" I asked.

She turned back, an urgency in her eyes. "John — come here!" I hurried over and she put an arm around me, pointing out the window with the other hand. "They're gone!"

And sure enough, not a single car sat on our street. Overnight, we had apparently ceased to be interesting. Without meaning to, Mom and I simultaneously breathed a loud sigh of relief. "Why?" I blurted, not knowing what else to say.

Mom turned to me with wide, happy eyes. "I have no idea. And I don't care. Good riddance to them all!" She hugged me.

Then I had an unpleasant thought. "Mom?"

"What, John?"

"What if something *bad* is happening?"

Mom considered my words for a moment, then shrugged. "Bad things happen all the time, John. At least, whatever it is, it isn't happening *here*."

* * *

A couple hours later, we all went for a walk. Just a simple walk around the block, down a couple of random streets, all very close to home. Something any family would do. Except we hadn't been able to for so long without being accosted. Our new liberty to do something so mundane was noticeable.

I don't remember much about that walk, because it wasn't meant to be memorable. Just *ordinary*. In fact, the one thing that I do recall was people — neighbors, friends — simply waving to us. "Hello!" Like nothing had ever happened.

It was totally normal.

Which is why it was so unusual.

* * *

By Sunday night, there had been no strange cars parked on our street for two full days. Something had changed, and we were all enjoying it. Even Holly said to me, during one of our mental conversations, *I'm happy it's quiet now. I didn't like the noise. Or the lights.*

I know, Hol.

I imagine it's the same for most anyone who becomes accidentally famous. One day, you're living your boring life. The next, you can't get the photographers to leave you alone. And the day after that, no one cares if you run naked through the front yard.

Well, Miss Janice next door might care. Check that. She would definitely frown on me streaking through the neighborhood. Anyway, you get my point. I think everyone suddenly thrust into the public eye is just as surprised when it all disappears as they are that it happened in the first place.

But by Monday, Bobby and I were heading to school, and almost reveling in the fact that no one cared.

Bus 73 picked us up at the corner of my street and drove us to Arthur Avalon High School. The bus was always crowded and hot in the early fall, when temperatures could sometimes still be in the high 80s or low 90s.

I had come from Thomas Edison Middle, where there was never a shortage of Thomas Edison–related puns and jokes — if there was a teacher who could flick on the lights without proclaiming himself or herself the inventor of the light bulb, I never had the pleasure of being in their class. So it was a little odd to go to a school named after someone I'd never heard of before. Who was Arthur Avalon, namesake of our school, emblazoned on every football/baseball/basketball/soccer/softball/volleyball/hacke ysack/horseshoes jersey, and the subject of every cheerleader's rallying cry? I have no idea. Sports star? Politician? Arborist? Let's go with arborist. Arthur Avalon, world-famous arborist. Sure. He could arbor the heck out of things. A fine man, he.

Have you ever played the game where you and your friends try to decide what superpower you would want if you could have one? Well, I had real superpowers, and yet there were still more I desperately wanted. The power to overcome acne. The power to talk to girls without breaking out in a sweat. Those would have been great add-ons. Come on, alien thorns in my cells. Help me out here.

Alas, it didn't work that way. That Monday, Bus 73 had no sooner appeared than it was squealing to a stop at our corner. The driver, Mrs. Worchart, swung open the (also) squealing door for us to climb aboard. Mrs. Worchart was a very nice lady, always chipper both morning and afternoon, giving every kid a hearty "Hello!" or "Good morning!" She was also rather large, so inevitably her bus became known as the War Cart, a tired play on her name.

We stepped up into the War Cart, and entered the fray of high school noise and mayhem. And who should I bump — literally — into? Carrie McGregor. She was sitting in the front row but turned around to talk to a girlfriend, so one of her knees was in the aisle. My knee touched Carrie McGregor's knee. I was dumbstruck.

"Oh, hi, John," she said, tucking a curl of red hair behind one ear and batting her eyelashes at me. Okay, that's a lie. She probably just blinked. But as I've said before, any movement of her eyelashes even moderately directed toward me caused heart palpitations.

"Carrie. Hey." A witty retort, no? Then Bobby pushed me in the back.

"Come on, stud. Seats open in the back." He gave a knowing smile, which was about the least subtle thing ever. Carrie looked away, but I think her cheeks had turned a little red. Ever since the time I had asked her out — and she had apologized but declined — I could barely speak to her. I wanted to ask her out again, but without the construct of a school dance coming up, I floundered. I couldn't just ask Carrie McGregor to go to the movies. That's something I would do with dopes like Bobby or Steve or Tom. I needed an *event*. And even then, I didn't think I had the nerve to try a second time.

Sitting in the back, I closed my eyes. Everyone was talking too loud, as always. I was lost in thought. Then I opened my eyes and saw Carrie, turned around to look at me. Just for a second. As soon as we made eye contact, she faced forward once more. But it happened, I swear.

Maybe I could find the nerve to ask her out again, after all.

4

Somehow I didn't hear the news until, I think, Wednesday or Thursday. Between classes, I was swapping books at my locker when suddenly my shoulder sluiced, all by itself, just a few inches. There was a loud bang as flesh and bone hit metal.

"Ouch, Jesus!" Steve Martucci had apparently felt the need to surprise-punch me in the shoulder when he walked up behind. Obviously, he missed. He pulled back his fist and clutched at it with his other hand. "Nice freaking ninja move, John. I nearly broke my knuckles."

I had to play it off. *"The supreme art of war is to subdue the enemy without fighting."* I waggled my eyebrows at him, just to increase the ridiculousness of it all, throw him off the scent. "Besides, I didn't ask you to try to suckerpunch me." As careful as I was to avoid having people find out what I could do, random acts like my shoulder sluicing about on its own were mildly terrifying. My body just did its thing. One day someone was actually going to notice. Then I'd really be labeled a freak and a weirdo. I wasn't looking forward to it.

"Thank you, sensei." Steve rolled his eyes, still rubbing his hand. "Hey, did you do the homework for seventh period...?" He gave me a cheesy smile that I assumed was supposed to win me over.

"Do your own homework, Steve." I closed the locker and started off to class. Steve trailed after.

"Come on, man. There's no time for me to read the assignment and write out the answers. It's already fifth period, and I've got gym. Just let me take a peek." Again with the smile.

I stopped and sighed, opening my folder to find the assignment. "You have 60 seconds." Steve snatched up my paper and ducked around the corner to a place of relative seclusion. "Make sure you change the answers enough that it sounds like you," I said. "You know, make them dumber."

"Very funny." He was already furiously scribbling words on his own paper.

"Can't you do it in the bathroom or something? No one had better see you."

Steve just waved a hand at me as he continued to write. "Like that thing in the ocean, I'm hidden in plain sight."

I furrowed my brow. "Oh good. That's very clear. What *thing* in the ocean?"

"The thing all over TV. The thing they're tracking." He kept writing, not looking at me.

I shook my head. "I have no idea what you're talking about."

Steve paused, just for a moment. "There's a thing. A big thing. In the ocean, somewhere out west. They don't know what it is. They can see it, well, sort of, but they can't really see it. Because it's underwater, you know? And it's moving toward land." He went back to writing.

"Oh, well that makes sense," I said, looking around to be sure no teachers had noticed Steve with my homework. "Are you done yet?"

He scribbled one more line, then handed my paper back. "All set — thanks!" Steve rushed off toward his next class, but a few feet down the hall he turned back. "What do you think it is? The thing in the water."

"How should I know?" I shrugged. "I don't know what you're talking about!"

"I think it's a whale, but they say it's too big for that. Maybe it's a prehistoric whale or something. Like the Loch Ness monster." With that, he was gone.

Was he just messing with me? Or was the Loch Ness monster headed to shore somewhere out west?

He's messing with me.

I checked my watch and saw that I had about 35 seconds before my next class started. And it was two floors below me.

Thanks a lot, Steve.

* * *

That night, I made a joke about it with my mom during dinner. "No, I don't think Steve was kidding, John. I saw some report about it. Weird, right?" She took another bite of chicken. "We can turn on the TV after we clean up and see if there's any news."

So we did.

And that was the first time I saw Mac the fisherman tell his tale. He talked about something swelling up below him. He said it looked like a giant head.

The reporters were skeptical. So far, they had footage of something large and dark moving eastward underwater. Radar showed it to be a big, solid shape, but offered few other details. The same loop of scenes played over and over. So-called "experts" were interviewed, each with their own opinion, but mostly just saying, "We have no idea. We have to wait and see." Mac was different. Not an expert in a suit, just a fisherman ranting on a pier about a monster in the sea. Telling the biggest fish tale of all time.

Nothing happened that first night. The story got old. No change.

Two days later, everyone was glued to the TV. The thing hit land.

* * *

Branding is a cultural phenomenon in modern society. Everything needs a brand. Every conflict needs its own name and clever graphic. Every scandal gets "-gate" added to the end. Without a name brand, things don't stick. So, not surprisingly, as soon as the creature broke the surface of the water, people raced to give it a name.

It rolled onto shore in a tight ball, like a meteor rising from the ocean rather than falling from the sky. Then it stopped, and unwound.

It was massive. It seemed to be made of stone. Simply put, it looked like a giant demon from hell. Someone — I think a Russian — tried to call it a gargoyle. Apparently *gargoyle* in Russian sounds sort of like "Gorgol," which in turn sounds exactly like the name of a monster in a Japanese movie. And there you go. But a gargoyle is a little dude up on a cathedral wall, staring down menacingly at the people below. This Gorgol certainly could stare down menacingly, but it would crush a cathedral to stone dust if it got near one.

The news channels all jumped on the name. The Gorgol had come. Rolled up, it was about 150 feet in diameter. That's like a 15-story building. It was covered in huge, dark, rough scales, like shards of mottled brown and black stone. Imagine eight full-grown elephants holding each other's tails, over and over. That's how wide it was. Imagine four city buses standing on their faces, stacked on top of each other. That's how tall it was. And that's just when it was rolled up.

Making land, the Gorgol unrolled and stood. It had four legs, sort of short and stubby, but thick and powerful, all about the same length. These too were covered with those rocky scales, and ended in round feet with spiked toes in the back and long-fingered hands with terrifyingly sharp talons in the front. When it started to walk, it did so hunched over, balancing on its back two feet. Because of that, it was actually a bit shorter unrolled. It didn't seem to be the most limber of creatures, but then we all watched dumbstruck as it stood to take its first good look at the world above the water's surface. Stretched out, it was nearly 200 feet tall. One big boy.

And its eyes... Deep reddish orange, and glowing with some sort of internal fire.

On live TV, the Gorgol lowered itself back to its hunched walking position. And proceeded to trample the seaside town where it had landed. It didn't look angry or vengeful. It was just big. Just as you could stomp an anthill without ever noticing, the Gorgol crushed houses and buildings without concern. People ran in every direction like the end of days had come. Maybe it had.

Watching the scene on TV, I was stunned. And that was saying something. Because I had seen some really weird shit before.

5

You won't be surprised to hear that people lost it. A giant monster rolled out of the ocean to destroy towns. There was general, widespread panic.

Still, to me, it seemed a world away. The scenes on TV were from places 2,000 miles away.

I actually resented the damned monster. With the paparazzi finally leaving us alone and Sol gone, I wanted nothing more than a normal life, at least for a while. The Gorgol changed all that, despite being so far distant. *Everyone* talked about it. *Everyone* was freaked out. Normal ceased to exist.

Bolstered by this doomsday atmosphere, I made a decision. I was definitely going to ask Carrie out again. Not to the movies. I had to think of something great. Underage, without a driver's license, my options were limited, which sucked. I had to be creative and go for style points.

I chose to ask her to a picnic.

Not a big, social picnic. Just her and me. I had the whole scene organized in my mind. I would pack a basket of food and stuff. I know, I know. I'd truly gone domestic. Deal with it. We do things to win the favor of someone we're interested in. You've done something, too, I just know it. So lay off.

Anyway, that was the idea. There were two parks in town. Frank Merrick Park was wooded and flat, and had great baseball fields, but wasn't terribly good for a date. Jeremiah Underly Park, however… that one had a lake. And if I could work it out — you know, get there before the families trying to do their recreational fishing and family cookouts — a few tables there overlooked the water. It was good. Like, romantic-comedy good. I was giving myself major credit before I'd even talked to Carrie. Come on, people. Work with me, here.

I walked up to Carrie on a Tuesday, between second and third period. She was at her locker, chatting with another girl, Tina Caleb.

"Carrie, can I talk to you?" Too dramatic, I know. Tina raised both eyebrows and faded away without a word. Carrie blushed. And her eyes… Okay, she just blinked. But to me, well, you know. "I was wondering what you were doing on Saturday."

She looked at me without saying a word. Time passed. It seemed like *eternity* passed. At some point, I felt like I was watching the movie of my life, not participating in it. "The John Black Story," rated PG-13 for occasional graphic language and sometimes death-inducing magical powers. She still didn't respond.

I had the horrible, awful feeling she was about to shout *Why did you close the door?* The trauma of that flashback made me turn red, I'm sure.

Then finally, she said: "Did you want to ask me something?"

I blinked twice, hard. "Um, I think I just did."

"You didn't."

"Huh?"

"You said, *I was wondering what you were doing on Saturday.* That's a statement, not a question. A question is a sentence worded to elicit information, ending in a question mark."

I blinked again.

And finally, Carrie laughed. "I'm just kidding, John." She reached out and gave a faux punch to my shoulder. Fearing what it might do, I flinched backward. "Oh yeah," she said. "Double-jointed." She laughed again, and then the laughter faded, and for a second time we looked at each other in silence.

Why, oh why didn't I write notecards or some kind of speaking prompts? I knew I was terrible at talking to girls, but I did it anyway, always unprepared. She was going to say no again. I was going to die.

Carrie blinked. Maybe fluttered. Maybe. "I'm not doing anything on Saturday, John. Why?" She smiled.

This is the point when my heart leapt into my throat. Then it bounced around and nearly choked me to death. I couldn't breathe. Carrie Mc-Freaking-Gregor was waiting for me to ask her out.

No. It was a trap. I would ask and she would say no again. I knew it. I couldn't proceed.

But I had to. I mean, otherwise, what? Say sorry and shuffle away down the hall? Believe it or not, that would actually be more embarrassing.

It was time.

"Carrie, I was wondering if you'd like to go on a picnic with me this Saturday afternoon. I know a nice place by the lake in Underly Park. I can bring everything, the food, the plates, napkins, utensils. You just need to show up. There are some tables there, I can make sure we get one. I'll get a tablecloth, you know the red-and-white-checked kind, and —"

She held up one finger. "John. Enough. Yes. I'd love to."

My mouth, which milliseconds before couldn't seem to shut up, failed me. I couldn't speak. Not one. Single. Word. I think I opened and closed my mouth several times. Nothing happened.

Then the bell rang. We were supposed to be in class.

Carrie looked concerned. "Oh no, my class is upstairs. I have to go — talk to you later, John." She smiled and waved as she left. I think my mouth opened and closed a few more times, like a fish on dry land.

I couldn't believe it.

I was going on a date.

6

The military response to the Gorgol was probably just what you'd expect: Kill the thing before it did too much damage. Some people had died, but they seemed mostly to be wrong-place/wrong-time tragedies. The Gorgol itself didn't appear to have an active desire to kill people or even to crush buildings. But that's what it did. And so in response, guns blazed, tanks fired, even aircraft zipped overhead, sending missiles into the stony scales of the Gorgol. None of it seemed to do much good.

The military had to be careful. As it was, the creature had smashed up most of the town where it landed. Now the counterattack was beginning to produce collateral damage. Given that our weapons weren't having any significant effect on the Gorgol, people were getting pissed that the few homes that remained standing were being blown up.

Watching footage of the Gorgol was baffling. The creature seemed to wander in circles. Sure, it smashed the heck out of everything it encountered, but why was it doing that? Some of the talking heads on TV speculated that it was looking for something. Maybe being drawn to something. Seeing the military bounce bullets and projectiles off its hard armor while the Gorgol just kept doing its thing... well, it reminded me of my dad, from some past summer. Single-mindedly grilling burgers while absently swatting away the hundreds of mosquitoes that were dive-bombing him. Only now, we were the mosquitoes.

For days, the Gorgol plodded around, looking for who knows what. I don't think it ever slept. Hell, maybe the Gorgol's biological clock had a much longer cycle than our human one. It would make sense, given the size of the thing.

The monster consumed every news channel, every commercial break, every pixel online. To avoid it, Bobby and I played more video games. In which we, too, blew things up.

"Johnny, this is it, you know?" Bobby sat beside me on the couch, mashing buttons on the controller as he ducked his character behind a wall, then lobbed a grenade overhead. There were multiplayer modes, of course, but we liked taking turns at the game, one spectating and commenting while the other dove headfirst into chaos. Ostensibly, the nonplayer was supposed to be watching and figuring out tactics for his next turn, but really we just practiced our sarcasm.

"This is what?"

Bobby didn't pause the game or even look over, just talked matter-of-factly as he continued to play. "This is the thing we need to do. The Gorgol."

"What about the Gorgol?"

"We need to be the ones to take it down," he said, jumping over a barricade and landing in an enemy bunker. Soldiers surrounded him, and in under a second, Bobby's character was down, dead. As the game started loading the last save point, Bobby tossed the controller to me. It landed against my leg on the couch.

"What, because we have powers we have to do *everything* now?" I said. It sounded whiny. I know.

Bobby just looked down his nose at me. On screen, the game stopped reloading and my character stood idly, watching war happen all around him. I didn't reach for the controller. The enemy soldiers began to move closer, and the screen flashed red as my guy took several hits. "John. Sol's dead, so now we're like the most powerful people on Earth, right? Do you think that happened so we could just sit around and play video games?"

I feigned indignation. "Oh, so now Bobby Graden is all about fate? Like, we have a predetermined purpose or something?"

Bobby rolled his eyes. "No, it sounds dumb when you say it like that."

"Then what?"

"I don't know, okay? It just seems awfully coincidental that you and I — and Holly — end up with some kind of power, and then all of a sudden the world is attacked by a giant creature from outer space or under the ocean or wherever it comes from." Shots were fired on screen, blinking red again. My character made a series of *oofs* and *args*.

"Bobby, I went after Sol because of what he did to me. He took Holly. I couldn't sit by when that happened. But this Gorgol thing? I mean, I don't want anyone to die, but that's not my fight." I reached for the controller just as the screen flashed red one final time and my character fell to the ground, dead.

"My turn," Bobby said, swooping the controller out of my hand.

We played for another hour or so. When we finally turned off the game, normal TV popped back on screen. A special report on the Gorgol. No surprise there.

The military continued its bombardment, but more carefully, more controlled. The all-out assault had failed, and throwing everything else at the Gorgol was just wasteful and dangerous to bystanders, I guess.

Meanwhile, something had led the Gorgol back to the sea, and the live footage showed it standing in the shallows just offshore from the town it had leveled. Then, for the first but hardly the last time, I heard the Gorgol scream. It opened its triangular mouth full of large, spiked teeth and emitted a shriek that seemed like it would destroy the news microphones, and maybe our TV speakers as well. The Gorgol just stood there, facing out to sea, letting loose its verbal fury.

Then I saw why. A naval vessel, some dreadnought with huge guns, floated off the coast with the Gorgol in its sights. As we watched, huge puffs of smoke went up from the ship's massive guns. A second later, the *whump whump whump* of the shells fired could be heard. Something hit the Gorgol, hard, and it staggered.

It fell. A huge cloud of dust blew up, and we couldn't see anything. But the monster was down.

We held our breath for a moment or two. I broke the silence. "Guess there's not much we need to do after all —"

"Wait! Look!" Bobby shouted, pointing at the screen.

The dust was thick, but something was moving. The camera zoomed in, and the black and brown shape of the Gorgol rolled over, countless pointed scales sliding past our view.

"Holy crap," I said.

"They didn't kill it."

I think this was about the time my mom walked in, pushing Holly in her chair. "What's going on, guys?"

Bobby chimed in. "They shot the Gorgol with some really huge guns and it went down. But... it's getting back up."

On screen, the Gorgol stood and faced its enemy again.

"This is bad," Mom said, pushing Holly ahead of her.

You see this, Holly? I asked.

Yes, but Johnny? Holly said.

Yeah, Hol?

It's like the old movies we used to watch. Saturday-morning monsters. You know, before I was... like this.

I laughed. *Yeah, it is, Hol. But a bit scarier in real life.*

Her eyes were locked on the TV.

The Gorgol screamed again, a piercing cry that was part locomotive horn, part banshee cry, and several parts of something so unnatural that I couldn't compare it to anything else. The sound was hell. And hell was pretty ticked off.

The news cameras tried to take in the whole scene, monster on the shore, ship at sea, squaring off. The Gorgol roared once more at its opponent. And then something really unexpected happened.

Something came out of the water and broke the ship in half.

7

All of a sudden, we needed two names, and some dude on TV was there to help us out.

The original, stone-clad monster that came out of the ocean was redubbed Gorgol Omicron — this was some reference to the O shape it made rolling onto shore. The new one was more like a sea serpent. The talking heads called it Gorgol Sigma.

Were they siblings? Besties? Enemies? Carpool buddies? Who knew. They were big and now there were two of them, and they were pretty angry at us.

Sigma was different. She — and, apologies, I almost immediately thought of her as she, despite the fact that I might have been completely wrong — didn't look a thing like her brother. Brother, you ask? That's just me, again. I had a feeling. In a way, Sigma and Omicron were sister and brother, alike and yet very different. Like Holly and me. But in reality, I had no more idea what their relationship might be than anyone else. Sigma was, essentially, a giant snake.

And when I say giant, that's no lie. Not even an exaggeration. Sigma could rear up taller than Omicron, maybe 20 or 30 feet higher when she was upright, like a snake about to strike. But unlike a snake, she didn't have to keep most of her body on the ground just to raise her head. Sigma had thin, spiky arms and legs that she normally tucked close to her sides. But she could use her legs to brace herself, so only about a quarter of her length supported the standing weight of the other three quarters. Yeah, that meant Sigma was about 300 feet long in total.

Like Omicron, Sigma could roll herself into a ball, only hers was more of a lumpy coil of rope, her head pulled somewhere inside for protection. That's how she came out of the water, moments after destroying the navy ship.

Her skin wasn't as rock-like as Omicron's, but still tougher than steel, with smaller scales that formed an interlocking system of armor over her entire long body, above and below. Where Omicron seemed to be covered with huge slabs of bedrock, Sigma looked like she was wearing chain mail.

If the first two things you noticed about Sigma were that she was very large and very tough, the third thing would be her speed. Where Omicron was lumbering and rigid, Sigma was fluid and fast. Keeping her four limbs tucked in, she slithered around like the fastest, biggest snake you've ever seen. In a way, her speed made her scarier than her brother. Like she could suddenly appear anywhere, without warning, in an instant. Well, without warning except for the path of destruction a 300-foot snake leaves behind as it passes by.

I want to say that Sigma was angrier, too, but that's projecting human emotions on her. Still, based on their reaction to the attack, the Gorgols must have had something approaching human emotion. One human emotion, at any rate. Anger. A lot of anger, it seemed.

As the TV cameras raced to keep up with her, Sigma smashed through the poor coastal town, crushing what few buildings Omicron and the military had missed. It didn't take long to notice something particularly unique about this new monster. Sigma's eyes looked like gemstones come to life. Each was a glittering ball with pointed ends, set unnaturally into her eye sockets. She appeared to have no pupils, so in every shot the news teams captured, she looked like she was staring you down. Or looking in every direction at once. In that way, Sigma was like one of those funhouse paintings where the eyes follow you wherever you go. But slightly more terrifying.

Mom finally just shook her head and wheeled Holly back out of the room. I watched Bobby study this latest round of destruction. "You still want to take on a monster?" I said.

Bobby smirked. "I liked our odds better two on one. This…" He waved his hand at the screen, where Sigma and Omicron continued on their rampage, bullets and missiles – hell, at this point, I expected the military to try sticks and stones – ricocheting off their armored bodies. "This looks like a problem."

Then, since the likelihood of Bobby pushing me to fight a monster had decreased, I became curious. "Exactly what the heck would you do against even one of them?" I said. "I mean, sure, *maybe* you and I could avoid being crushed to death if our bodies could do their shift-away thing or something. But that's just defensive. What could we possibly do to stop one of those?"

"You could use your mind to throw it back in the sea," Bobby offered.

"And then it would just swim right back out again."

Bobby paused, thinking. "You could freeze it. Like you did to Sol."

I had no response. Sapping the heat out of a living person and shattering him into a billion fragments, while effective, was also something that weighed heavily on me. Sol was an evil man, but that didn't absolve me. I had purposefully *killed* someone.

"That would work, wouldn't it?" Bobby asked.

I shrugged. "Maybe." At the same time, I felt remorse. And yet...

"Then teach me how. I can take on one, you do the other." Now Bobby was smiling.

"What happened to keeping quiet about our powers? Living with the paparazzi has been pretty awful. We do something like this, and they'll never leave us alone again, not for the rest of our lives."

"But we'd be famous."

"True," I said.

"And we'd be heroes."

"I suppose so."

Bobby looked me in the eye, still smiling. "*Girls* like heroes. Even certain girls." He took me by the shoulders. "Like Carrie."

I shook my head. "I told you already. I don't want Carrie, or anyone else, liking me just because I have superpowers. That's just... weird."

"But there's no way around it, Johnny. I mean, if we go out and stop these monsters, save the world, people are gonna know about our powers. They're not just going to forget about them once we're done."

I had a really stupid idea. "We could wear disguises."

Bobby laughed. "Now you're the crazy one, Johnny. You want to wear spandex and a cape?"

"No no no! Nothing like that. Jesus, what sort of nut job do you think I am? I just meant a mask or something, so no one would recognize us."

Bobby grimaced. "I don't know. Maybe." Then *he* had a really stupid idea, too. "Would we need code names? You know, in case cameras were rolling and we needed to call out to each other?"

I sighed. *Code names. Right.*

Super Dork. And his sidekick, Idiot Boy.

8

I woke up in a cold sweat. No, it had nothing to do with either of the Gorgols. It was Saturday morning. In a few hours, I was going on a date.

I had absolutely nothing planned. See, the *idea* of the date was incredible. I had it all pictured in my mind. We would have a checked tablecloth, a basket full of delicious food. Some bubbly (*sparkling* water; no flat stuff for this occasion). We'd eat off porcelain plates with fine cutlery. And of course, at the end, Carrie would throw her arms around me and declare her undying love.

So, problem. I had no tablecloth, food, bubbly, plates, cutlery, or even a basket. I'd be lucky just to score the picnic table on time.

"Mom!"

"Morning, John. How are you?"

"Good. Well, no, not good."

"What's the matter, honey?"

"I have a date today." Why did I say that?

Mom's eyebrow raised. "Is that so?"

"Stop. Mom. Please. I need help. I'm supposed to have a picnic all prepared before I meet Carrie at the park at one. And I have nothing."

"Carrie? Your science-fair partner? I had no idea…" I nodded. "And a *picnic*? How romantic!" I rolled my eyes. "Seriously, that's romantic. Nice choice, John!" She tried to punch me in the shoulder to make her point. My shoulder, of course, slid easily out of the way. "I keep forgetting that's going to happen," Mom said.

"Anyway, Mom. Can you help me?"

She looked at me, hard. You know the way your mom looks at you and you can tell there's something else, like she isn't just noticing your shirt color, she's doing something crazy, like thinking of every moment since you were born? It was like that. She looked wistful. "John, you don't know this, but your dad and I, well, our first date was a picnic. Please don't make a big deal about that. I'm not saying you're going to get married. I'm just saying, I *love* what you're doing. And I would love to help you." She may have teared up. I tried my best to ignore it. Even though it was incredibly sweet.

Mom got everything ready. I mean *everything*. She totally rocked it and saved my butt. Maybe even more than when she drove me across the country toward Sol. Well, no, that was probably a bigger deal. But this was a close second.

* * *

Let me just say that a picnic, or, more specifically, a romantic picnic date, is more than just the sum of its parts. Despite the fact that my mom got all the things I would need, I was still an inexperienced fool at dating. As you'd expect, considering this was my first time.

I did at least secure the table. We had a front-row view of the lake at Jeremiah Underly Park. It wasn't a sunset on Santorini, but it was pretty great for a 15-year-old's first date. Carrie seemed legitimately overwhelmed.

"John, this is…" She looked over the spread of food, slid her hand across the red-and-white checked tablecloth. "I don't know. Amazing."

"That's good, right?"

Carrie smiled. "Yes. Definitely. *Amazing* is definitely *good*." Then her face changed.

"What's the matter?" I asked.

"I just wanted to say sorry about the whole dance thing, and how I reacted when you asked me out the first time." She looked genuinely upset.

I probably turned a shade darker than the red in the tablecloth my mom had found for us. "Hey. Don't worry about it." I laughed nervously.

"And, that night. How'd you do it? How'd you put out the fire at the school?"

Carrie gazed deep in my eyes, and I felt the answer — the real answer — about to seep out. I shook my head to clear my thoughts. "Uh, just dumb luck. There were these big buckets of soap, like industrial strength or something, and I dumped them on the fire." I made a bursting gesture with one hand. "*Poof.* It went out."

"That's just amazing. You're a real hero. A lot of people could've gotten hurt. Including me." Carrie put her hand on top of mine. I nearly passed out. Breathing was labored. Pupils dilated. *Get control of yourself, John.*

Something about the gesture made me bold. I asked a question I hadn't been planning on. "I'm curious, Carrie. If you hadn't already been asked to the Middle School Prom by Larry, would you have —?"

"Yes, John. I would have gone with you," she said, batting her lashes at me for real. Now I thought I was going to throw up. My stomach was a rolling mess of nerves. I giggled. I actually freaking giggled. "Now, I want you to answer a question of mine," she said.

I gulped. "Okay, sure. What's the question?"

"Tell me something no one else knows about you." Still her eyes were locked on mine.

I had to say it. Because, you know, nerd conquers all. And throwing someone else's joke back at them when they least expect it is the height of comedy. "That's not a question."

"You know what I mean," she said, laughing.

I wanted to do it. I really, really did. To tell her about the powers. "I have —" I started.

"Have what?"

No. She was going to think I was a freak. I couldn't tell her. No way.

But.

Carrie had told me that she *liked* the idea that I was double-jointed. Maybe she'd like it even more to know the truth. Since it was actually an infinitely more awesome truth, in many ways.

"I can, um. Well, how do I put this?" Carrie leaned close to hear what I had to say. I could smell her perfume. Something floral and sweet and intoxicating. "I can —"

And then people started shouting.

The first thing I thought was *Cut it out, I'm trying to say something important.* That didn't matter.

"There's someone fighting the Gorgols!" Two people were huddled close together, staring intently at a phone.

Um. Of course. The military has been fighting the Gorgols all along, I thought. But no, wait, did this person literally mean there is some*one* fighting the Gorgols? A single person?

No, stop. I was about to say something.

"What's happening?" Carrie said, leaning away, starting to stand. The moment seemed to be over. As she stood and turned, I sighed deeply. There would be no truth told on this day after all. I followed Carrie into the crowd of people.

"Look!" the man with the phone said, pointing at the screen. As if we were going to look at something else, given the commotion. "I can't believe it! Some guy is fighting the Gorgol! The slower one, *Armigon.*"

"*Omicron,*" someone else corrected. "Like the Greek letter?"

"If you say so," phone man replied, eyes still glued to the screen. He chuckled in an *I'm stupid and I don't care* kind of way.

We pressed close together, all of us strangers. On the screen, live news footage showed Gorgol Omicron standing on the rubble of some seaside building. And something tiny was standing before it. Something human. In a red mask.

Oh my God, what is Bobby doing? That was my first thought. *Dammit, the mask was* my *idea!* That was my second thought. But the figure seemed different. Thinner than Bobby. And whoever he was, he held a sword or long stick. Like he knew how to use it.

Omicron swooped down with one massive, clawed hand, and common sense told you that the human figure was going to die. But he didn't. His body sluiced and shifted. And as it reformed just to the side of the blow, he struck hard with the long weapon in his hands. It shouldn't have done anything to the giant monster. But again, that was wrong. Omicron was slashed. The creature screamed in anger, a pained cry.

"What the hell?" someone in our group yelled. "How did that guy do that?"

"This isn't real. This is special effects. It's gotta be," another person said. "Where'd you find this video?"

"No, it's real. This is live from 24News."

"He's hurt the thing!" someone shouted. A cheer went up. People were rooting for the masked human warrior fighting the giant creature.

Bobby was right. We should have gone and fought it. Easy to say when you're a couple of thousand miles away, watching someone else do the dirty work.

In pain, Omicron slashed again, and again the fighter's body shifted.

"How is he doing that?" a person behind me asked. Beside me, Carrie clutched at my arm, maybe in fear or maybe just to angle for a better view.

The person slashed at Omicron once more, and the monster screamed again, definitely wounded. Then, gesturing with one hand, the fighter sent large rocks heaving off the ground and crashing into the creature's newly gaping wound. Physical and mental powers, basically the same that I possessed, had just been demonstrated on live TV. This was more than Sol's little shows. This was the whole package. I was simultaneously relieved and really pissed.

Someone who had powers like me had revealed it to the world. Which meant that I could, too, maybe.

It also meant that, when I did, I would be... I don't know, *unoriginal*.

Shit.

Still, this masked person, who I no longer thought was Bobby, looked like he was hurting the monster. Could he kill it?

Then, as if to answer my question, from nowhere Sigma crashed into the masked person and sent him flying through the air, to be dashed on the large, jagged rocks of the shore.

For a moment, he didn't move. News cameras zoomed in. Was he dead? People held their breath. And we noticed... something had changed. The red mask had been knocked partly aside.

Long hair spilled out.

Curls of red.

Familiar hair.

"Pip?" I said aloud before I could think better of it. I don't know why, but I was suddenly *sure* this person in the red mask was a she — and I knew her. It was Pip, one of Sol's students. All my memories of her came streaming back, even though I'd never truly met her. I had a lot of dream memories of Pip. In fact, I thought of her as my redheaded dream girl. Which was awkward, because I was standing next to my very first date, who was also a redhead (and rather dreamy). It was a conflicting moment, I can tell you that.

"What?" Carrie said.

"Oh, nothing. Sorry," I said in a lame attempt to cover up. "But I don't think that's a man. Look!" Now everyone was noticing the red hair.

"It's a woman!" a lady next to us shouted. "A super woman! Everybody — some kind of super woman is fighting the Gorgols!"

Which was technically incorrect, because at that very moment, Pip turned tail and fled.

9

Bobby tried to punch me in the arm, but of course, that didn't work. He just rolled his eyes. "See? I *told* you we should have taken on the Gorgols!"

"She didn't beat them," I said.

"She?"

"Oh, come on, Bobby," I said, rounding on him. "You know who that was."

"Pip?"

"Um, yeah."

"I thought that was just my imagination."

"Nope, it wasn't."

"Then it's even more important to go fight. Pip will need our help. I know she was a student of Sol and all, and that may make you not want to help her, but I was one of those students for a while, too. Besides, Pip was different. She was never mean, like the others could be. I honestly think she saw something good in what Sol was trying to do, and she wanted to stick around to make sure that came through."

"Is that why she was the one he left in charge of Holly?" I asked, almost spitting the words.

"Yes, actually. She didn't approve of that whole thing, but she stuck around to be sure that *someone* was taking care of Holly. Ask your sister."

"I plan to," I said.

"Besides, you… you had a thing for Pip, right?" Bobby said. His tone was off, softer than normal. He sounded unsure.

With Carric still fresh on my mind, I bristled. "I never even *met* her, Bobby." That was true, but the underlying secret was that I *did* have a thing for her. Having just been on my first-ever date, I suddenly felt like I was cheating.

Bobby shook off whatever he'd been feeling and smiled. "Somehow, for people like us, I don't think that matters as much. You *know* her. She may even know you."

I walked away. We were grabbing a snack in my kitchen after school. Kicking Bobby out of my house would be extreme. Walking into the other room was a mild but notable protest.

So I turned on the TV. And of course, the main topic of coverage was the Gorgols. Pip seemed to have disappeared, but the monsters continued to traipse through seaside towns, wreaking havoc. The newscasts were keeping a tally of the dead. It was getting worse. The Gorgols were beginning to push inland, and that really freaked people out. Folks who lived along the ocean had migrated to the hills, and now the hills suddenly were unsafe as well.

The funny thing, though, was how the people on TV tried to rationalize everything. *Rationalize* a couple of giant monsters from the sea, and a superhuman woman who had fought them. They pontificated on the origin of the Gorgols. Some said they were creatures from the distant past, dormant for thousands or millions of years, now awake. Like underwater dinosaurs that somehow had eluded our notice. Others said they were aliens.

And the news channels brought in martial-arts and sword-fighting experts who tried to analyze and define Pip's technique. Despite the fact that you could see her body deform and sluice past Omicron's attacks, they offered up video experts who tried to say it was something related to the speed of her motion versus the frame rate of the recording. *Blah blah blah.*

Almost immediately, Pip gained a cult following. They called her *Red Hope*. That was simultaneously hilarious and terrifying. If people knew about me, what would they call me? *Please, make it something cool*, I thought. I had to wonder if Pip was watching the news, hearing this name. What did she think of it? I didn't truly know her, but those dreams were so real, full of people who were real. So I knew a little bit about this girl. I thought she'd be embarrassed by the name.

So Red Hope, aka Pip, got a fan base. People, especially those along the coast where the Gorgols were destroying everything, held rallies, begging her to come to their aid. She became a sort of mythical figure overnight.

I had to wonder what her plan was. She had done some damage to Omicron, but it seemed like there was still a long way to go to kill even one of the monsters. Pip against both of them seemed impossible.

I felt sorry for her. I guess that left me open.

"There's no way she can do it alone, Johnny," Bobby said, reading my mind as he entered the room munching on potato chips from a bag.

"I don't think so either," I said.

Bobby nudged me and held out the bag, so I grabbed a couple of chips. "See? We need to do it."

"You still haven't answered my question — how is this really our fight?"

Bobby crammed another chip in his mouth, dropping crumbs all over his shirt. "Johnny, think about it. If Sol had never taken Holly, would you have fought him?"

"No."

"Are you sure? Don't forget when he was in the capital. People *died*. You would just let that happen? Especially knowing now that you *could* beat him. You'd just let him go on killing people?"

Damn it. Bobby had a point. "Well, I know *now* that I could beat him. That's not something I knew before."

"But you tried anyway. Because it was the right thing to do." I couldn't meet Bobby's eyes. "But there's one more thing. They're coming. We can run, we can ignore them, but that doesn't change the fact that some pretty big, pretty destructive monsters are stomping around, and people are getting hurt. Regular people. People who don't have power, or the option to stand aside that we do."

Bobby was serious. Crap.

"Plus," he said, "Pip needs our help. We need to find her, make a plan. It would be three on two, Johnny. Decent odds." Bobby offered me another potato chip. "Come on. Go with me. I'll be your best friend."

I grabbed the bag forcefully, in frustration and maybe mock anger. "No." He gave me a long look. I didn't change my answer. Though I couched it, a little bit. "Besides, I'd have to ask my mom."

10

Bobby went home, and I figured that was the end of that. The creatures were across the country, and yeah, they were a problem, people had died. But everything can't fall on my shoulders, right? That's what I told myself.

Still, inside, I knew what I *wanted* to do.

Walking around the house, I daydreamed of fighting the Gorgols. Maybe I sashayed a bit. I was a swashbuckler.

Yes, it was ridiculous looking.

And it was just a fantasy. I wasn't going to actually *do* that.

I envisioned myself stabbing into the heart of a Gorgol and standing victorious atop its giant, fallen body.

I kinda liked it. I kinda liked the idea of doing that. To save the day? Yes, to save the day, that was the reason.

Not just to show off my power. No way.

As I walked past Holly's room, my head suddenly exploded with a sound like bells and thunder and chimes and a thousand gongs smashing into each other. I grabbed for my head. Was this a migraine? Were my powers finally killing me?

No. Holly wanted my attention.

Oh my God, Holly, stop!

She was sitting in her chair, looking toward me in the hall. I held one hand against her door frame as the sound continued to incapacitate me. *Sorry, Johnny. I just needed to talk to you.* Abruptly, there was silence.

Okay, okay. But you don't have to blow my brains out to do it.

She looked indignant. *I said sorry. Just wanted you to come here.*

All right. I'm here. I shook my head. *What's up?*

I want to try again, Johnny.

I knew what she meant. The powers. Since we returned from the desert, since she came back to us more than she had in so many years, Holly had to get used to the idea that she had powers.

Given all the time we had trapped in our house, and the fact that we shared these abilities, I tried to train her.

Well, *train* sounds important.

What I mean is, every once in a while, we would spend a little time trying to see if she could exercise her power on purpose. That was the big thing — *on purpose*.

So far, no luck.

I pulled a quarter out of my pocket and placed it on the table in front of her. *Okay, Hol. Try to move it. And remember what I've told you. Relax. Just imagine the quarter moving, just a tiny bit. You don't have to strain about it. Calm.*

She tried.

And tried.

But honestly, I didn't expect anything to happen. We must have tried this exercise three or four times before, with no success. I didn't expect things to change all of a sudden.

Until they did.

The quarter didn't shake. It didn't slide a few millimeters across the desk. Nope. Not my Holly. That quarter leapt up onto one edge and started spinning.

Jesus, Holly, you did it!

She laughed, out loud, as the quarter spun and spun and spun. Gradually, its energy dissipated and the quarter slowed, then entered a loopy wobble before collapsing to the table. I watched it the whole time, grinning.

Holly could use her power.

Holly?

I turned to see that she'd lapsed into one of her fades. Not really all there.

Holly?

She blinked, and returned to me. What did that mean for her using her powers? Did they take too much out of her? Would using them put her at risk of falling back into the locked world she'd lived in for so many years?

I can feel them, Johnny.

Feel who, Hol?

The monsters. The ones on TV. I can feel them even now.

I could feel others with the power, like Sol or Bobby, even when they were far away. But I couldn't feel the Gorgols at all, so how could Holly? Despite her struggles with control, I knew she was incredibly strong with her mental abilities, stronger than I could really comprehend. Maybe she could sense others with the power more than I could.

But if that was true, it meant the Gorgols weren't just giant, ultra-strong wrecking machines covered in impenetrable armor. They were giant, ultra-strong wrecking machines covered in impenetrable armor, *with superpowers.*

Oh no.

Holly gasped. "Johnny?" she said aloud.

Sorry, Hol. I was just connecting the dots. I can feel people with our powers — people like Sol. If you can feel the Gorgols, does that mean they have power, too? If they do, I don't think I can stop them. I don't think anyone could stop them.

You could feel Sol? she asked.

Well, not really feel, *but sense. Almost like I could hear him. It's like each of us with power has a beacon. I've learned how to make mine quiet, but I can find others. Like I usually can tell where Bobby is. He's not so careful about making his sound quiet.*

Holly thought for a moment. *Do I have a sound like this?*

Yeah, you do. But I almost never hear it. Almost like you have it locked deep inside and it only comes out once in a while. Like just now when you tried to reach out to me.

Oh. And that was painful for you. Is mine loud?

Very.

But I don't hear you, or Bobby, or even HIM. Even when he took me. Ever. I never have.

I can't explain that. Maybe it's similar to how your beacon is usually completely quiet to me. Maybe the transmitter and receiver are connected somehow.

I don't understand that.

I tried to come up with another way to phrase it. Sometimes it was hard to remember that, from a developmental standpoint, Holly had lost a lot of years. She was catching up, but sometimes things I'd say didn't make sense to her. *I just meant that maybe the thing that makes your sound — that makes it so strong, but usually silent — is the same thing that makes others silent for you.*

Again Holly paused to think. *But, Johnny. I can* feel *the monsters. Not hear them.*

I shook my head. *I don't understand.* Was this just phrasing that she didn't get, or were we actually talking about different things?

Make your sound — your beacon — for me now. Can you? Holly asked.

Okay, I can try. But if your receiver isn't working…

Try.

I tried. Holly grimaced, twisting like she was trying to look over her shoulder. *Oh. Oh! Really?* She smiled and made a little giggling sound. *That's you, Johnny? I've heard that before. I didn't know that was you!*

I laughed, too. *Yep, that's me. I'm going to turn it off now.*

Okay. I'll remember that's you in case I hear it again. But Johnny, that's not like what I mean. I can feel *them.*

The Gorgols?

Yes!

Tell me what you mean by feel them.

Holly pursed her lips, thinking. *When I was little, before… you know. Well, I remember one time at the beach getting a sunburn. You know what sunburn feels like, right, Johnny?*

Of course. I was as pale as they come, like most of my family. "Sunburn" was our word for "tan."

It's like that. Like a sunburn, but really light. And it doesn't stay in one place. It's on the side of me facing the Gorgols. If I turn around, it moves over my skin, but stays pointing the same direction.

Okay, so Holly had a Gorgol tracker built into her body. Was that useful? They were 200-feet tall and kind of hard to miss, so I doubted we'd need to resort to complicated methods to find them. *Weird.* That was all I could think to say about it. I didn't really know what other use her ability would have.

Then I noticed that Holly seemed scared.

"What's wrong, Hol?" I said out loud.

"Johnny…" she said. *Johnny. The feeling. The sunburn feeling. It's been getting worse.*

I frowned, not sure what to make of that. *Uh-huh.*

"Johnny!" she said again. *Johnny, I think something bad is going to happen.*

What do you mean?

Holly's eyes widened with terror. She crossed her arms, and with one hand began idly scratching the other arm. *I*

*think I know what the monsters are looking for. I think
they're looking for me.*

Why would they be looking for you, Hol?

Her voice in my head went quiet. Looking at her face, it
seemed like she was trying to work out a math problem.
Solve for Gorgol.

I think they're looking for me because I brought them here.

I blinked and pulled back. *Huh?*

*Those fires from the sky. When you and I flew and I nearly
killed us. I tore open the sky and those things came out.*

11

Holly. I need to talk to you and Mom about the Gorgols, okay?

Okay, Johnny.

I wheeled her into the kitchen, where Mom was ready with dinner. *I'll speak to Mom out loud, and if you don't understand something, let me know. Tap on the table or something to get my attention.*

Okay, Johnny. Are you mad at me about them? Because I brought them here?

What was I going to say? "It's fine that you brought killing machines down from the sky, little sis!" *No, Hol, of course not.* I pressed my forehead against hers.

What are you going to say to Mom? Is it bad?

Maybe.

I don't like that, Johnny.

I smiled, trying to reassure her.

So we sat down and ate together, and as we were finishing, I tried to subtly shift the conversation. "Mom, what do you think of these Gorgols? What do you think should be done about them?" See? Subtle.

Mom froze. She had cut a piece of roast beef, stabbed at it with her fork, and was about to put it in her mouth, but after my question, she placed it back on her plate. She looked at her food, in a way that told me clearly both that she was not looking at her food and that she had probably expected this conversation. "Tell me what you plan to do, John," she said, head down.

"Mom? Are you okay?"

"Not really, John. And honestly, I'll probably never be fully okay again, knowing what I know. I'll always be afraid that your powers — that Holly's powers — make you both have to take risks. Make you targets. Put you in danger. As a parent, that's terrifying." She finally looked up, and there was a tear slowly falling down one cheek.

I swallowed. Did I really want to do this? Not really. Did I think I had to anyway? Probably. "Mom. You know what I can do, what Bobby can do. Holly is *incredible* —" I looked at Holly with a smile, reaching out to pat one of her hands. "— but I don't think she's ready. But, Mom, Bobby and I feel like we need to help. To stop the monsters and keep them from killing a lot more people." It wasn't much of a convincing argument, but it was the point I needed to make.

The fork rose and my mom finally ate her roast beef. She chewed, slowly, looking nowhere into the distance. "You know that person?"

"Who?"

"The person who fought the Gorgols." Mom took another bite, without looking at it, probably not even registering what she was doing.

"Yeah, well, I think so. I think it's a woman — I mean girl — well, I don't know. She's like 18. Her name is Pip." I felt Holly tense beside me.

Hold on, Hol, let me explain.

"*Pip?*" Mom said. "The woman who is trying to save the world from two sea monsters is named *Pip?*"

I nodded. "Her real name is Phillipa, but she goes by Pip."

Mom nodded. "Okay, so this Pip. How do you know her?"

"She was in Sol's group of students," I said, and Mom jerked to attention. "It's not like that, Mom. She's not like Margrethe." Mom was well aware of the dangers of Margrethe, having watched Aunt Cindy's car get nearly destroyed by that woman. "Pip... I think she's okay. She was the only one who took care of Holly when Sol had her." And then she disappeared into the hills when I'd finally found my sister, but Mom didn't need to know that.

"Holly?" Mom asked, looking but not expecting a response.

Holly's eyes welled. "Mommy," she said, unable to add anything else out loud. I reached out to her, in case there was something else she needed to say.

Hol. Okay?

Johnny. Tell Mommy you're right about Pip. She stayed with me. Gave me food. She tried to be nice. Well, maybe not really nice, I don't know, but a lot nicer than HIM.

I patted Holly on the hand again and repeated what she'd said to my mom.

"That's not much of an endorsement," Mom said. "But why you? If this Pip character is fighting them, let her fight. Why do you need to be the one?"

I shrugged. "Because of Holly."

"What does that mean?"

So I explained what Holly told me. About feeling them. About bringing them to Earth.

And about how the Gorgols were looking for her.

Mom was silent. For a long time.

"Mom?" I asked.

"How will you do it?" she replied.

I was confused. "Um. We'll go there and fight the Gorgols."

"Johnny. No." It was Holly.

What, Hol?

I don't like this idea, Johnny.

I understand, but, you know, I can't just sit back and wait for them to find you. And besides, every day we wait, people are dying.

It's not that, Johnny.

Then what, Hol?

I'm just worried that if you start — if you start fighting the Gorgols — you can't un-start. I had no reply to that. I was afraid of that possibility myself.

Mom looked at me with a pragmatic sort of seriousness. "You said *we'll go there.* Go to the Gorgols. That's all well and good, John, but let's look at the facts. If you disappear now, we'll be all over the news again. The reporters and all those cameras..."

Holly shuddered.

I hadn't thought about that. School had just started. If Bobby and I went missing again, Mom might be strung up, by the media at least. Hell, they might think she'd kidnapped us, or worse. I shrugged. "I don't know."

A conspiratorial kind of look appeared in Mom's eyes. "To be blunt, I don't think your sister can take anymore of their flashing lights and yelling. So if you need to disappear, we need a plan."

"What?" I asked.

To my right, Holly tapped the table. She didn't understand, so I reached out. *Mom wants to help.*

Holly looked confused, still. *She wants you to go?*

No, Hol. I think she just knows we have to.

I still don't like it.

"John," Mom said, looking concerned. "Say what you will, but you're 15. If you disappear again, people will freak out. If you *and* Bobby both disappear, well…" She paused, looking around. "I don't even want to think about what they'd do if we all went together."

"Bobby and I could just sneak away…"

Mom laughed. "That would be worse. The media would have a field day. I don't know how they'd blame it on me, but they would." She looked at Holly, and the implication was clear — if I left and that brought attention to my mother and sister, Holly would suffer.

But if I didn't go, the Gorgols would come to Holly.

"Then what?" I said. "How can we go across the country, again, without people losing their minds?"

Mom thought quietly. "There are three possibilities. One, like you just said, we all disappear. No one knows where we are. That seems unlikely to work, and will just cause another sensation, and I have no idea how all of us could hide from everyone. Two, we figure out a reason that's so believable that no one questions it or follows us. That seems impossible. I have no idea what the reason could be, and people are just too cynical to buy much of anything these days, even if it was the God's honest truth. But, three…"

"What?"

"We don't go anywhere."

I blinked. "How's that going to help? Do nothing? Let people die? The Gorgols will just come to us anyway."

She turned to me directly, dinner forgotten. "What I mean is, we make everyone *think* that we haven't gone anywhere. How long do you think you need?"

I hadn't actually thought about that. "Um, I don't know. A day? I mean, not counting the time to get there and back. But the Gorgols are big, so it's not like we have to hunt for them. And once we fight, I think it'll be quick." Mom looked at me closely, gauging what I meant. Trying to see if I was that confident. And I wasn't. "One way or the other," I made myself say. She looked away, but before she did, I saw the lines of worry deepen on her face.

Mom shook her head slightly. "You *have* to fly. Otherwise, it just takes too long. Train or bus would be *days*. But flying is complicated. Security, lots of people around. I don't see how it can be done. Someone will notice you. They'll remember you from the news."

"Mom. When I went to the capital, I *pushed* a lot of minds. At the bus stop, on the bus, in the city." Suddenly, I was certain. "I think I can do the same at the airport. All I need to do is make sure people don't recognize me. Recognize *us*. So Bobby can help, too."

"John, a single airplane can have hundreds of people. In the airport, there will be thousands."

"Yeah, but I only need to push the ones who are near me. You know, like when we flew to see Grandma and Grandpa that time, and we sat in, like, row 68 or something? I didn't have any idea who was in row 10, did you?"

"No, unless I walked past them on the way to my seat."

"And that part's fine. I can push people as I move past them. Once I'm sitting somewhere, I just need to make sure the people around me don't recognize me. So, I think I can do it. Airport, plane, city, whatever."

Mom relented, but just barely. "Okay, but what about buying a ticket? That's going to cost a fortune. I don't know if I even have the money. Since your Dad passed —" She stopped for moment, unsure. "Anyway, if I buy a ticket, your name will be on it. There'll be security…"

"For security, I can just push their minds again. Easy. I've done it to cops before."

"That's hardly something to be proud of," Mom said.

I just shrugged. "And I don't want you to spend all your money on me, Mom." It was true. I never so much as asked her to get me a phone, even though every other kid had one. Well, except Bobby, but his parents were just jerks. "I mean, I think what we're going to do is really important, but we might fail. I couldn't bear it if I failed *and* sent us to the poorhouse."

"There's no such thing as a poorhouse, John. If I don't pay the mortgage, we're homeless."

"Well, I couldn't bear that, either."

"And if you fail, they're coming here anyway, right? Home or no home."

"Gee, no pressure," I said.

"Okay, how are you going to get a ticket? No, *two* tickets. Without what little money I have."

"I don't need a ticket. I just *push* here, *push* there, and everyone lets me right on board. No questions asked."

"That's stealing."

"I know, but I won't do it unless we're sure the seats will be empty. We can find flights in the middle of the night or something — besides, that'll mean less people around. And we're doing it to try to save lives. Including our own." I looked at Holly and saw the fear in her eyes. I smiled at her with what I hoped was winning confidence.

"What about a place to sleep, if you need it?"

I reminded her about the night I'd spent in the hotel suite when I'd gone to meet Sol in the capital. She shrugged. "More stealing." But she got very quiet, considering everything.

Holly tapped on the table again, so I explained the idea to her. Still, she was confused.

But won't people still notice that you're gone, Johnny?

It was a good question, and one I didn't have an answer for, so I repeated it to my mom. A mischievous look spread across her face. Like she was going to enjoy pulling the wool over the eyes of the world. "John, you don't look well," she said. "I think you might be coming down with the flu."

I grinned back at her. The simplest ideas were often the best. A little time locked away in the house, where no one would see. Or so people would think. But this meant I was going alone. Well, with Bobby, but, you know, not with my mom. Then I realized, I *had* to do it alone. Even if my mom came along, she couldn't face the Gorgols. I had to do that. I didn't want her bringing my sister any closer to those monsters anyway. So it was time to learn to do more on my own. My grin turned into a smile. Despite the fact that the whole thing scared me, a little. At the same time, I felt a little bit of a fire starting to burn. There was a fight coming, and part of me was saying *Bring it on.*

"Yeah, you look sick, John. And come to think of it," Mom said, "Bobby didn't look too good today, either."

Interlude

Reaching out. Reaching.

The signal is lost.

No, the signal is not there. Has never been there.

Scanning. Searching. Something, like static in the air, makes the transmission waver.

Wait. Another. There is another signal. Not the one sought, but something new.

And the signal sends feelings.

Hurt.

Worry.

Anger.

Frustration.

Determination.

A second new signal appears, blending the two. It does not send feelings.

It has none.

12

Sitting in row 35, seat B, with Bobby next to me in the window seat, I thought, *Well, that was easier than I expected.*

Bobby took a sip of the soda the flight attendant had brought to him and gave a little grin. I could tell he was really enjoying himself. To be honest, so was I.

It was the middle of the night, what they call a "red eye." We chose the flight because it was half empty, so we weren't technically stealing, just stowing away. Which was stealing from the airline, but, you know, they were going to fly the plane whether we were on it illegally or not, so the theft was at least minimal. Plus, we cut ourselves some slack for trying to save the world.

"Dude, this is amazing," Bobby said. And I remembered that he'd never been on a plane before. He stared out the window at the dark country below like a kid waiting for Santa Claus. Lights glowed in patterns unrecognizable from the ground, showing the rigid structures of our cities and towns.

Rather than gawk at the sights, I thought of the Gorgols. A single Gorgol walking through any of the little towns we could see below would result in hundreds dead, dozens of homes destroyed.

And I felt fear. Sol was a man, an adult. That was fearsome enough for me. But the Gorgols were giant monsters. And there were two of them. And, well, if we failed... I didn't want to think about that.

What the hell was I doing? All the effort, all the secrecy. Just to fly us to our deaths? I started to hyperventilate.

"Johnny, stop," Bobby said.

I turned to him, not even realizing how fast my breathing had become. I'm sure I was flush and red in the face. I tried to calm myself.

"Johnny, seriously," he said. "Have you heard of a no-win situation?"

I nodded, still breathing heavy.

"Yeah? Well, this is a no-lose situation. You and me together. Two superpowers!" He held up his hand for a high-five, but I just kept panting. After a moment, he lowered his hand, dejected. "Anyway, here's the deal. We watch each other's backs. And worse comes to worst, we bail. Fair?"

Between breaths, I tried to speak. "What?"

"I mean it. We bail. This whole monster-killing thing doesn't work out, we get the hell out. Okay?"

I appreciated what Bobby was trying to do. Calm me, give us a semblance of a plan, a way *out*. I was just pretty sure that we were *in* no matter what. Once we attacked the Gorgols, they wouldn't just let us go. I could feel it. "But they'll just come to us anyway, come after my sister."

"True. But if we have to bail and think up some new plan, we can, okay? And don't forget Pip," Bobby said. "It's three on two once we find her."

Find her.

Yeah, we needed to find her, as soon as we landed. Before we even thought of going after the Gorgols. "I know how we can do that." My breathing was calming.

"Good, Johnny. How do you want to find Pip?"

Inside my head, I pulled away the shroud that covered my beacon. Bobby immediately leaned away from me. I guess it was that strong.

"That should work," he said with a grin. "Assuming she wants to be found." A second later, Bobby's own beacon became stronger.

From Pip's vantage, it must have sounded like two bells ringing, far away, but getting closer by the second. Maybe she would feel like the cavalry was coming. The idea made me chuckle.

"Feeling better, Johnny?" Bobby asked.

I shrugged. "For now."

* * *

Between the time of night we left, the length of the flight, and the time zones we were passing through, it would have been a really smart idea for Bobby and me to get some shut-eye.

Instead, we drank a lot of soda and watched movies.

They had four movies to choose from. Some sappy adult drama that looked like it would make my mom cry. An animated movie for babies or possibly toddlers, but no one even a day older. Then there was one about a football team no one thinks can win, but magically does. (*Yay! What a surprise!*) And a monster movie.

Bobby watched the football movie. I wanted to see the monsters.

Maybe I could learn something.

The movie was called *The Sword of Atys*, and it was about some muscle-bound swashbuckling swordsman saving a kingdom from the tyranny of a large and rather grumpy dragon. I'm not really sure *why* the dragon was attacking the kingdom, even after I'd finished the movie, but maybe it was just bored.

Our hero, a chap named *Volteer* or *Vulture* or something like that, began as an innocent farm boy. My first eye-opening moment came when Volteer had his initial fight against the dragon.

He lost.

Beaten, battered, sent away to lick his wounds. Mocked by the dragon as he ran away.

Oh shit. I hadn't considered that option with the Gorgols. That I might just be headed for Round 1 of a longer fight.

After that, Volteer began to listen to his mentor, a wizened old dude named Merwin. And, yes, I noticed that was a clear ripoff of Merlin from King Arthur. This was not Agrade material. Anyway, by the middle of the movie, Volteer was blocking and thrusting as well as any other movie swordsman I'd seen, even carrying on lengthy conversations (did I mention the dragon talked?) during his final duel. Volteer's learning curve was somewhat mysterious. I think they edited out most of the parts where he was in Swordsman School for the sake of brevity.

But there were scenes of great majesty, Volteer poised with sword at the ready, awaiting the attack of the dragon, then deftly parrying claw or tooth. The *clang clang clang* of the battle went on for what seemed like forever. Eventually, Volteer remembered the dragon's prophecy, which predicted a single fault in its otherwise flawless armor. Yes, I know, they ripped that off, too. With a dramatic swirling move that was more ballet than combat, Volteer spun in and thrust his sword into the heart of the beast, and it fell dead around him, leaving behind nothing but dust, a most likely very smelly dragon carcass, and a hero.

I found myself both smiling and deeply concerned. I didn't have any swirling ballet moves to defeat the Gorgols. But I wanted very much to be the hero, despite the fact that I knew a certain arrogance came with that. Still, that thrust, into the dragon's heart. I liked that.

Maybe too much.

A silly grin on my face, I realized Bobby was watching me. He didn't bother saying anything or even taking off his headphones. He just smiled, pointed at the heroic Volteer on my screen, then pointed at me.

After the movie, I dozed for a short while, my ears filled with the ceaseless hum of the jet engines, a sound that was both annoyingly monotonous and strangely calming. The cabin was lit by only the dimmest of lights for the odd person who might stumble to a restroom in the middle of the night. I'd stayed up too late, jacked up from the excitement and soda and strangeness of the whole experience, and finally I crashed. And in my dreams, a dragon spoke, flying around me on updrafts of air.

But the dragon's voice wasn't the one from the movie I had just finished, the one with the over-the-top British accent and impossibly low bass growl. It had an accent, but I knew it was Portuguese. One I'd heard before.

In the voice of Sol, the dragon circled above me, saying, "John, my old friend."

Old. Friend.

13

I popped up with a start, head throbbing. The lights were up, people talking and milling about. Bobby, thankfully, had woken before me and was actively pushing minds to ignore our presence. Flight attendants were shifting through the aisles, giving out trays of strangely plastic-encased breakfast.

But I didn't hear any of that. I just heard the tone.

Pip had unleashed her beacon, calling us toward her. It had an odd, wavering quality to it. Like a Doppler effect on repeat.

I looked at Bobby, and he smirked. "Wondering when you were going to notice it. You slept through it for like 10 minutes."

"Does her beacon always sound that way?" I asked. "It seems strange."

"I don't remember the warble, or whatever you want to call it. I don't remember it having that… I don't know, interference?" Bobby didn't seem too concerned about the difference, though.

The voice from my dream still buzzed in my head, spinning around. I rubbed at my eyes, trying to clear my head.

And I realized I was about to land in a place ruled by monsters, and I was planning to fight them to the death. Not their death, *the death*. Which could mean *my* death. For the first time I could recall, I wished I drank coffee, or just understood why people drank it. It seemed desirable while I rubbed at my temples and tried to wake up. The pilot announced 20 minutes to landing.

"Ready, Freddie?" Bobby asked, dry-rubbing his hands together.

"No way, Jose," I replied. It was one of two standard responses, the other being "Yes, indeedy, feed the needy." But at that particular moment, I wasn't feeling very ready.

The airport was on the eastern outskirts of the state capital, a good long drive from the coastal towns the Gorgols had mostly flattened. So we still had a healthy car ride ahead of us. Nonetheless, landing felt important.

After the flight attendant collected our breakfast trash, which consisted of a large amount of the food-like substance they were calling breakfast, I used my mind to raise my tray table into its upright and locked position. No hands.

"Are you trying to get someone to notice you?" Bobby asked.

"No, I just feel like I need to do *something* to practice."

"How about this?" Bobby said. "When we get near the shore, we can stop some place and you and me can spar. Cool?" I nodded. "It'll be like old times." He grinned.

"Like what, the time you tried to kill me?"

"Ah, memories," he said, one hand over his heart melodramatically.

"Ass," I said. Brevity in insults is often best.

"If I'm an ass, then you're friends with an ass. So what does that make you?" Bobby tilted his head in a sort of jaunty way.

I looked out the window to see the ground approaching, knowing that somewhere out there, two 200-foot-tall monsters were waiting for me. "It makes me stupid. Really stupid."

* * *

Despite having his mind pushed to both fail to recognize us *and* be willing to drive us toward the Gorgols, we could tell the cab driver was getting uneasy.

"This will have to be close enough," I said to Bobby as we sped through a deserted area of dense pines. "It feels like Pip is close by, maybe really close. And besides, you said we were going to spar."

Bobby nodded, and we had the driver pull over. We didn't have any money, so we sent him on his way with another little push to forget the whole thing ever happened. I wondered if he'd get halfway back to the airport to find his next fare and wonder why the heck he was so far out. We couldn't worry about it. We were on foot in the land of monsters. We had exponentially bigger fish to fry.

Standing beside the road, the mental throb of Pip's beacon seemed so loud that it might have been truly audible. She was close. She must have felt us coming and decided to meet us. There was still an odd quality to the tone, but we estimated its direction as best we could and began walking toward it. That led us into the thick pine forest, deeper and deeper, until we could no longer see or even hear the road. Finally, we came to a clearing. Well, not a clearing, but a place that had been cleared of normal growth in favor of crops. Orange trees grew in long rows, the fruit adding dots of bright color to the otherwise unbroken deep green extending into the distance.

We passed between orange trees, walking row to row, until Bobby stopped just ahead of me.

"Okay," he said, turning around, smirking. "Let's go."

"Here?"

"Would you prefer a steel cage or something?" He dropped down into a fighting stance.

What the hell did I know about fighting stances, or technique? I had fought three people with power: Bobby, Petrus, and Sol. Of those, the fight with Bobby was a brawl, but in a way, no different than the random fistfights kids our age had. Petrus and Sol were different. In both cases, I never landed a single blow. In fact, I never threw a single punch. And I won both fights. Still, I couldn't imagine a fight with a Gorgol that wouldn't be full-contact. Sparring was going to be necessary. I raised my fists, halfheartedly. "Okay."

We stood, nearly toe to toe, and I steeled myself, not sure when to start sparring, or, when I did, where I should strike first.

Something shot out at me and I was sent sprawling to the ground. Bobby laughed.

I shook my head, pointlessly swiping at my now dirty clothes as I started to get up. "I guess we're starting now?" I said.

I felt him coming, felt something shooting out at me again. It was Bobby's right fist, so fast it became a blur. No, that's not right. So fast, his hand and arm actually blurred in real life, extended, sluiced. Like a liquid version of a person, Bobby struck at me.

This time, my body took over. Apparently, after the first knockdown, the rest of my cells decided they didn't trust my mind to do the right thing. My head and upper body shifted, sluicing away from the blow. But Bobby didn't relent. His left fist followed quickly, trying to catch my body in its new position. Again, I slid away.

We stood there, inches from one another, Bobby's fists flying impossibly fast, with inhuman moves, my body dodging instinctively, sliding left and right, up and down.

I felt glancing hits, but nothing direct. Bobby tried harder and faster to punch me, but my body moved faster and faster to avoid it.

Anyone watching would have seen two pairs of nearly motionless feet and legs, with nothing but a shape-shifting mass of color atop each.

We kept on that way for what seemed like an hour but was probably no more than a minute or two, tops. When you operate at hummingbird speed, time seems different. Finally, I came to realize, as I dodged and slid, that I needed to do more than simply evade and defend. And a little fire lit inside me. A desire to change the fight.

I had to attack.

In the middle of a roundhouse Bobby was attempting to land, I swooped my right fist upward.

And Bobby sailed through the air, slamming against a nearby orange tree, shaking its limbs and sending a few green leaves scissoring to the ground. Bobby shook his head. "Ow," he said. "Snuck one in on me."

"Yeah, sorry," I said with a grin that spoke to exactly how sorry I was. Undaunted, Bobby jumped to his feet and lunged at me.

This time, he led with his left. My body sluiced, bending around his outstretched fist. My right hand punched at his face, but Bobby's neck bent backward and I missed. Punches and dodges, back and forth, most of them missing or glancing off without effect. We were learning how our bodies could move, like flowing oceans of cells somehow kept together as a human form, but able to slide and sluice in unbelievable ways. Slowly, both Bobby and I started to smile.

And just when Bobby thought I was getting too complacent, he pulled up and froze for just an instant, throwing off the rhythm of our liquid fighting dance. Then, without warning, he put all of his effort into a double-fisted thrust into my abdomen. My body had almost no time to adjust, to slide out of the way, and so, although I was in the middle of a dramatic dodge, Bobby's hands struck me, hard.

Letting out a harsh *oof,* I was sent through one row of orange trees, then the next, to skid to a stop in the moist, deep brown soil.

Bobby must have enjoyed his sudden success, because he didn't pursue, but just left me to dust off, again, and come back to find him. Which, after a moment to shake off the cobwebs, I did. I honestly don't know if it was the hit or the show of confidence that irked me more, but I knew one thing had changed. The fire inside me was no longer little, it was raging.

I was angry at Bobby. And I wanted to do something about it.

A static sound grew louder in my head, and for a moment I didn't know if Bobby had knocked something loose inside me. Even more upsetting, Bobby had his back turned to me. The nerve. I leapt up beside him, then quickly stopped dead in my tracks. Instinctively, I tensed when I saw the object of Bobby's attention.

There was a man in a short-sleeve green shirt and khaki shorts standing as if watching us. At first glance, he looked like a Boy Scout, but in adult form. I didn't see or feel it, but Bobby must have tried to push the man's mind to ignore us, to move along. Because Bobby suddenly shook his head and gasped.

"Don't do that," the man said.

14

"How'd you do that?" Bobby asked, standing tall and stiff. I immediately realized we had a problem. Although we'd spoken to people all along our travels, every conversation had been heavily laced with mental pushes to guide the outcome. This was our first *real* conversation since we had left home.

The man before us raised one tanned hand in a gesture of peace that still felt like a veiled threat. "Settle down, you two. I just came to see what's going on. Between the sounds in my head and all the crashing around fighting, you guys make a lot of noise." He could hear us, in his head. He was like us. If I were to write a book report about it, it would be titled *What I Didn't Expect to Find on My Summer Vacation.* Another person with powers. Right in front of us.

The stranger smiled, but his eyes stayed cold. Calculating. He was in his early twenties, shorter than average but muscular. He had close-cropped, light-brown hair, and his exposed skin was evenly tanned, all the way down to the thick khaki socks poking out of his leather hiking boots. Everything about him seemed to speak of a life led mostly outdoors.

Bobby took a step forward. "Who are you?"

The stranger shrugged. "I'm Jake. Who are you?"

It was oddly straightforward, and caught both of us completely off-guard. "Um. Bobby?" Bobby replied.

The stranger, Jake, gave a half smile. "'Bobby?' Like, you're not sure if you're Bobby or not?"

I stepped beside my friend and saw his face reddening. Bobby cleared his throat and spoke again. "I'm sure. My name's Bobby."

Jake nodded slowly toward Bobby, in a reserved, *nice to meet you* kind of way. "And you?" he said, turning to look at me.

Something happened when he looked at me. Something cold ran down my spine, like a bad omen. Like I was walking on the spot where I would some day die. I didn't answer.

"Cat got your tongue?"

"Huh? What?" I said, eloquently.

"Your name?" Jake said with raised eyebrows, waiting for the reply.

"John. John Black," I finally said.

Again, Jake gave a nod. "Nice to meet you, John Black," he said, slowly looking me over, the way someone at the slaughterhouse might examine a steer or pig. Unconsciously, I slid a little bit behind Bobby, not liking the feeling of Jake's eyes on me.

"If your name is *Jake*, why does your shirt say *Weissman*?" Bobby asked. At which point I noticed that Jake's shirt did indeed have a patch on his left breast pocket that read WEISSMAN in neatly embroidered capital letters.

Jake seemed bemused by the question. "Do you have a last name, Bobby?"

"Um, yeah. Graden," Bobby said.

Jake tapped at the patch on his shirt. "Well, I do, too."

Bobby sighed. "Oh yeah. My bad." He laughed at himself.

Something was different about Jake. Not the idea that he had powers. He had rejected Bobby's push — but that wasn't the odd thing. It was his beacon. It didn't sound like any other beacon I'd heard, not even Holly's erratic blast of sound. His was like a radio station fading into static as you drive too far away from the source. There was a normal beacon in there somewhere, it was just obscured. Slightly, ever so slightly, it seemed to pulse or waver.

Knowing all this, knowing that we had met a potential partner or foe, I asked the most important question I could think of. "But why do you have your name on your shirt?"

Jake eyed me, and once again I felt the cold pass over me. "I'm a park ranger," he said. "Well. Was. I *was* a park ranger. Probably not anymore."

"What happened? Were you fired or something?" Bobby asked.

Jake laughed. "No, no." Then he thought about it for a moment. "Actually, probably so. I haven't shown up to work for, like, I don't know, several weeks. I doubt they'd be thrilled to welcome me back. Running off without notice isn't the kind of behavior they look for in a young ranger." He laughed again.

Bobby wrinkled his forehead. "Okay, so you used to be a park ranger, but not any more, and now you're here." He looked to me once, then back to Jake. "But why? And how did you push back when I pushed?"

Bobby didn't need to explain, Jake understood instinctively what *push* meant. "I came because I could hear you." He pointed to his head. "In here. Not out loud." Bobby and I both nodded. "You guys were so busy trying to beat the crap out of each other that you didn't notice me walk up." Jake paused to look past us, toward the west. "She's nearby, too, you know?"

"Pip?" I said before I thought maybe silence and secrecy were better ideas.

"Yep. Her. I've talked with her, once. We don't see eye to eye on things, unfortunately."

"On what things?" Bobby asked.

Jake rolled his shoulders, like a fighter loosening before a boxing match. "The Gorgols. I'm assuming you saw her on TV, right? Seems like they played it back a million times." Again, we nodded. "Yeah, I don't like her doing that. The Gorgols may be big, but they're just animals trying to live their lives. Stay out of their way, and you'll be just fine."

"That's your solution to the Gorgols attacking people? *Stay out of their way?*" I asked. "What if that's not an option? What if you *are* their way?"

Jake's glance toward me turned the thermostat from *cool* to *ice-cold*. "The park, where I was a ranger. It's in the desert. Most people avoid it, especially in the summer, which was just fine by me. But in the spring and fall, people would come out from the nearest cities in droves. Minivans with four TV screens, brand-new hiking boots, loud voices, kids running all over, destroying things, and everyone leaving their plastic junk-food wrappers when they finally left. You know what happens if one of their little rug rats bumps into a den of rattlers or some other animal that lives in the desert? No matter what — no matter if one of the kids gets bit or not, they want to kill everything. Exterminate the natural creatures. It makes me sick."

Bobby looked confused. "Yeah, but with the Gorgols, aren't *they* the ones who don't live here? Who are running all over, destroying things?" Seemed like a logical extension of what Jake just said. I puffed up my lower lip, looking at Bobby. *Nice work, friend.*

Jake just shrugged it off. "I'm not so sure. I think those creatures have been on this earth for a long, long time. Much longer than any of us. They're like bears that just woke up from hibernation. Can't blame a bear for coming out of its cave after the winter and looking around for something to eat, can you?"

"I don't think they're from this —" I started.

Jake raised a hand. "She's almost here. So… I'll see you around, I guess." With that, Jake gave a polite tilt of his head, then turned and ducked into the trees.

"Hold on!" Bobby called. "Why don't we all talk together? Figure this out?" But Jake was gone, his fuzzy beacon diminishing even as another one got louder and clearer in our minds.

"I guess you boys have a choice to make," a voice said from behind our backs. A voice I had only ever heard in a dream. Amazingly, it sounded just as I remembered.

Pip.

15

She spoke to Bobby almost exclusively. Like she had nothing to say to me at all. Maybe it was because she didn't know me, or maybe somehow she knew I knew things about her and she didn't like that. Her red hair flowed in waves down over her shoulders and her untucked flannel shirt. Jeans and boots completed the outfit — rugged, but, you know, in a kind of attractive way. Something dark poked above one shoulder,. The hilt of the sword she'd used when she attacked Omicron. Despite my powers, I found her self-assured demeanor intimidating. Not because of veiled threats like Jake, but instead from the sense of her calm certainty that she could kick both of our asses if she wanted.

Pip and Bobby talked. Around me, sort of like I wasn't there or didn't exist. It got me a little pissed off. She brought up our *choice* — what were we going to do about the Gorgols? Fight them with her, or let them go like Jake was doing? I tried to interject. To say the whole reason we came across the country was to try to stop the Gorgols.

Then I told her how the creatures were coming for my sister. And I saw a strange gleam in her eye. Compassion?

But she simply turned to Bobby and said, "Is that true?"

"Yep."

She looked Bobby up and down, even spared a quick glance at me. "Did you bring weapons?"

Bobby struck a mock-confident pose and smirk. "We *are* the weapons, babe." For a moment, he seemed very pleased with his joke.

Then a blur passed from where Pip had been standing to where Bobby was suddenly sprawled on the floor. When it cleared, Pip was leaning over him, sword raised over her head.

"*Ow*," Bobby said, rubbing at his left leg. "What'd you do that for?"

I realized then that her sword was still in its scabbard, completely encasing the blade. She hadn't *slashed* at Bobby's leg, she had *bludgeoned* him.

"I am well aware that you have powers, Bobby Graden —"
For a brief moment, she acknowledged me again. "That
you *both* have powers. But fighters across the centuries
have understood that weapons are a tool to *enhance* the
power you already have, even to overcome the odds. Take
the biggest, toughest wrestler, and put her up against a
person with a sword and average ability, the wrestler
loses."

Bobby stood up, wiping dirt from his pants and shirt.
"Well, I didn't bring anything. Sorry."

I cleared my throat. "I have —" I remembered something
from my travels to find Sol. A sort of a weapon I'd made
by accident. There were these dogs. I thought they were
big, so I was scared. They turned out to be nothing, just
little things. Still, I made a weapon somehow. *Made* it. But
it was ridiculous. Why did I open my mouth? I froze,
saying nothing more.

Pip squinted a look my way. "You have *what*?"

Well, I had really put my foot in it. I had two choices.
Make up a lame excuse or just say it. What the hell did I
care? We were three people with very strange abilities. I
figured I would just plow forward and accept their ridicule.
"When I was traveling, trying to find Sol, I did something
accidentally. I think I could do it again if I tried." I found
that believing you could do something greatly affected
whether you actually could, at least for me. For me and my
powers.

"What are you talking about?" Bobby asked.

"This." I unbuckled my belt. That was when Pip's eyes grew *really* wide. "Wait," I said, raising my hand, palm out. "It's not what you think! Anyway, well. Just watch." Since I was already making a fool of myself, I decided to do it with some style. I whipped the belt from around my waist in one quick motion, snapping it out straight. And it froze, solid, mirroring the sword still in Pip's hand. "Heh. It *worked.*"

Bobby and Pip held their breath.

For like a second.

Then they both cracked up, nearly collapsing to the ground in laughter. "Johnny, what the hell are you going to do with that?" Bobby said. "Give the Gorgols a spanking?"

I knew it looked nuts. A belt, hardened to a solid weapon by my mind and the thorns in my cells. But I wanted to prove my point. So first I willed the weapon to be *sharp*. Then I swung the belt — now technically a sort of belt *sword* — in a wide horizontal arc toward the trunk of the nearest orange tree. It must've been eight inches thick.

But my belt sword sliced all the way through it, and all three of us had to leap out of the way of the falling foliage.

"What the —?" Bobby shook his head. "Dude, that's just… *weird.*"

* * *

We walked for some time, heading west. Pip was 20 feet or so ahead, leading us to the Gorgols, I assumed. Or her secret underground lair, or a trap, or a fast-food restaurant, for all I knew. She didn't say much to me, didn't really look at me. So I had no idea.

"What's her deal?" I asked Bobby. It was obvious that I was unhappy with how she ignored me.

He laughed. "You don't get it, huh?"

"Get *what?*"

"Johnny, she's *scared* of you. You *killed* Sol. She was one of the group, in fact the one that stayed right to the end. She knew what Sol could do. Maybe she stayed with him partly out of fear. Then you walked up and killed him. And you're a couple years younger than her — meaning she thinks you're just a kid. If you can kill Sol, I guess she really doesn't know what to make of you. And that scares her."

"I know she took care of Holly, but still, like you said, she *stayed* with Sol. Is she crazy, too?"

Bobby gave a nod. "Maybe. Maybe we all are. What sane people sneak across the country to try to kill two giant monsters? Besides, it doesn't really matter any more, does it? Sol's gone. That ship has sailed. Now we're all on our own. Or, you know, we are unless we choose to work together, like now. I think she knows she needs our help against these things. And if she's afraid you're stronger than her, then she wants you here most of all. She just doesn't have to *like* you or *talk* to you too much, right?"

"I suppose," I said.

Ahead, Pip stopped walking, holding up one hand but not even bothering to look back toward us as she spoke.

"We're here."

16

"You have a secret underground lair?" I said, turning to take in the room.

Pip huffed, tossing her sword onto a low table. "I have a *place to stay*, asshole."

"Children, please!" Bobby interjected. "*Language*." He smirked, too enamored with his own joke.

My eyes widened as I took in more and more of Pip's "place to stay." Maybe at some point vacationers or college-age beach goers had rented it for cheap. She told us it was several miles from the water — a small, basement apartment, embedded under a house that seemed abandoned. Whether said abandonment was recent — in other words, Gorgol-induced — I had no idea, but I assumed so. The walls and appliances were intact, and seemed well-kept. More importantly, there were working lights, which meant electricity, and a phone in the corner that still had a dial tone. Someone had bugged out in a hurry.

The apartment opened onto a small living room with a narrow kitchen. Past a closet that might have been a pantry, there was a short hall that ended on two doors — a bathroom in front, and a bedroom to the right. The furniture was worn but not worn out. Still, the whole place had the feel of my Aunt Cindy's place. A sort of time warp of patterned decor and rounded corners in colors that shouted, "This stuff has been here for a while!"

But that wasn't what stood out. Around the living room, Pip had made some modifications. Every open wall had been adorned with peg board, and every peg board held weapons. Swords, daggers, knives, machetes. But no guns. In fact, nothing that fired a projectile of any kind, not even bows or crossbows. All blade weapons.

"Why no guns?" I asked without remembering how *anything* I said seemed to annoy Pip.

She got annoyed. Shocker.

"For people like us," she said, flipping a curl of red hair out of her face as she gestured to herself, Bobby, me, "guns are useless. We need hand weapons."

Bobby beat me to the obvious question. "Why?"

"We can dodge bullets. We can even throw bullets with our minds, but what would be the point? The Gorgols seem impervious to them. And anyone else like us could just throw them back." Pip pulled out her sword again, eyeing it as she guided it in slow arcs before us. "But a weapon in your hand. A sword. It takes on some of your powers. It's a natural extension of *us*."

"*A natural extension*," I repeated. It had to be true. After all, my department-store leather belt wasn't normally capable of chopping down trees.

"Yeah."

I pondered the idea for a moment. "What can you do with it?"

It seemed that the simple act of me speaking was enough to grate on Pip. I had to try to remember Bobby's words, that she might be scared of me. It didn't seem that way at all, talking to her. She looked like she wanted nothing more than to buy me a one-way bus ticket to somewhere far away. Still, she explained. "You can fight. If you try very hard, study, maybe you can win." Pip eyed me a moment, twisting up her mouth. That curl of red hair drooped over her face again, and she tossed it aside with a tilt of her head. Pip was pretty, make no doubt. The hair flip was, well, *interesting*. It suddenly came back to me that at one point, when she existed only in my dreams, I thought of her as my dream girl. Then she asked a perplexing question. "Have you read the Codex Wallerstein? Talhoffer 1467?"

I wrinkled up my forehead. "You might as well have just said *banana, banana, banana*."

Pip sighed, heavy and hard. Then she walked to the only chair in the room and dropped into it. "This is impossible. We have to act now, before more people get killed, and you guys aren't ready. You're worried about these things getting to your sister and yet you don't know anything, can't do anything. Why did you even come out here?"

I looked at Bobby in a sort of *what the heck is her deal?* way. Bobby shrugged and tried to smooth things over. "Listen, Pip. We came to help. If we have to read the Talisman 1492 or the Wolfenstein Code, you know, we'll do it." I raised an eyebrow at him, both for his butchering of the titles and because I knew he was more likely to use a book to prop up one corner of a table than to read it. "Well, we'll try. Honest." He put his hand over his heart and made some sort of salute.

Pip sniffed at the air. "What's that smell? Oh, yeah, it's bullshit." She sat there a moment, looking back and forth between us. Then she must have decided something. "Fine. Come outside," she said.

* * *

Pip led us to a backyard ringed by a high fence. The neighboring houses were farther away than I was used to back home, meaning that rather than seeing adjacent windows looking down on us, it seemed we were 100-percent private. In all honesty, I was glad. We looked pretty stupid.

Bobby, Pip, and I each held a long sword. A freaking *sword*. I kid you not. As a guy who grew up in the suburbs, I'd only seen swords in museums or at the Renaissance Festival. Sure, like everyone who attended the Ren Fest — you do, don't you? — I always picked up the demo swords at the booth where they were sold, and I would play-fight with my friends, quoting movies like a dork. But despite my demonstration with the belt, the idea of actually swinging a sharp metal object with the intent of cutting or killing someone was completely alien to me. I didn't know if I had it in me. Plus, I just felt like an idiot.

"Try to hit me," Pip said. To me. *Why do I have to go first?*

"Me?" I said, stalling for time.

"No," she replied. I sighed with relief. "Both of you together."

"Pip, I don't think that's such a good idea," Bobby said. "We don't want to hurt you or anything."

In response, Pip lashed out with the flat side of her blade, hitting Bobby in the head faster than his body could react.

He flew across the yard and slammed into the fence, rattling the wood slats. Though unharmed, Bobby certainly looked ticked off. He stood and raised his long metal blade with both hands. "Have it your way," he said, just before launching himself straight for Pip.

She met him halfway, dropping her own sword and reaching out for Bobby's blade with both hands, using his own momentum to pull and carry him too far, then wrenching the sword free. As soon as she gained control of it, Pip swung the sword by its blade, clobbering Bobby with the hilt end like a hammer. Bobby's body shifted, but not far enough, not fast enough. The blow sent him crashing straight down, face first in the dirt and grass, with a loud *Oof.*

"That's called the *murder stroke*," Pip said, still holding Bobby's sword by its blade. "Effective, don't you think?"

I grinned, a silly, pandering grin toward Pip. "'Murder stroke'? That's... lovely."

She relaxed, letting the sword fall to her side, and allowing Bobby to get up. "And that's your first lesson, boys. The point of it was this: You don't know anything. Nothing at all. Take a breather, we're doing this again soon."

17

"Where'd you learn this crap? It wasn't from Sol," Bobby said as we snacked on peanut-butter-and-jelly sandwiches in Pip's kitchen.

Pip huffed. "Sol was a pompous ass. He was powerful, but..." For a quick moment, Pip looked my way. "You need to think about this, boys. You can learn from *anything*, not just from people like us. There are hundreds of years of warfare strategy written down. Read some of it."

Bobby didn't respond, he just smirked and nodded. An expression we all knew meant *Thanks, but no thanks*.

Pip dropped her sandwich. "Do you think your enemy — maybe not this one, but the next, or the one after that — is so blissfully unaware of war tactics? If that's the case, you'll win every time. But what if she or he or it's not? What if your opponent has spent a bit of time *learning*?" She raised the sandwich and took a healthy bite, chewing slowly. "Worst-case scenario: What if your enemy is as powerful as you, John Black?" I was stunned she addressed me directly. "You need something else on your side. I think knowledge and tactics are the difference makers." Pip swallowed. "Without those, you're dead."

It was the first time Pip jump-started my anger. That little fire started up inside. "But I beat Sol without studying tactics," I said.

Pip took a final bite, leaving nothing but crust. Then she tossed the remainder of her sandwich into a white plastic trash can on the side of the kitchen, in a huff. "Did you ever think you just got lucky? Sol underestimated you. Don't expect that from every opponent, or you won't live much longer."

"Look," I said. "I don't plan on having more fights."

"Then I hope your luck holds, because you don't have anything else on your side any more." Again, she brushed a lock of curls out of her eyes. "People with power… they draw attention. Why do you think Holly has needed you? Because she *draws attention*." Then Pip ducked out to the backyard again.

* * *

"Why do you want to fight the Gorgols?" Pip asked, sun glinting off her red hair as we stood in the afternoon light of the back yard.

There was a long pause. We were tired and sweaty from fighting each other. Well, Bobby and I were tired of getting our butts kicked. Pip seemed fine.

"For my sister," I said, lowering my sword to the ground.

Pip blinked sweat out of her eyes. "And that's all?"

"To stop the killing. To save people," Bobby said.

"To be a hero?" Pip asked.

Bobby scratched the side of his head with one ruddy hand. "Sure, I guess."

"With superpowers. You want to be a superhero?" Pip smiled. And she looked at me.

I almost answered. Almost.

Yeah. That's what I wanted. I wanted to slay the dragon and have someone look at me and say *Wow, nice job!*

Which was a lie. I might be flattered by that, but it wasn't the real why.

I wanted to fight because something about the idea of fighting was appealing to me.

I almost answered.

Then Pip shifted and asked Bobby the same question. "You want to be a superhero?"

"Well, it sounds kinda ridiculous when you put it that way," Bobby said, shoulders drooping.

"Why?" Pip asked, with renewed energy. "Before, with Sol, you and I were absolutely lining ourselves up to be super villains. You know that, right?"

"Yeah, but I didn't think *you* did. I always thought you were trying to bring out the good in Sol."

Pip laughed. "Maybe I was for a while, but that was a losing battle. At some point I realized he was always going to be a villain. Just listening to him talk, especially the way he talked to normal people, and you knew he was just *bad*."

"And that's why I left," Bobby replied. "But you didn't."

Pip's face darkened and wrinkled with anger. "I made a *choice*."

"The choice to stay with evil?" I asked.

Pip wheeled on me. "The choice to help *your* sister, John Black. Everyone else had left. Bobby, Petrus, Margrethe. If I had left, too, your sister would have been alone with Sol. Would you have preferred that?"

"No," I muttered, not sure of what to say. "Thank you. Thanks for what you did." I looked at my shoes.

"You don't need to thank me. I did it because I thought it was right. Just like I think fighting the Gorgols is the right thing to do now. It's just interesting how both choices amount to the same thing, helping your sister. But now..." She turned to Bobby and started to smile. "Rather than being villains — or worse, just being some villain's henchmen — we have a chance to be heroes. Doesn't that feel... *better*?"

Bobby started to nod, a smile growing on his face like Pip's. He laughed. "Yeah, I suppose so. But calling *us* superheroes still sounds ridiculous." Then Bobby thought of something. "You know what they call you, right?"

Pip rolled her eyes. "Sadly, yes. *Red Hope*. But you guys better get ready. Once we do this thing, people will see you. They're gonna call *you* something, too." She laughed, jabbing a finger in our direction. "But if you don't want them knowing who you are, you're going to need masks like mine. Come with me." Pip led us inside, to the pantry-closet thing, where she pulled open the accordion-style door. Lining the shelves inside were boxes and cans of food, bottles of soda, bags of snacks. She knelt down and picked up two things from the lowest shelf, tucked back far where we would never have noticed them — a black hooded mask and a yellow one. "I figured we'd meet, especially once you started making all that noise in my head. I figured you'd need these."

"*IWANTTHEBLACKONE!*" Bobby and I said simultaneously, hands reaching for the same mask. Pip pulled the masks back before we could start fighting over them.

"Jinx, you owe me a soda," Bobby said with a half-hearted laugh.

"I guess you boys are going to need to work this out," Pip said.

"Nah," I said, taking a step back. "You can have the black mask, Bobby." So gracious of me. Inside, I was kicking myself.

"Yes!" Bobby snatched the mask from Pip's hands and raised it to his head to try it on. But he never did. He stopped. And then he held it out to me. "You earned it, Johnny. You took down Sol."

It was such a silly thing for us to argue over or even care about. A black piece of cloth versus a yellow one. And why the hell didn't Pip just get *two* black masks? *Probably to test us. To see how juvenile we are.*

"Besides," Bobby said, shaking the mask in his hand for me to take it. "You're John Black. You need the black mask." I nodded a thanks.

What had we become? A trio of superheroes. Or wannabe superheroes. It was utterly laughable. So of course, we tried on our masks. "You look ridiculous, by the way," Bobby said. We stood in the living room, admiring each other's absurd appearance. Bobby's yellow hooded mask covered his entire head except for a generous opening around his eyes, presumably large enough to ensure decent range of vision.

"I know what they'll call us," I said, tugging off my black mask. "Blackbird and Canary Man."

"Those names don't really work with mine. Red Hope is so much more majestic," Pip said, unable to stifle a laugh.

In a moment, we were all laughing.

* * *

Forty-eight hours later, all we had done was eat, sleep, and train. I can't say it was very helpful or effective. I mean, I had no idea how long Pip had trained with a sword, but I was pretty sure a few sessions for Bobby and me wouldn't make much of a difference. The only benefit I noticed was that the sword felt less alien in my hands.

"How are you so good at this?" I asked Pip at one point when Bobby excused himself.

I could tell Pip was a little embarrassed by the question. "My dad," she said. "He was a big nerd. Into all sorts of medieval fighting techniques. He taught me from a pretty young age. When he was in a good mood, that is." Pip effortlessly slipped her sword back into the vertical scabbard on her back. I didn't know much about medieval fighting, but I assumed her back-scabbard was a more modern adaptation. "What about you? Your dad teach you anything cool? Anything useful?"

I thought about my father, and was unable to meet Pip's eyes. "I think so."

"What?"

"One time when I was using my powers for no good reason, I accidentally killed my father." I didn't say that to be dramatic. It was the truth. I didn't feel like hiding it or beating around the bush.

Pip looked down. "I'm sorry." She let the words hang. Maybe she didn't know what else to say. Maybe she was letting those two words hold their own weight for a moment. "My dad's gone, too. Just so you know."

"How?"

"Lung cancer. It took a while. At the end it was really… terrible. If I could use my powers to cure lung cancer — well, any cancer, really — I'd do it. Even after he was…"

Was what? She trailed off and I thought of the thorns. Were they cancer-proof? I had no idea. There was a long and rather uncomfortable silence, until I finally spoke. "Morality."

"Huh?" Pip replied.

"That's what my dad taught me. To try to do what's right."

Pip and I held each other's glance for a long time. Finally, she nodded. I think at that moment she accepted me. Her gesture wasn't just the vacant pleasantry of casual human interaction. She nodded to someone she respected. Something had changed between us. "And that explains why you're here. You're doing what's right. Not just for your sister, but for the world."

At just that moment, we heard the muffled sound of a toilet flush. Water ran, easily for three seconds, then Bobby opened the bathroom door. "All right. I'm ready for day 468 of Pip's Master Classes in Nuking Hot Dogs and Learning Sword Fighting. Who's in?"

"Very funny, jerk," Pip replied.

Two days. We've been here two full days already. She'll think we're dead. And what if the cars full of photographers have come back? "That reminds me," I said. "I need to call my mom."

18

"Hi, Mom."

"John!" Clearly Mom was anxious. "You're okay? I
haven't... you know, seen anything on TV."

"We haven't quite reached the Gorgols yet," I said. I
explained about meeting Pip, staying with her.

"You boys are sleeping in that girl's apartment?" Mom
asked, with a tense tone to her voice.

I had to laugh. Of all the things to worry about. We were
attempting to defeat giant monsters, and my mom was
concerned about a little hanky-panky. "It's not like that!" I
said, face flushing. "Remember, you were the one
concerned about us stealing things like plane tickets and

hotel rooms. Here, we're just Pip's guests." Bobby shot me a look and I rolled my eyes.

"I'll be outside, nerds," Pip said, walking out. Clearly she had inferred the gist of my conversation.

"John, it's been days. What's your plan? Are you all still going to…?"

"Yeah, we are. Soon."

Mom paused. Her next words sounded embarrassed. "What have you all been doing all this time?"

"Training with swords," I replied. "A lot."

"Swords? Really? Do you think that will help?"

"Pip seems to think so. Personally, I wonder how a three-foot metal sword is going to help me kill a 200-foot, armor-plated monster." I chuckled at how ridiculous it sounded. "But I suppose it's slightly better than the *just show up and wing it* plan that Bobby and I had in mind."

"Not funny, John. You be careful. *Both* of you. No, *all three* of you. And watch each other's backs."

"We will, Mom."

"Thank you for this. For your sister."

I didn't say anything. We both knew what the other felt.

"And John, remember. I can't keep fooling people that you're home sick forever. School isn't waiting on us. Too much longer, and people will start asking questions."

"Okay, Mom." *Hurry up and kill the giant monsters, son. It's a school night.* But I knew what she meant. We wanted to stay anonymous, and we were about to do the most public thing possible. Still, a part of me wanted to be public — had wanted to be public for a long time. But I knew instinctively that being public with powers like we had would only lead to unwanted attention. The paparazzi would look tame in comparison. "Love you. Tell Holly I love her, too."

"I love you, too, John. Come home safe, soon."

I didn't reply. Well, I nodded. As if she could hear that. I just didn't want to promise anything.

* * *

"So how's your mom?" Pip said with a smirk.

"Don't mock," I replied.

"I'm not. It's, I don't know — kinda sweet."

"What about you? You've got a mom somewhere, too, after all."

I could tell right away I had said something wrong. "That's not always true, you know?" Pip turned and walked into the yard, then faced us again, raising her sword. Her face looked cold, hard. "It's time to learn the last trick I have for you, boys. Attack me."

Bobby looked at me, shrugged, and then immediately leapt toward Pip. I started to follow, but before I took even two steps, I saw Pip lash out with her sword. No, it was something different. A staff maybe. But where did it come from? Bobby took a blow to the side of the head, even as his body tried to sluice away from it. The force redirected his energy and sent him tumbling to the ground in a heap. "What the hell was *that*?" he said, already reaching for his head.

Pip pulled back and stood straight. In her hands was the same sword she'd been holding a moment before. "That, lads, is what *we* can do with a sword."

"But something changed," I said. "You weren't holding a sword when you hit Bobby."

Pip smiled, enjoying knowing more than we did. "But I was. I just made it *more* than a sword. Well, technically, that's wrong, since it seems to be the same mass. I just reconfigured it into something longer."

"How?" Bobby stood, more curious than hurt.

Pip held her sword with both hands in front of her, angled upward. Then, as we all watched, the sword slowly grew longer while it simultaneously got thinner. "It's like the way our bodies shift, only you're telling it to happen. I've seen you two shift your bodies on purpose — I was watching you spar in the orange fields, and I've seen it here in training. And because the sword is in your hand, you can make it do what you want, too." She paused, glancing back and forth at us with just a bit of a haughty look. "Before you even ask, I tried doing this with things I wasn't holding and it never works. But in my hand, I can turn a three foot sword into a sharply pointed six foot metal rod, maybe bigger."

"That's incredible," I said. "But… is it enough to beat something 200 feet tall?"

There was a long moment of silence. "It'll have to be. But I want us all to try something. Follow me."

* * *

She led us down the street, to where an old wooden fence blocked the way. Turning, she followed the fence before finally stopping at an unremarkable section. Reaching out, she pulled at the wood slats and they moved aside, making a hole large enough for us to enter.

Inside we saw a parking lot. Most of the spaces were empty, but a few cars and trucks were scattered about.

"We're stealing a car?" Bobby asked.

"No, of course not, doofus," Pip said. Something about how she talked to him... I couldn't figure out if she thought nothing of Bobby, or an awful lot. "See that rusted red truck, in the last spot?"

"Yeah? What about it?"

"This is a commuter lot. That's why it's mostly empty now. But that truck," she said, jabbing a finger toward the old rust bucket. "That truck has been here for weeks. It's never moved. I've noticed."

"So?" I asked.

"It's abandoned."

I waited a moment, still trying to grasp the importance. When I couldn't, I repeated: "*So?*"

"So, we're going to slice it to pieces with our swords. It's the best thing I could think of to emulate the Gorgols' armor. If you can use a basic sword to slice apart the metal of a truck, well, that'll be a start."

Bobby and I both shrugged.

We walked toward the truck, slowly circling it. On the far side, I saw a long, thin gash in one of the doors, and another on the rear panel. "You've been at this before." Pip nodded. "Okay, so how do we do your little trick?"

"Clear your mind, raise your weapon, then reach *through* it with your mind. That's about the best way I can describe it. Stretch it with your mind. Like you're a little kid trying to reach the cookie jar on a high shelf. Reach as high as you can. *Stretch*."

Bobby and I raised our swords, as Pip did the same. Pip's sword stretched easily out in front of her, growing longer. After a few moments, Bobby's began to slowly extend as well. Mine, of course, was stubborn.

"John?" Pip said. "You okay?"

I nodded. "Sure, I'm okay, but I've never been the one to learn new things fast. Not with these powers. Not like Bobby."

Pip's sword shrank back to its normal size and sagged toward the ground. "You've gotta be kidding me."

I shook my head. "Nope."

"He's not kidding," Bobby added.

"You beat Sol, somehow, and you can't do *this*?" Pip was dumbfounded.

"Hey," Bobby said, stepping between us. "Just give him a minute."

"It's okay," I said. "I'm bad at learning new things. I accept that."

Bobby turned back to me. "But that's not true, Johnny. Sure, you seem to struggle with the things the rest of us master fairly quickly…" I was hideously embarrassed, but Bobby just shrugged with an inaudible *sorry*. "But you *create* these things — these *solutions* — none of us ever even dream of. You destroyed Petrus, and Sol. I have no idea if I could've done either of those things."

"I'm not terribly proud of killing people," I said, my own sword dropping.

Oddly, it was Pip who spoke words of encouragement. "But sometimes, you have to." After a moment, I nodded, knowing it was true. "Try again," she said.

I raised the sword a second time, and concentrated.

Nothing.

Nothing.

It would never work. I could never make it work. There was no point in trying.

I gave up.

And the sword suddenly stretched into a thin metal beam, at least 15 feet long, razor sharp along its edges.

Finally, Pip spoke a word that encapsulated the thoughts of all three of us. "*Whoa.*"

19

"Well, I think you've got the basic idea down," Pip said after we'd finished slicing the rusty red truck into about 6,000 small parts.

Bobby lowered his sword, allowing it to shrink back to normal size. "What do we do now?"

Pip eyed us, back and forth. "We take down some monsters."

* * *

"Um, where do we go? How do we do this?" I said.

"You just have to follow me. It'll take nearly an hour to walk there, but the Gorgols have been along the shore. Unless they suddenly left, they'll be there."

"You mean unless they suddenly decided to go pay Holly a visit?" Bobby asked.

Pip nodded and shrugged at the same time. "I don't think that's happened yet. They keep returning to the shore. It's like they want to head east, but something keeps drawing them back."

So we walked. We walked forever in the heat.

Did I mention we were carrying swords on our backs and wearing large, hooded masks? If there was one way to make a warm day feel like a blisteringly hot day, it's to cover your head with a mask and lug around a heavy metal object. At times, I felt like I couldn't breathe from the heat inside the mask. But we didn't dare take them off — we were walking into a place saturated with media, and we were wearing swords. The three of us wouldn't remain unobserved for long. So I kept my black hood up, Pip wore her red, and Bobby had his yellow one.

We walked, and walked, and walked. We nearly collapsed.

Okay, we walked for maybe 45 minutes. It was warm, but still, it was autumn, so the heat could've been much worse. As we crested what amounted to a rise in the flat lands near the western sea, Bobby spoke. "Where the hell are they?" he said.

Pip scanned back and forth across a land that looked like it had been utterly devastated by the monsters. "I have no idea." Below us, houses, buildings, cars, telephone poles — anything that normally would stick up from the ground — had been trampled down. The Gorgols had been very thorough. Whatever the town used to be called, it wouldn't need a name anymore. This town was gone.

"Maybe they went back into the sea," Bobby offered, with a hopeful tone. Pip tugged her sword from its scabbard. Bobby tried again: "Maybe they don't want to bother with us people anymore."

Pip turned, raising an eyebrow. "Cold feet, Bobby?"

Bobby flushed. "'Course not." He pushed past Pip, over the ridge, and led us into the desolation of the Gorgols.

"Hold on," Pip said, raising her voice to stop him. "We need to fan out. No use making it so that one measly swipe crushes all of us." There was only so much she could teach us in a few days, so we just had to accept that we were pawns waiting to be shifted on a chess board, ready to go where Pip directed. We formed a wide triangle, with her in the center, out in front leading the way. Bobby was behind and to her right, maybe separated by 50 yards. I took up a similar position off to the rear left. Then we slowly walked forward, picking our way through the rubble toward a tall cliff that edged the sea.

"You know," Bobby shouted from his side, "it might have been smart to turn on a TV or check online this morning, to figure out where the Gorgols are."

"I did," Pip yelled back. "They've been circling into the sea, sometimes underwater, sometimes making a wide arc on land. I'm guessing they're in the water now, since I don't notice any giant monsters around, do you?"

"Negatory, mornin' glory," Bobby replied.

"Look!" I shouted, pointing at a helicopter racing toward us from the northwest, on a vector that was about halfway between Pip and Bobby from my angle.

Even from far away, I could see Pip sigh. "Get ready, boys. You're about to become famous."

Famous. The word was exciting and terrifying at the same time. But who was I kidding. *I* wasn't about to become famous. Some masked superpowered guy was. *Oh God, the nickname thing. Please please don't make it lame.*

The chopper zipped toward us, then made a wide circle overhead, a large camera locked on us the entire time.

Pip turned back to us, pausing our march to the sea momentarily. "No names now, boys. Go by color." I nodded as Pip looked my way. "Spread out a bit more, Black." Then she turned to Bobby. "Yellow, ready?" He also nodded, then Pip continued to lead us toward the cliff.

It was the slowest, most surreal march of my life. From afar, the landscape looked flat as a pancake. Up close, it was littered with all sorts of debris that we had to work around, over, or through, some of it much taller than us. All the while, the helicopter circled overhead. We were no doubt the ratings magnets of the day for the 24-hour news channels. After a short while, two more helicopters joined the first.

"I don't like this, Pi— I mean, Red," I said. "I feel like I'm in a fishbowl." I looked up at one of the choppers. "And I get the feeling that everyone knows what we're walking into except us."

"Feeder fish," Bobby yelled, so I could hear him over the *whump whump* of the rotors.

"What're you talking about, Yellow?" Pip replied, still inching forward. The edge of the cliff was getting close.

"When you have a predator fish as a pet, like an oscar or even a piranha, you drop feeder fish into the tank from time to time. To keep the predator fed."

"You think *we're* feeder fish?" I asked.

Bobby walked silently for a moment. "Well, I really hope not."

Ahead of us, Pip reached the cliff and stood looking down into the sea. She raised her sword defensively, ready for anything. Bobby and I instinctively paused, swords mirroring Pip's. Almost all of our focus remained on her, but I noticed that one of the helicopters was peeling away to race back toward the northeast, behind us on Bobby's side.

Pip turned around, sword lowering. "Nothing. So I guess we wait until the monsters show up."

Be careful what you wish for.

I didn't even have time to think that, as the tightly tucked, rolling form of Omicron smashed into the cliff below Pip, flipping over the edge and directly into her. Pip's body sluiced, but I couldn't tell if it was enough. Omicron rolled over her and cut between Bobby and me like a giant bowling ball leaving a 7-10 split.

There was no time to think about Pip as Omicron unrolled behind us, wheeling his massive form around. Bobby and I spun, swords up. I can't speak for him, but for me, the few days we'd spent training disappeared completely from my mind. I felt like I'd brought a butter knife to a bazooka fight, and I didn't even know how to butter bread.

Up close, Omicron was terrifying. All teeth and claws and stone-like scales. *Oh God. What exactly were you thinking, John? You're going to get yourself killed.*

First puffing up, then pushing down upon itself, the monster gave its cry, and where before the sound had been like hell unleashed through our TV speakers, now the blast was directed at me. A wall of sound crashed into me, making me flinch back. With the deafening roar came a foul wind, the breath of the beast, like seafood left in the trash for days on end. It was almost enough to turn my stomach. Somewhere in the back of my mind I realized that even Omicron's breath was too much for me. I could see the sword shaking in my hand. I was frozen and shivering, facing my doom.

The monster was incredible. There was no way we could beat it. Gorgol Omicron towered over us, even when he was hunkered down. Looking up toward his tapered, stone-like head was like staring at the sheer face of a tall building. Omicron's back was even worse, scaled with massive, pointed, rocky armor, but that didn't matter at all. I would never even consider attacking from the back. Besides, he was facing me. And having his attention was enough to instantly make my blood turn cold. His massive underbelly towered above me, framed by his outstretched forearms with their spiked fingers. Remembering the dragon movie from the plane, I knew the underbelly was typically a monster's soft spot, so I scanned Omicron for any sign of weakness. Instead, I came away with the feeling that his armor was flawless and impenetrable. His underbelly looked like the chest plate a baseball umpire would wear, if that plate was made of solid, brownish-black stone. Maybe there were soft spots, the underarms perhaps, but how could I get to them, when they were behind Omicron's powerful arms and claws, ready to rip me apart and crush me to death?

It was utterly hopeless.

Just then, a yellow blur zipped in toward Omicron's far leg. There was a flash of something — Bobby's sword — and suddenly the Gorgol's voice changed from rage to pain. The big creature swept its claws toward where Bobby stood, only to tear into the rock. Bobby had sluiced away.

He's actually fighting it, I thought. Dimly, another idea came to me. *I could actually fight it, too. Maybe, together, it won't be hopeless.*

We can do this!

I raced in to join my friend. And like the hapless first wave of infantry in every war movie I'd ever seen, I became cannon fodder. I was immediately sent flying through the air by a single well-timed swipe from Omicron. My consciousness picked up its punchcard, slipped it into the time clock, and checked out. It was quittin' time.

20

Flipping end over end through the air, the tangy mist of sea-salt air filling my nose, I thought of my father.

Is this what it was like? Those last horrible moments?

I felt like something inside, a light, my fire, popped off and was gone.

It must have taken no more than a second, but for me it seemed like minutes, maybe hours. My mind's eye saw my dad. Not the friendly face of the father who taught me to ride a bike, helped with homework, grilled burgers. Not even the dead face I remembered from his wake the day before we buried him. Instead, I saw a face of *horror*. A face that knew what fate had in store.

I saw the face of my father moments before his death, the
way he must have looked, grimacing in fear, flipping end
over end, gripping the steering wheel as his car did its last,
terminal acrobatics.

No.

Then…

Yes. I deserve it.

This must be how I died. Why else would I have this
vision? In ultra-slow motion, a part of my brain knew that
my flying body would soon hit something hard and painful.
Something that would end my life.

And I deserved it.

I killed my own father. That was called patricide. I was
guilty. A sin I would carry to my rapidly approaching
grave.

And it wasn't just him. I carried the weight of other deaths,
too. Walter Ivory. Petrus. Sol. Despite what they were,
what they tried to do, they were human, they had lives.
Maybe even loved ones. I knew Petrus had Margrethe, until
I robbed them of each other. Was Margrethe still out there,
mind altered by me to forget all about what I had done? Or
had my mental push worn off? Did she live every moment
wrapped in grief and anger?

Phillip Black. *Phil.* Dad.

Sol. Jose do Branco.

Walter Ivory.

Petrus.

Margrethe.

The lives I had snuffed out. Human lives. With my powers. My blessing, my curse.

If any part of my superpowers was controlled by a simple and pure desire to live, I extinguished that desire. The fire went out. I welcomed the impact, still flipping through the air.

In real time, barely an instant had passed. And then, I hit.

The feeling was worse than any I could remember, worse than when Sol had dashed me into the desert canyon wall. Gorgol Omicron had hit me with an unbelievable force, sent me reeling at an unbelievable speed.

The sharp, volcanic rocks of the shoreline tore my body. I knew my physical powers, to sluice and shift, to form and bend and reform. What if I were ripped to pieces? I didn't think there was any way to recover from that. After all, I had blown Sol to bits, and he was gone.

Through eyes that were blurred with blood or maybe tears, yet somehow still held a form, I looked at the sky, the brightness of the blue, the white clouds blending into a glow that I could barely tolerate.

Forever passed, and slowly my eyelids began to fall.

"John," she said.

Mom?

I couldn't speak. With waning effort, I reached out with my mind. *Mom?*

"John, use your powers. Will yourself back together, back to life."

No, Mom. It's too late. And... I deserve this.

"You can do it. You have to do it. Quickly."

No, I can't. I don't want to.

Her voice came closer. "You *have* to do it, John. *Now*."

Hands slid my mask upward, just enough. Then, she leaned close and kissed me.

Somewhere in my mind, a spark reignited. The kiss. It was not what I expected. Not the tender, loving kiss of my mother, the kiss I had known my whole life.

This was not my mother.

Which was good, because the kiss, her lips on mine, lasted for some time.

And something was *happening*. A warmth flowed from the kiss, into my brain, down into my body. Like an infusion of life, the kiss changed me. It ran through me, heightening my senses. The pain increased, but so did the burn of my powers healing me. My vision cleared.

The little fire inside popped back on. Tiny, but there.

"Pip?" I said, blinking.

She leaned backward, breaking the connection, her mask falling back down to cover her mouth. "Good. Come on — help me help you. Will yourself back together. I *know* you can." Still, her voice sounded far from confident. It sounded more like pleading.

The look in her eyes was one of deep concern. I could only assume based on that look that I was in very bad shape. I couldn't feel much of my body. I could see, barely hear, but touch? There seemed to be almost nothing. Was this shock, from all the pain? Still, the warmth burned through me. What had Pip done to me?

The little fire got bigger, just a bit.

Was it possible to combine powers? Or transfer them? There had been many surprises, learning my abilities. Pip had those abilities, too. Maybe...

"How...?" I started.

"Come on, John. Quickly. You're getting there, but we need you. Bobby's in trouble. He's all alone out there. Against both of them. Hurry!"

In trouble. Against both.

The Gorgols. In my state, they had seemed a million miles away. And at some point while I was out, Sigma had appeared. Sneaky little bastard. Well, she wasn't little, but you know what I mean.

I had given in to death, but death had eluded me, because of Pip. And then... if I let my friend die, and I lived, another death would be mine to carry.

My little fire suddenly puffed larger, not the tepid flickering of a single flame but the raging blaze of anger.

I shuffled one foot, pulling it under me, though I felt nothing. Not my shoe, not the ground. I simply willed it to happen.

Pip's eyes went wide. If I could have seen through the red mask she wore, I bet her mouth was agape. "My God...," she said.

I pulled the other foot, then pushed with both, forcing myself to stand. But somehow my point of view flipped upside down. I could feel my body, bent impossibly. Then it compressed. I guess those little thorns in my cells were doing their magic tricks. My body sluiced back to a standing form, and the world righted itself.

Pip stood before me, still in shock. "That was incredible."

I flexed my fingers, making and releasing fists. Then I shook my arms, made circles with my neck, reaching up to orient my mask so I could see. And finally, like all the gears had clicked into place, I was me again. "Where's Bobby?"

Shaking her head slightly, Pip turned, rushing off with sword in hand. "Follow me."

Sword.

I scanned the rocks around me, but my sword was nowhere to be found. "Pip! My sword!"

She paused, turning back. "Over there!" She pointed at the ground to my right, past a pile of cement rubble that once might have been part of a patio or sidewalk. Then, not sparing another moment, she ran again.

I had no choice but to follow, snatching up the weapon that I suddenly felt I must have. Why did I feel naked without it? I had trained for such a short time with the thing, why did I care?

Because it was *something*. Something that might stand between me and the monsters.

But I knew the only thing that could really help me — besides Pip, besides Bobby — was me.

And I was angry.

21

Running, dodging rubble, we could see the distant forms of Omicron and Sigma, their focus clearly on something.

From where we were, the two monsters seemed to be dancing, circling each other, almost like the gunslingers in the Westerns my dad showed me now and then when I was younger. As if someone was shooting at their feet and yelling *Dance!*

So much of this was like revisiting Saturday-morning movies. War movies, Westerns, monster movies.

My life was surreal. This, of course, was not the first or last time I thought such a thing.

I stopped running for a moment, watching. Sucking in air, Pip paused, too. "They're too big to attack something so small at the same time," I said. "It's like they're getting in each other's way." Then it dawned on me, and I grinned. "He's *playing* them!" I laughed out loud, looking to Pip.

But she didn't smile. If anything, she looked more determined than before. "He is *for now*. But he can't do it forever. Dodging those things even once is tiring. Bobby's gotta be exhausted." *Oh shit.* She was right. "If we don't get there now, any tiny mistake could be Bobby's last." She bolted, and I followed.

Coming over the next small rise, we could see more clearly, although we didn't stop to gawk. Bobby — his yellow mask a bright spot in the blighted landscape — was sluicing and jumping between the feet of the Gorgols, running dangerously close to one to avoid the other, back and forth. It truly seemed like he had worked out something to keep them at bay, yet it had to be wearing him down.

As soon as I thought that, Bobby stumbled. Sigma, standing upright on her thin legs, had swiped at him with one spiked claw, and Bobby had lost his footing at the exact wrong time. The monster's hand swept into him, sending him crashing backward, directly into one of Omicron's legs. The second creature wasted no time, punching downward. Bobby sluiced just in time to miss the brunt of the blow, but still took a sidelong glance. Again, he was sent flying, a yellow streak in the air. The Gorgols must have smelled blood. Sigma tucked into her lithe, snakelike form, slithering to one side to intercept Bobby, and caught him in her mouth, notched between two razor-sharp teeth. I knew Bobby was down to his last option.

Come on, Bobby, do something — we're almost there! And as if I willed it, Bobby's nearly lifeless form lurched, and he grabbed at the teeth on each side of his body. Sigma shook her head, but rather than letting himself be flung away, Bobby held on.

My fear and concern for Bobby made the anger inside me burn even brighter.

Pip and I ran, closing the distance. A cold fear spread down my spine as I thought about my first, extremely brief encounter Omicron just moments before. If I was taken out as quickly a second time, it seemed certain my friends would die. But I wanted the fight this time. I wanted to dive in head first. *Just don't be stupid, John, okay?* Running and slashing and simply hoping seemed futile. We were tiny, the Gorgols massive. Anger alone wasn't going to cut it.

We needed some kind of plan.

"Red!" I shouted, still running. I actually remembered to use her code name. An idea had come to me — limited, but better than nothing. "We need to separate them — together, they're too much."

Pip nodded. "I'll hit Sigma, you get to Omicron!"

Great. Omicron. That worked well the first time. Nonetheless, I nodded, angling myself toward the bulkier creature ahead. "Okay!" Pip peeled off toward Sigma. Fear and uncertainty filled me, but the burn inside tempered them both. I wanted this fight. *Omicron. Time for a payback.*

Ahead, Sigma, with Bobby still in her teeth, slammed her head toward the ground. Apparently he had found a way to hurt her, and she wanted him gone. When Sigma's head once again came up, Bobby was no longer in her mouth.

Nor were two of her teeth.

Way to go, Bobby! I thought, watching the action as I neared Omicron. The big, brown, stone-scale beast was distracted, watching his sister deal with Bobby. So I had an opening. A chance to attack Omicron where I wasn't just careening headlong into him. My only chance to deal a blow without the possibility of being hit first… of possibly being knocked out first, again.

I ran, my sword held high. And the world slowed.

As if time had been trapped in honey, everything passed by in muted, strangely dense air. I had a moment to think. *What do I expect to accomplish? Omicron is nearly 200 feet tall, and I'm not even six feet tall. At best, I give him a nasty cut on his toe.* There had to be some better idea.

My anger wasn't listening anymore. It was a desire to destroy this creature. The fact that the Gorgols were heading for my sister, for Holly, was just an idea, an abstract one. The fact that the monsters could kill Bobby or Pip at any moment was concrete and immediate. I needed to kill the beast, and I needed to do it *now*.

Higher. I need to get higher. Soft tissue. Internal organs. Maximum damage.

But how? The landscape had been smashed nearly flat wherever the Gorgols had tread. Except for some rocky outcroppings here and there, the valley provided no opportunities to meet Omicron at eye level. The edge of the valley was maybe a half-mile behind the creature, where the hills climbed upward. If I wanted to strike a real blow on Omicron, I had to reach the rocks.

But first things first.

I needed the Gorgol's attention. I needed to hit him, hard. And not in the toenail. But there was nothing to climb, no way nearby to get higher, unless…

Unless I can fly.

I laughed as I ran forward. *Fly?*

But Sol had done it, in a sort of hover. Bobby had done it, behind the shops that night. Could I? I failed the last time I'd tried. I remembered words my dad had said to me, so many times when trying to get me to do something I didn't want to do that had to be done. *No time like the present.*

So I tried again.

Finding the largest nearby rock as a launchpad, I leapt into the air, sword raised.

And beyond all belief — or maybe specifically because I wasn't *disbelieving* — I flew. Up and up in an impossible arc, one that should have already had me back on Earth, feet still running through the rubble. Instead, I floated upward toward the right side of the creature. My eyes were glued to the area below Omicron's right arm, the hopefully delicate side of his torso, the joint. I flipped my sword around to point down, both hands on the hilt ready to drive it deep into the gut of the beast.

I flew with a spiteful gleam in my eye, determined to kill.

I've heard the term bloodlust before, but I'm pretty sure this was the first time I ever felt it. I would bury my weapon in the side of the beast and he would die. The smile on my face must have looked twisted and frightening. I flew, a grimacing angel on wings of death. Or maybe just a dopey teenager in a silly mask with an outdated weapon. But, come on, I was going for the kill. Allow me to think I was a tiny bit cool, okay?

That is, until my arc began to decline.

No, come on! Higher! I demanded my body to fly upward again, and instantly dropped a dozen feet or more. Guess who wasn't smiling anymore? *Gah! Stop it, John, just go!* Thinking about it was bad. Thinking about it made me doubt myself. Thinking about it made me go down, not up.

I tried to clear my mind. Somewhere to my right I heard Pip cry out — not in pain, but a battle cry. I had to hope they were handling Sigma, that Bobby was okay.

My arc continued to fall, past the mid point of Omicron, down. Toward his right leg, directly at his knee.

That's fine, I thought with a renewed viciousness. *Taking out that joint might be enough.* I held the sword above my head with both hands, willing it stronger, willing it to dive deep into the knee of the creature. It grew and its point became more defined, looking more deadly. *It might be enough.*

Then I hit, and my sword bit into the stony flesh of Gorgol Omicron, just at the base of his knee. The creature's body sliced open and a dark viscous liquid poured out around me. I continued to fall, sword still in hand, cutting downward like a swashbuckler riding a stage curtain to the safety of the deck below. Only I didn't cut cloth, I cut skin. Hard, knobby, stone-like skin, but still skin. The bloodlust increased seeing, well, *blood.*

Omicron tensed. Then he shrieked, head facing down toward the pain, toward me. The sound seemed to shatter my eardrums.

Still my sword cut as I slid downward, opening a long vertical gash starting from my impact point near the knee. Omicron stumbled in pain, starting to topple.

It's working! My maniac's smile returned.

Then something hit me like a massive hammer to the back of the head. A hammer that my body once again could not avoid — despite all those silly hammer tricks Bobby and I had once dished out on one another. I was ripped away from Omicron by a downward swipe that sent me through the air, this time toward Omicron's short and scaly tail, over it, and beyond to the ground below.

But, thankfully, there were no rocks. No wall to be dashed against, just the relative flatness of the rubble. I hit the ground and rolled unceremoniously to a stop.

I was intact, but without a weapon — my sword must have remained jabbed into Omicron's leg. My body was in a heap, but compared to the first hit I had taken, I was okay. I pulled myself together and stood, looking toward the back of the monster.

It started to turn.

And there, in its right leg, I saw the gash I had made, my sword still poking out of the bottom of the bleeding cut. It must have been 25 feet or more, straight up and down, with the sword hilt at the bottom like the dot on an exclamation point. It seeped with the nearly black blood of the Gorgol.

Soon, a very angry Omicron would be facing me.

I stared, eager to see the damage I had done. Proud of myself. The anger inside feeding off it, loving it.

But Omicron was gigantic. Without a weapon, I had a serious problem. I either needed a way out or a new plan.

Over my shoulder, I spied the rocky edge of the valley, the only place I would find any place to hide. If I wanted to get away. If that was even possible.

And if it wasn't? If this was a fight to the death, no exceptions, no way out? It was also the only place where I could climb upward, meet Omicron face to face.

Face to face with nothing in my hand. Doofus and the beast.

It was a prospect that I both feared and welcomed.

22

I reached the pines at the base of the valley wall, climbing between large rocks, making my way up.

Behind me, Omicron wailed, so close that the pine needles shivered in the foul-smelling wind as I cringed against a boulder, expecting his massive jaws to clamp down on me and end the farce of my fight. When they didn't, I kept moving. I needed something. Some way to kill Omicron. Because that's what I really wanted to do. Kill. That meant going up, despite the fact that I had no idea what I intended to do when I got there. Look him in the eye, just before he devoured me? Maybe so. Anger is an interesting motivator.

I wasn't far into my climb when the earth exploded behind me, dirt and debris kicking up in a huge cloud, accompanied by a deep curtain of sound that I felt more than heard. I shielded my eyes, and covered my mouth and nose so I could breath in the sudden wall of dust. Coughing, I pulled myself up the hill, trying to escape the billowing mass. For several minutes I struggled to get higher, to a place where I could breathe. And see.

What the hell was that?

As I reached a flat section of rock, the air cleared somewhat, and I gasped, both from the effort of the climb and to bring something other than dust into my lungs. The slab of rock jutted upward at an angle, so I followed it until it ended at a platform just above the slowly dissipating cloud.

There, I stood on an outcropping, my feet just inches from a drop of 100 feet, maybe more. And below me, only a short distance away, Omicron was splayed on the valley floor.

My cut had felled the monster.

Oh my God. I did it! I laughed. "Ha! Take that!" I even did a little dance. I was positively gleeful over what I'd done. Little ol' me. Taking out giant creatures. The overwhelming desire to kill my foe was a drug, and I was high on it.

Had I severed some important ligament, made it impossible for the Gorgol to walk? It was the only thing that made sense. But he was down, and that was all that mattered. I laughed again.

At the epicenter of the dust cloud, I saw movement. Omicron's head turned and he looked up. His glowing amber eyes seemed to latch onto me, and he began to pull his massive forearms underneath his body. Then, with obvious effort, he pushed himself off the ground.

It wasn't over. Omicron was trying to stand.

Laboring, clearly favoring his left side, Omicron rose. The massive scales of his back approached the height of the rocky ledge where I stood, then continued to rise. His head went up and up, eyes still locked on me.

Where moments before I had been standing above my enemy, now the Gorgol towered over me, staring down with what seemed to be a deep and painful hatred. Where moments before I felt tall, now I felt, once again, my true insignificance in comparison to the creature.

It was hopeless. I'd given it my best try and, while my cut clearly hurt Omicron, it was a manageable injury. And without a sword, I wouldn't be dealing another such blow any time soon. The Gorgol was simply too big.

That was the sensible side of me.

The other side of me roared. "Come on! Come on!" I wanted to fight. I wanted more.

Omicron puffed up, filling himself with air. Then he howled directly at me, a near-deafening sound that hit me like a certain red car in the snow, from a day so long ago that now it seemed like a dream. His massive jaws hung open, the stench of his breath washing over me.

I had a moment to wonder to myself: *Where did you come from, Omicron? How old are you? And for God's sake, when was the last time you brushed your teeth?*

Still bellowing, Omicron made his move, lurching face first. His head rushed toward me at blinding speed, mouth open, tall spiky teeth moving to surround me, devour me.

Moments away from being eaten by a giant monster, I yelled in defiance. I don't remember what I actually said, but I like to think it was something grand. *Chew on my bones and spit out my blood if you must, but damn you to hell and bring it on!*

Defiance aside, at that very moment, I suddenly learned to fear my powers. What good would they do me in an unwinnable situation? Sluice out of the way of the teeth? Still Omicron's jaws would hold me. What about when I was swallowed? Writhing around in his stomach acids until my powers gave in and I finally expired? That sounded remarkably unpleasant.

So that's why your breath is so bad, eh? Dead, rotten people like me inside you. I imagined some future prey, also staring into Omicron's maw of death, smelling my foul remains. I pitied that person. I seriously doubted that I smelled very good alive at that moment. Dead, I was certain I'd produce a stench that would, well, wake the dead. Maybe that was a good idea. I could save myself.

I thought all of these things, things a person shouldn't be thinking milliseconds from death or massive, prolonged agony. And still I shouted back at the beast, like a tiny mirror image of him. A giant monster descending with huge open mouth, and a tiny monster — that's what I felt like — mimicking his fearsome expression.

The mouth opened wider, coming for me. Time flowed slowly, strangely.

I had to do something. I pushed. I mean that I tried to use my ability to move objects to push Omicron away. That, friends, was the saddest of all jokes. If the Gorgol even moved an inch, I couldn't tell.

The teeth came closer, blazing fast in real time.

I pushed again, this time on Omicron's mind.

And…

It might have worked. If I'd had time. But Omicron's mind was *big*. Maybe not excessively complex, but it was no small thing to delve into an alien mind and try to revise its thinking. I didn't know where to start. And I had no time to experiment. Deep within him I sensed something — echoes of ideas or feelings. But I didn't know what to change, what switches to throw, so I stabbed randomly at his mind, flailing in my rage, but missing any real target.

There was nothing else I could do. Physical push, no. Mental push, no.

In my mind's slow motion, the teeth surrounded me, the mouth closed over me.

And I had lost my sword.

Realizing the futility of it all, my anger flipped backward, away from Omicron and onto me. *What the hell is so special about the sword anyway? I've only trained for, like, six minutes. How could I possibly be any good?*

But I knew that wasn't the point. Pip trained us on techniques, I think, mostly so we didn't cut ourselves or drop the damn heavy swords. Which is essentially what I had done. Only, I'd left mine jutting out of Omicron's right leg.

In our hands, the swords were more than swords. How else could we slash a truck to pieces? How else could I have injured the Gorgol so badly? It didn't even matter that my sword was metal. In my hands, it became something more.

Just like the belt.

The belt.

It was the dumbest of all possible ideas. To attack a 200-foot monster with a leather belt.

But it was my last hope.

In the infinitesimally small space between the thought and the moment when Omicron's jaws would close around me, I reached down, flicking the buckle on my well-worn belt with ease. With a smooth motion, I whipped it from around my waste and brandished it overhead in one hand, aiming straight into the soft internal tissues of Omicron's open mouth.

The belt was not a belt. The belt was solid. It was sharp. It compressed into a fine-pointed thing, almost a spear. A sword-spear.

And in that blink of an eye, Omicron's teeth dug into the rock around me, shearing me, my new weapon, and about a quarter ton of stone off the top of the outcropping. Swept up, inside the monster's mouth, I pushed forward. Somehow, miraculously, I wasn't impaled on one of those teeth, but instead managed to squish myself into the wet, putrid, slimy space between Omicron's tongue and the roof of his mouth.

My sword-spear stabbed upward, penetrating more easily than my real sword had cut through the outer flesh. Deeper and deeper the belt went, and I began to realize there was a warmth coming from it, like an electric current. Still it went deeper.

Then, like closing the circuit to a battery, the current hit something powerful, and the warmth and energy increased tenfold.

Immediately, I felt it.

Pain.

I could feel the Gorgol's pain.

Confusion.

An unnamed emotion, raw and powerful and true.

Anger.

Fear.

The ideas, the feelings, were like clouds of mental energy, and I felt my mind hopping from one to the next to —

LOST.

MOTHER.

HOME.

What the hell? There were no words, but still the ideas rang through my head. The crying rage. LOST. MOTHER. HOME.

What did it mean?

The spear thinned and grew and penetrated farther. Slowly, I was skewering the brain of the beast.

The pain and confusion and fear increased. And so did the three words, more passionate, more urgent. LOST! MOTHER! HOME!

Was this Gorgol lost? Beyond all belief, did this 200-foot-tall monster have a *mother*? Where was its home? The sea? Somewhere else?

Suddenly, the feelings spiked. The pain and confusion turned to desperation. Omicron was dying. I was killing him. And yet he repeated, softer now, like echoes fading into the distance. LOST. MOTHER. HOME.

I thought of ants and gnats and flies and mosquitos. Was that all we were to a Gorgol, human insects? Sometimes a pest to be swatted, but normally not even that. How often had I trampled an anthill without knowing, or stomped some unsuspecting bug by simply walking or running or playing? Was it possible that none of Omicron's actions had been fueled by malice? Was it possible he just didn't pay attention to something so small and insignificant as a human being? But we human beings fought back. I'm certain I would notice if a legion of ants suddenly opened fire on me with little ant machine guns.

But when insects do attack, what do we do? How exactly do we respond to swarms of gnats or bees or mosquitos? By trying to kill them all, before they hurt us again. I thought of my sword, sticking out of Omicron's leg. I was the mosquito.

The bloodlust waned. My rational mind started to return.

What was I doing? I was killing him, and he was lost. I was killing him, and he was seeking mother. I was killing him, and he was seeking home.

More than anything, I realized just how little I could possibly understand about the Gorgols. What right did I have to kill Omicron? Maybe Jake Weissman was right, after all.

In my hand, the sword-spear pulsed with warm electricity, delving ever deeper into the delicate tissue of Omicron's brain.

No. I tugged, pulling back. *No.*

From my primal cave deep inside the creature's mouth, I suddenly felt the entire world falling. Well, not that. Omicron was falling, with me inside. His energy had hit a critical point. The wound in his leg, in his brain. He was falling.

No! I pulled on the belt again. *No, stop it!*

But we fell, and fell, and fell. And then we crashed, a tidal wave of mass propelled by gravity into the harsh and unforgiving earth. Inside the beast's mouth, I was cushioned from the initial blow, pressed between Omicron's tongue and the roof of his mouth, until his jaws fell open and I tumbled away, surrounded by another massive cloud of dust.

I rolled to a stop, covering my mouth and nose, needing air, looking for a way out. But my energy, too, had been sapped. I cowered, hoping the air would come soon.

I sat on the ground, just feet from the glowing eyes of Gorgol Omicron, within a haze of dust that painted everything a dim grey, that limited my world to only the 20 feet or so in which I could make out any detail. Then the sphere widened, and slowly I could see more. More dust was pushed away by the labored last breaths of the Gorgol. Soon, the air began to return, and the cloud settled.

Before me, the amber eyes of Omicron dimmed and went out, and his body lay still. But I waited for him to arise once more. I wanted him to arise. Part of me did. LOST. MOTHER. HOME. In some ways, I had lost the will to harm this creature, at least not without knowing more about him. To find out his true nature. Was he really a force of hatred and destruction, or simply living on such a larger scale that we were overlooked?

Get up. Please. I'm sorry.

No, I've killed you. I am more than you.

Two sides fought within me.

One wanted Gorgol Omicron to stay dead and gone. The other wanted him to get up.

But he didn't. The creature shuddered, and a long slow breath rolled out of him, a final release, the last of his living force.

What have I done?

I looked into Omicron's now-dark eyes, trying to understand. But understanding eluded me. Something was gone. Something more than Omicron had been taken away.

Still, there was the fire.

Good riddance.

After a time, motion to one side, past the dead Gorgol, caught my eye. Flashes of red and yellow, Pip and Bobby, approaching fast. Above, I noticed a helicopter circling, realized it had probably been there all along, its rhythmic *thump-thump-thump-thump* just a natural part of the landscape, like the debris and the rock. And now, a new landmark. The massive, lifeless form of Omicron.

With one hand, I absently touched at my mask. Sure enough, it was there, although it was torn and ragged on one side. My belt was once again just a belt, hanging limply in my hand, and I was covered in the thick saliva of the creature. I doubted even my mom would have recognized me in such a state, and I was exhausted. So I didn't care too much about possible news cameras hovering overhead.

I tried to blink away the daze I was in. The circling helicopter began to remind me of a dream. Of a circling dragon with a familiar voice.

Then, higher, nearly behind me, another form appeared, its khakis and boots hard to mistake. Jake Weissman glared at me from above, as I stood beside the dead body of Gorgol Omicron. The look in his eyes was anger, maybe hatred. All for me.

One part of me rued that look.

The other part wanted to smack it off his face.

Then Jake's head turned sharply, and I saw his mouth fall open. He started west toward the setting sun as the helicopter overhead suddenly tilted in the same direction and sped away.

Keith Soares

1

"You did it!" Bobby shouted as he ran to meet me, Pip only slightly behind. I didn't reply, my eyes instead tracking Jake as he began to head west across the rocky hilltops above, as if running he could catch the helicopter in flight. "Joh— I mean, *Black* — you did it!" I had nearly forgotten about our color-code names. Bobby slowed to a jog before coming up and giving me an enthusiastic bear hug.

"Nice work," Pip said as she joined us, standing just feet from the motionless forest of Omicron's teeth. "How'd you manage to do it?"

So I explained, as quickly as possible — slicing open the monster's leg, then climbing the hill. And Omicron chomping down on me, only to get stuck through the brain by my improvised weapon. Bobby and Pip seemed impressed. They couldn't see my face, with the mask and all the creature slobber covering me. They couldn't see how I felt. I had killed, and afterward I regretted what I'd done. And yet, there was still a strange cocktail of pride and happiness bubbling within me.

Pride.

What is pride? If my anger had been a thick, juicy slab of steak, my pride was the full belly afterward.

I slayed the beast. I was proud of what I'd done.

Pride. I messed with some kids once, because of my pride. My father died.

Suddenly I was unable to stop the tears. With Pip there, I remember being embarrassed, although why, after the fact, seems unimportant. Like Omicron, my dad was dead. Sure, if the creature was coming for my sister, I was doing the right thing. "Then why doesn't it feel right?" I said aloud. Bobby and Pip both looked at me, but didn't say anything.

Guilt.

How much of the stuff could one person rack up?

Maybe Jake Weissman was right. Maybe the creatures *should* be left alone. Who knows? Maybe they could even be reasoned with. I hadn't tried to connect with Omicron's mind until the very end, when it was too late to do much more than lash out. What would have happened if I had spent longer trying to reach him? Could a human mind reach a Gorgol mind?

Lost. Mother. Home.

I thought so.

It was bizarre and senseless to feel such guilt, killing a monster that destroyed everything in its wake. But lying next to us, Omicron looked… *pathetic.* A sad, lonely shadow of the once ferocious creature it had been.

Bobby, my friend, must have sensed some of what I was feeling, realized the weight of more than one death now pushed firmly down on my shoulders. He sucked in a breath, standing up straight before me like friends do at funerals. "You okay, Johnny?"

I was glad he forgot to use my code word, and figured, with the helicopter gone, no one was there to overhear us anyway. The tears flowed as I wrinkled my brow and tapped the side of my head. "I touched his mind, Bobby. Omicron's. I felt what he felt. There were these feelings… *Lost. Mother. Home.* He didn't say the words, not even in my mind, but those *feelings* were there. Those three specific feelings."

"And you think Omicron was a *baby*, looking for his *mommy*?" Pip said.

I wheeled on her, too emotional to stop myself. "Maybe! What would you know? You just want us to *kill, kill, kill!*"

Pip was taken aback. "No, John. I wanted us to *stop* the killing." She nodded toward the Gorgol's body. "The killing that thing was doing. People were dying, innocent people, dying for no reason. Besides, you said yourself that these things are looking for Holly. Are you just going to let that happen, let her and a bunch of innocent people die?"

Thinking of my father, I lashed out again. "Innocent people die all the time!"

Bobby stepped forward, between Pip and me. "Yeah, they do," he said. "But not for no reason."

"Really?" I said, raising my voice. "What's the reason my dad died?"

Bobby looked at me without blinking. "To make you," he said, pointing a finger at me. He lightly tapped me, in the center of the chest. The way I had tapped Sol, but with a completely different intent, and completely different results.

I laughed, a single harsh sound, tears still streaming down my ridiculous mask. A mask I wanted nothing more than to rip off. "Right. Bobby, he *made* me when I was born. All he did when he died was *leave*, and for no good reason. I caused that accident. If anything, the whole thing made me a killer and an idiot. Just like now. There could have been another way." I wiped at my eyes through the ragged hole in the mask. Still, at least part of me felt differently. *No, there's only one way. These Gorgols need to die before they get to Holly. You know it's true.*

Bobby put a hand on my arm. "Johnny, you're wrong. With your dad, it was an accident, and it was only an accident. Good people *do* die. But it always has a point. Even if it's just the same point, over and over. To remind the rest of us that we *all* have to be good, or else good will die out from the world. Today, you tried to be good, to help *other* good people from dying, to help your sister, so their good and hers wouldn't die." Bobby turned, looking at Omicron's lifeless body. "Johnny, you have a choice, every day. You may not even realize it, or care, or whatever, but you do. You have power, real power. You don't have to be the nice guy. If you chose to be bad, I don't know if anyone could stop you. I couldn't. But you choose to be good, because of people like your dad before you. And, I don't know... I think because he died, it means more. You're more likely to be like him. To be a hero like him."

I wiped my eyes again. *Don't have to be the nice guy?* I thought. *What if I'm not? And what if I don't really choose whether I'm good or bad?*

"Johnny," Bobby said. "It might just be that, because of your dad, you saved the world from Sol. And now, from Omicron, too."

I felt so conflicted. Pride. And guilt. "But what if Omicron wasn't bad? What if Omicron was just lost?"

"Then all of this sucks, and I'm sorry," he said. "But that creature was still killing people, even if it was just by accident. Something had to be done. Our world doesn't really have room for giant monsters to roam around, smashing things and hurting people."

Monsters…

Wait.

"What happened to Sigma?" I asked.

Bobby looked back at Pip and shrugged. "We were fighting her hard, making some ground, losing some. She's fast and difficult to land a hit on, that's for sure. But then she just stopped. Balled herself up the way the Gorgols seem to do and rolled away."

"Rolled away? Where?"

Bobby pointed west, the same way Jake had gone, the same way the helicopter had gone. "Back to the ocean, I guess."

I thought for a moment. Why was everyone and everything suddenly so keen on going back to the ocean? I seriously doubted that Sigma was giving up and running away. *Oh, maybe there's a surf competition. Or a bikini contest. Luau, perhaps?* I was trying to lighten my own mood, but it wasn't working very well.

From the west, we heard Sigma's cry, higher-pitched than Omicron's, but still strong and echoing. And like a distorted mirror of sound, there came another. A second cry overlapping the first, deeper, louder, and even stronger. Bobby looked at Omicron beside me, still and silent and gone, then turned to Pip and me with awe and fear.

"There are *three* of them?" he asked.

Three fireballs in the sky.

"Of course there are," I replied.

2

Pip, Bobby, and I, masks still covering our faces, crested
the last rise before the ocean and immediately froze.

At sea, the water roiled. Not just in one place, and yet not
in every place. Not in a small isolated area, as if from a
dolphin or whale, and yet not so widespread as to be natural
to the water itself, as if from the weather. No, something
was stirring the ocean, and stirring it in a very width swath.

Something even larger than the two Gorgols we knew.

Closer to shore, Sigma was putting on a strange display,
slipping in and out of the surf, letting loose deafening cries.
My heart sank. Sigma's calls weren't angry, or threatening.
They were the pathetic howls of a dog left chained up in the

cold. A baby crying for milk that isn't coming. A sister who has lost a brother.

LOST. MOTHER. HOME.

"It's their mother," I said, to no one in particular.

Pip turned to me, her eyes too big and white within the opening of her mask, like there was nothing but eyes underneath. "*That?*" She pointed just as something large and dark broke the surface.

The new Gorgol was still mostly hidden by the surf, but she was coming ashore fast. I say "she" because I believed — and still believe — that she was Omicron's and Sigma's mother. And she was big.

Visually, their mother looked like both of the younger Gorgols, despite the fact that they only loosely resembled each other. She had the thicker, stony-scaled back of Omicron, but her long, thin tail, trailing off behind her to make a snaky S in the waves, mirrored Sigma. From the sides of her head down to her wide shoulders, she was hooded like Sigma, but that hood was solid and dark, looking completely impenetrable. Momma was a mashup of both Gorgols, on steroids.

I didn't hear it until the next day on TV, but Mother Gorgol soon had her own name, in keeping with the others: Alpha. It fit her perfectly. Not an alpha male — who needed that?

This was an alpha female. She was simply *Alpha*, the first, the biggest, the strongest, the one.

Below us, Sigma issued a staccato bark, and for a moment Alpha paused. Then she reared up and shrieked at the darkening sky.

"She knows, now," I said. "She knows I killed Omicron. And that means she'll be after me."

Bobby put one hand on my shoulder. "After *us*."

To my surprise, Pip rested a hand on my other shoulder. She didn't say a word, but the meaning was clear. We were a team. Three of us versus two of them. Even if it meant a death sentence for us all.

The thought of killing again flared, the fire lighting once again. It intrigued me. Too much. It was a lure, a drug. Anger fueled the fire. Pride justified what you did with it. I tamped it down, forcibly. "But I don't want to fight them anymore," I said in a low voice. At first I didn't think Pip or Bobby could even hear me. A moment passed when nothing happened.

Then Bobby clapped me on the back gently. "If that's the case, well...," he said, turning his back to the scene below, where the Gorgols were reunited. "We'd better run."

I gave Pip a sidelong glance and could tell she didn't want to leave. But something had changed. We'd somehow become a true team. When Bobby began to lead me away, Pip followed without complaint.

Not one of us noticed Jake, who must have been standing atop a nearby cliff, looking down on the same scene at the beach we had seen. But Jake, he definitely noticed us.

3

The hardest part about getting home was not getting caught. Funny, considering how we pushed so many minds while traveling across the country. Yet when faced with hovering helicopters, their pilots too far overhead to reach with our minds, we had to revert to simpler tactics.

We split up, took the most obscure routes we could think of, and paused for lengthy, random breaks. Frankly, I think I was lost for most of the night, since I wasn't familiar with the area at all. Luckily, I could keep tabs on Bobby and Pip from their beacons, giving me a general sense of direction, and I knew Pip would be the first home.

Hours later, under cover of darkness, with our masks thankfully tucked away, we finally met up once more at Pip's.

Bobby, last to return, sighed dramatically as he entered, squinting as he stepped across the starkly contrasted line between the dark outside and the brightly lit room. "Ah, back in the secret underground lair," he said.

"Will you quit it with that?" Pip hardly looked up from the book she was reading on the faded couch, pretending not to care, but her left foot twitched with irritation. It was like she was keeping beat to a song that no one else could hear.

"With what?" Bobby said, tossing his yellow mask onto the short counter. "Calling it your secret underground lair?" Pip nodded sharply, so Bobby turned to me for backup. "Johnny. Is this place a secret? I mean, do we want anyone to find us here?"

"No, we don't," I said, not really wanting to be dragged into Bobby's needless teasing of Pip, but still amused in a juvenile way.

"And, are we or are we not underground?"

I scanned the basement room, where two doors exited to the street outside, although most of the apartment was indeed underground. "Sort of." I waggled one hand.

Bobby grasped onto it anyway. "*Sort of* counts. And finally, Johnny. Answer me this. Can you call this our *lair*?"

I started to roll my eyes when a blur streaked across the room. One of Pip's daggers, plucked from the rack on the wall, tossed Bobby's way with deadly accuracy, causing his torso to bend into an exaggerated C shape. Behind him, the dagger thumped deeply into the frame of the door, shivering like a diving board just after the diver jumps.

Bobby's torso slowly reformed. "Feisty one, isn't she, Johnny?"

Pip stood and turned toward the back room, and we knew this was her way of declaring lights out in 10 minutes. Not that either of us complained. We'd had a rather exhausting day.

Nine minutes or so later, with Pip closed in the bedroom, Bobby on the couch, and me on a blanket in the middle of the floor, we called it a night, each of us quickly falling into a sound sleep.

Superpowers or not, when you're really tired, you're really tired. In moments, I was out cold.

* * *

There was a sound. A very strange sound. I barely had time to pull open my heavy eyelids.

The front door splintered, ripped from the hinges. Something flashed past me, over me. Then someone pressed two of Pip's long swords across my throat, an unholy metal cross against my jugular vein.

"If I do it, do you think the powers can save you?" he said, a frothing male voice that whispered in anger. I blinked, trying to understand what was happening, to really wake up. "Do you think your head will jump back on your body if I cut it off?"

"Jesus, Jake, settle down!" Bobby shouted, leaping up from the couch. Pip was already in the doorway, the light in her bedroom spilling into the living room. From my left and right, Pip and Bobby both crouched slightly, in ready poses. But they didn't move forward.

I realized that Jake Weissman was asking a really good question, one for which I didn't have an answer. It occurred to me that he might be able kill me. It was completely possible that Jake was about to end my life. "Jake, please. Can we talk?"

His hold on the swords tightened, and I felt them cutting into my neck. "Tell your friends to take a seat."

"Sure, sure. Guys?"

"No way! Get the hell out of here!" Bobby said, inching closer.

The swords tensed, narrowing the space between the two blades, the space where my living flesh was. "Bobby!

Don't! If he cuts — I… I don't know what will happen."
Although he tried to remain focused on Jake, Bobby spared
one quick look at my eyes. Instantly he knew what he had
to do.

Bobby sat down on the couch, gesturing for Pip to do the
same on the chair next to her. "Fine. We're sitting. But let
me tell you something, Jake. If you do *anything* to my
friend there, it won't be half as bad as what Pip and I will
do to you next."

Jake chuckled, just inches from my face. "That's a bet I
might be willing to take…" I felt the blades tighten. Had it
not been for my body's innate ability to sluice and morph
away from trouble, I'm certain I would have been bleeding.
A sort of trembling feeling came into my neck, telling me
that my physical powers were ready to kick in. But to what
end? Could I really reattach my own head, even if it was
only separated for a millisecond?

*How did I miss this? What else have I missed? And does it
even matter anymore, if Jake decides to cut me?*

All at once, I felt afraid — not just in that moment, but for
all the other times I might have been randomly decapitated.
Such as by Gorgol Omicron only hours before.
Involuntarily, my body shook with the knowledge that I
might have been near death so many times in my
recklessness.

Having superpowers really distorts your sense of infallibility. Regular dangers fail to hold their normally distinct weight. The instinct to avoid putting your hand on a hot stove disappears when you know it can't hurt you. But realizing that I might have been overlooking a rather significant and simplistic loophole sent the whole feeling of immortality crashing around my feet.

What can I do?

Fire. I can use my fire. Because one thing is for sure: I don't have to sit here and wait to die.

The bloodlust came again. The urge to hurt, maybe kill.

Jake's attention was partially focused on Bobby, concerned that he might leap forward at any moment.

Good, keep looking at someone else. I like being underestimated.

I snatched at the blades, taking one in each hand. Jake tried to react in time, but once my fingers were wrapped around them, he couldn't undo what had already been done. He pressed down, but that just helped me. Leveraging his weight, I pulled and flipped my body backward, swooping the two swords in large circles from down to up again.

And in a second, I was standing over Jake, his body sprawled on the floor. I hovered above him with the two swords, hilt out. Without a pause, smiling insanely, I dealt the murder stroke — the upside-down, hilt-forward blow Pip had shown us from ancient times.

I figured that if Jake was like me, he might have the same fear of being decapitated. I told myself, in that instant, that it was a feint, that it was all about making him afraid.

But part of me wanted Jake to die.

Jake's body moved like liquid, away from me, toward the shattered front door. In an instant, my sword hilts had splintered the floorboards, but Jake had pulled back, clearly panting from the effort.

I released the swords and stood in a ready pose, knees bent. "How about a more fair matchup?" I said, with Bobby and Pip stepping up to each side of me.

Jake Weissman turned and ran into the night.

4

I don't care who you are, there's something decidedly weird about sleeping in a room where the front door has been ripped away. It's like walking around with your fly open — sure, you're probably gonna be fine, but if anything does pop through that opening unexpectedly, you'll be having a bad day.

So I couldn't sleep the rest of the night.

I don't know about Pip, off in her room with the door closed, or even Bobby on the couch above me. But me, well, I was on edge.

I think I was asleep — I think — when Pip appeared over me.

"When are you going to finally wake up and do something right?" Pip said.

I felt cold. Very cold. I wanted to reply, *What are you talking about?* Some sort of reply. But my voice didn't work. Pip looked at me in anger.

"Well? Are you planning on answering me?" she said, before turning and making a disgusted face. From somewhere, she pulled out a cigarette and lit it, sucking in then exhaling a puff of smoke.

Pip? What's —?

"Your father is going to be furious at you," Pip said, breathing smoke like a cinematic dragon.

My dad? You know my dad is...

Blinking, I shook my head. *Something is wrong. Pip looks... older.* "But, Mom!" I said. *What? Why did I call her that?* But my voice sounded strange. Not me. I wanted to look down at my hands, body, ensure I was still me, but my viewpoint wouldn't change. And that's when I realized that I was only watching, not participating.

A movie in my mind, seeming so real. I had done this before. The vivid dreams of Sol's team, moments plucked from other people's minds.

I'm seeing into Pip's head. The feeling was remarkably awkward. I felt like a peeping tom. At the same time, it was fascinating.

"But, nothing, young lady! Go inside and get ready for bed!" Older Pip — Pip's mother, I assumed — huffed, and a huge cloud of smoke jetted from her mouth. She turned away, dismissing me. Or Pip. If I was watching one of Pip's memories, her mother was dismissing her. In fact, Pip's mom didn't seem like the nicest person.

My view changed, turning and dashing through a screen door, up a flight of stairs, into a brightly lit yellow bathroom, closing the door. I looked in the mirror and I was Pip. But this Pip was younger, maybe 13 years old.

She was crying.

I didn't want to watch anymore. I wanted to stop my eavesdropping mind, but since I hadn't done anything to start the connection, I had no idea how to cut it off. I willed my mind to look away, stop seeing the weeping face of Pip.

Then there was the loud *pop* of a door slamming somewhere in the distance. Low thuds of someone climbing the stairs. My view turned toward the bathroom door, and I could feel the fear. Pip's fear.

The door flew open, and a man stood facing me. He was pale, but his skin was flushed from some sort of exertion. His hair was close-cropped and light, and it dribbled down his cheeks into stubble that was tinged orange and brown with bits of white. From the side of his mouth, a lit cigarette dangled. "You just can't do as you're told, can you?" he asked, with the quiet kind of anger that's so much more frightening than actual yelling.

It must have been Pip's father. He took a step forward, blowing too much smoke into the small bathroom, filling the air with the haze and smell of it.

I shut my eyes, Pip shut her eyes, willing him away.

Don't.

When I opened them again, I was descending along a rugged hillside, orange rocks growing dark and grey in the fading light. The wind whipped around me, so hard it hurt. Small stones and debris broke free of the hill and spun in the air. Sand rained on me from seemingly every direction at once.

Sand?

Sol.

I was in a desert, and all around me, a powerful sandstorm raged.

Sol, will you just die?

I struggled down the hillside. The sky darkened as I reached an impassable section, where the path seemed to have been cut off by a vertical wall that stretched high above me and sank deep below. I was stuck. Still, without hesitation, I moved toward the cliff. Mentally, I steeled myself for the fall, but as my mind's eye approached the edge, I saw my boot easily find a rock for support, then another. I moved with an ease that said I expected this path, I knew it was there.

No, this isn't Sol's mind, this is someone else. Someone who knows this desert place.

Two more awkward steps and I left the vertical chute behind, stepped back onto a normal path. I started to run, hard boots crunching along, kicking up orange dust to join the general swirl. "Come on... Come on..." I said in a familiar voice.

Of course. Jake. Jake was still somewhere near the secret underground lair, and I was picking up his dreams, too. A vision from his time as a park ranger.

The wind gained force and blasted against me, against Jake. My view swiveled as he faced directly into a shower of orange dust.

And smoke.

The smoke and dust and wind blew, turning yellow. A man stood before me. Pip's father again.

"Your mother told me everything. Got anything to say for yourself?" He took a long pull on his cigarette.

The view darkened to orange and brown as the wind raged again in my face. I could feel Jake's fear as he raced against the weather. He kept running, trying to turn away from the storm, although the storm seemed to be everywhere.

Finally, he rounded a tall outcropping of rock, where the path bent down toward the canyon floor and, with luck, some kind of safety. A feeling welled up — excitement, relief? Then, as Jake turned the corner, those feelings fell away instantly, like a popped balloon. Ahead, the darkness intensified, to the point of becoming nearly black.

The wind rose to meet me, to meet Jake, and we turned away, but behind us was the same. Darkness pressed in from all sides.

There comes a time in every overwhelmingly tragic situation when the best advice is probably *Stay where you are and pray.* We reached that moment.

Milliseconds before the dark walls of wind crushed together with us in the middle, Jake shouted, "Ohhhhh, shhhiiiii—"

All senses blurred together. Vision became an endless array of darks and lights, like static on a TV tuned to nothing. My ears heard an endless scream, the wind howling, relentless and swift. And I felt pain. Like a million wasp stings, a million crows' beaks pecking at me, pushing yet pulling me apart.

Then, as the dark wind threatened to tear apart everything, I smelled tobacco. Somehow I managed to blink. To release the manic squint enough to let in light. I saw Pip's dad before me again. Too close. Eyes bloodshot, wisps of smoke still curling through the large gaps in his teeth. Pip closed her eyes and my view started to go dark. "Just remember," he said, leaning in. "You brought this on yourself."

5

Without moving my body, for fear of giving something away, I opened one eye and scanned the room. The ruined front door, formerly a gash of darkness peering out into the night, was now a blot of growing light.

Jake's dream and Pip's rattled in my head. *Pip is in the other room, so that makes sense. But where's Jake? He must be close by for me to —*

Something moved in the doorway.

I couldn't help it. I inhaled, quickly and loudly, which woke Bobby. "What is it, Johnny?" He rubbed at his eyes, but sat up quickly. Then Pip appeared in her doorway. I guess we were all tense from the night before.

"Outside…" In unison, Bobby and I stood, and I stepped closer to the hole that used to be our front door. I could hear the sound of paper flapping in the light morning breeze. I stepped through the opening and into the light. Laying on the ground in front of me was a note, weighed down by a rock the size of a softball. I pushed the rock aside and retrieved the note, unfolding it.

JOHN BLACK —
I'M GOING TO MAKE SURE YOU REGRET WHAT
YOU'VE DONE. JUST WATCH ME.

It wasn't signed, but, you know, the morning after someone rips down your front door and tries to kill you, it's pretty obvious who might be leaving you threatening notes. Well, I suppose the note could have been from the Gorgol family, but as far as I knew, they couldn't write.

Just watch me. Pretty dramatic, huh? What was that supposed to mean? What did Jake have planned? Or was he just mouthing off because I got the best of him? Probably that. Hopefully that.

And still, one small corner of my brain kept thinking, *Bring it on, Jake. Just try me.*

From inside, the phone rang. "John, it's your mom," Pip called to me.

If there is any quicker way to quell bravado than having your mother call, I don't know what it is. "Hi, Mom," I said as I took the phone from Pip with an embarrassed nod.

"John. Are you okay? I saw..." I guess she couldn't bear to describe my fight with Omicron, which must have been on rapid repeat on every news channel.

"Yeah, Mom, I'm okay. I just... I'm not proud of what I did. I think it was the wrong thing."

The line was silent for a moment. "John, *you* know *you* better than anyone, better than even I do. And these powers you have, they're yours, to use or not. For whatever you want, good or bad. But I'll tell you this. That creature killed a lot of people, crushed their homes, ruined a lot of lives. People were terrified. You may feel bad for what you did, but you stopped any more of that from happening. Besides..."

"Besides what, Mom?"

"Holly. She felt it. Like a wave of relief. Like it had taken away some burden or pain. I believe her, John. Those things are looking for her. Stopping them was what you had to do."

I sighed. "Yeah, I know, but Omicron had *feelings*, or something like feelings. Before he died, I could sense it. Besides, there are still two more of them." *And I'm afraid that if I kill again, this feeling that right now is only part of*

214

me now might become all of me. But how do you tell that to your mom?

"I understand, John. It makes perfect sense with what the news has been playing, too."

"What do you mean?"

"You haven't seen?" she asked.

"No. We had, uh, kind of a rough night." My mom didn't need to know about me nearly being beheaded, right?

"Sorry. But as you can imagine, the news is going crazy with all this. Replaying the footage over and over. You in the black mask."

"Uh-huh. Must be an excellent disguise if you could tell."

"Well, I *am* your mother, and I think I can see through you wearing one little mask. Besides, don't forget that I had the benefit of knowing where you were going."

"Oh yeah, right," I laughed.

"Have you heard what they've started calling you?"

Oh God, no. "Please tell me it's not ridiculous. *Please.*" Of all the things, *this* was making me nervous. Finding out what people nicknamed me.

"Black Sword."

I had to let that sink in for a moment. *Black Sword? Is that cool?* Maybe it was, kind of, but I felt decidedly unlike any person who should be called *Black Sword*. Though I suppose the name made sense, considering I wore a black mask and fought with a sword. It was just... weird. "And Bobby?" I asked.

"Well, he has a particularly frantic way of fighting, according to the talking heads analyzing this whole thing."

"And...?"

"They call him Yellow Fury."

I laughed out loud. *Black Sword, Yellow Fury, and Red Hope.* If the world was going to be saved from Gorgols, apparently it was going to be at the hands of three complete dorks. The only thing worse would be if *we* started calling *ourselves* these names.

"What's so funny, Johnny?" Bobby said, coming inside.

"Oh, nothing, *Yellow Fury*." I laughed again.

On the phone, Mom stepped in. "John, behave."

"Sorry, Mom," I said.

"Oh, shit. They call me *Yellow Fury*?" Bobby asked.

I nodded, giggling.

"I…" he started, suddenly beaming. "I *love* it! Yes! I sound bad ass!" He pumped a fist. Across the room, Pip rolled her eyes. "Wait — what about you?" Bobby said, rounding on me.

I looked away. I should have seen this moment coming. In a low voice, I said the nickname like a punishment. "Black Sword."

"Black Sword?" Bobby pondered it for a moment. "Yellow Fury, Black Sword, and Red Hope. Us." He thought about the names, looking back and forth at us, once again breaking out in a smile. "We're awesome! We have awesome names! And — oh wait! Now we need a team name!"

"No way, shut up!" I yelled.

"The Triangle Gang! No, wait. Force Three?" Pip threw a shoe at Bobby to express her displeasure.

"No, Bobby!" Thankfully, to my knowledge, no one ever again called us the Triangle Gang or Force Three. I hope.

"John? Are you still there?" Mom said on the phone.

"Yeah, Mom, sorry. Bobby got a little excited."

"I understand. But there's more. The news has been showing some other footage, too. Strange footage. The Gorgols, all together. Alpha — that's what they're calling the new one, the really big one — and Sigma, standing over Omicron's body."

A wave of guilt hit me, as powerful as one of Omicron's swipes. Swipes that, to him, were just like human hands waving at a mosquito. "They really do feel," I said quietly.

"I guess so," my mother replied. "But that's not the really weird part. There's a man, too. The helicopter cameras show him up on the hillside, looking down at the Gorgols."

"A man?" *Jake?*

"Yeah, a man in khakis." *Okay, definitely Jake.* "And the three of them — the man, and the two living Gorgols. They seem to be in a trance or something."

A million thoughts ran through my mind, looping and turning and flipping over one another. The Gorgols, in a trance? Maybe peaceful now? They mourned their dead. The one I killed. And now, Jake. Had he subdued the monsters? Succeeded in peace where I had used only war? Jake was right, the Gorgols were just nature's creatures. Or did that make any sense? They still seemed so alien, so much out of place. But if he could reach their minds... "Could he be talking to them?" I pondered aloud.

"Maybe, John, I don't know."

I gave it very little thought. I had traveled so far, and, from all the evidence, done exactly the wrong thing. And a part of me even enjoyed it, which turned my stomach. I needed to think about what to do next, either way. If the Gorgols could be reasoned with, I needed to think that over. If they couldn't, well, I needed to think about that, too. Because my anger, my want to fight, was a fire. And that fire was changing me.

Like a phoenix. Reborn from fire.

But was that a good thing?

What if, when the fire died out next time, I didn't recognize myself anymore?

If the Gorgols were under control, I could go in peace. And if they weren't, I could hold off deciding what to do for a bit longer if I went home.

So that's what I did.

And Force Three or the Triangle Gang or whatever you want to call us broke apart the same day we were formed.

6

Pushing minds once again, we flew home without Pip, our fledgling team soon to be separated by the entire width of the country. Bobby and I said all the right words, so did she. *We got your back. We'll meet again soon.* But we were leaving, Bobby and I.

Honestly, I was surprised Bobby was willing to go. I think it was just our friendship that swayed him. I don't really think Bobby cared whether people found out about him or not. And it seemed unlikely that he was going home because he missed his parents too much. Maybe he realized that if he was outed as Yellow Fury, it wouldn't take much to pin Black Sword as me. And then what? I had already been through the whole paparazzi thing once, and didn't like it. It was too hard on Mom, and even worse, maybe dangerous for Holly. We weren't ready to go public.

Not for the first time, not for the last time, I wished none of this had happened to me. Not the powers, not the crazy thorns in my body that changed me. I could have lived a life without knowing Sol. Without killing him. Without killing Omicron. I could have lived a normal life and been happy. I think. I hope.

Does it matter, though?

The taste for killing, for not just exercising my power, but *over*exercising it. Showing off. I could feel it, deep inside, and it scared me. I wanted a normal life instead.

An hour into the flight, I scanned the movie options. That dragon movie was still available. So I turned everything off and went to sleep instead.

* * *

When we landed, people were standing around a TV monitor at the gate. The endlessly blaring news channel most airports leave on, to try to distract passengers' minds from the endlessly boring nature of travel.

What caught my attention were the words *Black Sword* and the almost absurd realization that they were talking about *me*.

For the past several hours, there has been no sign of the three heroes known as Red Hope, Yellow Fury, and Black

Sword, so we don't know how they might react to this truly unexpected development. Back to you, Jim.

Thanks, Todd.

The news show continued with other analysis and banter, but unfortunately failed to recap what "this truly unexpected development" might be. And since it was pretty clear from what we did hear that we might want — or need — to know what was happening, Bobby decided to ask someone nearby.

"Ma'am. Excuse me, do you know what this *unexpected development* is they're talking about? We've been on a plane."

The woman turned to answer, then, noticing Bobby's age, wrinkled up her forehead. A quick push from me helped smooth away the concern. I looked around to see if anyone else had a similar issue, noticed a few stares, and pushed accordingly. I didn't make the woman ignore us, just stop being concerned.

"Well, it's most peculiar. After all this time those monsters have been by the ocean, they're now headed inland, east. With that man."

"Man?" Bobby asked.

"The man they're calling *Ranger*. Because he wears those clothes." *Jake, of course.*

"The man is with the Gorgols?"

"Oh, yes. The creatures are walking east and — "

"Walking?" I asked. "Not that rolling thing they do?" The Gorgols must not have been in much of a hurry.

"Yes, walking." The woman looked at me, a little annoyed by the interruption. "I suppose they have to walk, because the man, Ranger, is up on top of the big one. Of course, rolling or walking, they're still smashing everything wherever they go. And nobody knows where they're headed. People are terrified. I just glad it's all so far away."

"*Up on top…*" Bobby echoed. Shaking his head, he thanked the woman and we slipped away.

"What do you think that means, Johnny?" Bobby asked as we headed toward the cab line. One more stolen ride before home.

I grimaced, not sure what to say. "Somehow Jake has gotten through to the Gorgols, communicated with them. Come to some sort of agreement."

"He's *riding* one of the damn things? What the hell?" I just nodded and shrugged. Since we had once again taken the red eye, the cab line was deserted. The taxi attendant eyed us suspiciously, but Bobby gave him a quick push and that was gone. "They're headed east. To us. You think this plane ride we just took was all for nothing?" Bobby said.

I shook my head. "No idea. But maybe it gives us some time to think."

"Right." Bobby chuckled.

One of those rental-car shuttle vans slowly motored past. "Bobby?"

"Yeah, Johnny?"

"If Jake has somehow determined how to talk to them, he must be light years ahead of us."

Bobby shook his head. "After talking to that guy, I don't believe that. I don't think he was all there, Johnny. I kept feeling him, I don't know, *pulse* back and forth. Like he couldn't decide who to be at that moment. It was weird. Anyway, I don't think massive feats of intellectual skill are suddenly going to be Jake's thing, if you know what I mean." Bobby Graden, the town bully, was questioning someone else's smarts. That was saying something.

Finally, a taxi pulled up. Push, push, in we went. In the back of the car, we talked freely. The cabbie would never remember, thanks to a little of the influence we provided.

"Bobby," I started. "Maybe it's Jake we need to talk to. Learn what he knows."

"Johnny, he tried to *kill* you," Bobby said.

"Because of what I'd done. What I might have done *wrong*." I let the word hang in the air.

Bobby turned to me, more serious than he usually was. "Was it wrong, though, Johnny? I mean, I didn't *kill* Sigma, but I gave her some wounds she won't forget. Those Gorgols are strong. Dangerous. You said it yourself that they're here to come after Holly. And they don't belong here, anyway. This isn't a new normal, this is just crazy. Jake talking to them — if he is doing that — doesn't make it normal, either. It might just mean he really is crazy. Either way, the Gorgols need to go, and if they won't leave on their own, they need to be dealt with. You took out Omicron. I came pretty close with Sigma." He sounded… boastful.

"You want to kill them?" I asked, afraid of Bobby's answer.

He nodded, slowly looking up to me. "Yeah, I think I do. If they show up here, then definitely."

Oh God, I thought. *Oh God.* Not for Bobby, not for what he'd said. For myself. *I want to kill them, too.*

7

I pressed my forehead against Holly's. *Hi, sis. Missed you.*

"Johnny!" Holly said. *You're home!*

It was mid-morning before I woke up, but still, I was exhausted. I mean, I'd had a pretty exhausting week, wouldn't you agree? "Yep — I'm back."

I saw what you did. And... I felt it, too. You know?

The sunburn feeling? It changed.

Yeah. Part of it turned off.

What about the new one? Alpha? Didn't that make the feeling increase?

No, Johnny. I could feel her all along.

"Oh," I said aloud. "You never mentioned that."

Sorry.

It's okay, Hol.

But, Johnny?

Yeah?

The sunburn is getting worse.

What does that mean, Hol?

I don't know. It's like I'm closer to the sun, or something. Holly curled her arms in, using one hand to scratch at the opposite forearm.

I'm not following you. Like it's warmer?

She considered it for a minute. *Maybe? I'm not sure.*

What do you think it means?

I'm afraid, Johnny.

Why?

Because I think it means they're coming closer.

* * *

The next morning, I went back to school. Having been "sick" for four days, I got a lot of attention. Some people were happy to see me again. Others tried to gauge if I was still hideously contagious. For those jerks, I gave a few fake coughs to send them running.

After second period, I ran into Carrie. I offered a sheepish little wave. "Hey, Carrie."

She smiled and came right up to me. *At least she doesn't think I have the plague.* "Feeling better? You had me worried." She squeezed my arm to emphasize her concern.

Now, look. I have faced down 200-foot monsters. But girls are another story. I nearly fainted. "I'm okay, a lot better now." I faked a little cough. Very little. A cough that said, *I really was sick*, while at the same time saying, *You don't need to back away from me*. It's tough to pull off just the right fake cough, but I think I managed.

"Oh great, the sicky John Boy is back," a sneering voice called out in the hall.

Jesus, really? John Boy? Why are the stupid so predictable? I turned to see who it was, although I was pretty sure I already knew.

Lawrence.

The same empty-headed bully jackass who dumped a bottle of beer and ash and spit on my head. Who made me lash out on that awful day.

In a way, this was the kid who made me kill my father. In the pit of my stomach, a fire, that fire, the thing that was maybe consuming me… it started to burn. "Oh, hi, Lawrence."

Dark and hairy and meaty and stupid. Those were good words for Lawrence Blatnik. Looking at him, I thought only of the car accident. My dad, killed.

"Carrie, you should wash your hands," he said, looking contemptuously at Carrie's fingers wrapped around my bicep. Lawrence curled his lip in disgust. "He's carrying something."

"Oh, shut up, *Lawrence*," Carrie said.

And here's where things got bad.

Lawrence *leaned in* to Carrie. And he said, in a low and serious voice, "You watch your mouth with me, *Carrie*."

And that was it. The full-blown feeling returned. In force. Maybe worse. I mean, against the Gorgols, I had other feelings. Fear, worry, confusion. Against Lawrence Blatnik, there was just one: bloodlust.

So I hit him. In the jaw.

Normally, a guy my size hitting a guy Lawrence's size, well, it would have an effect, sure, but probably a limited one. But my hand *solidified.*

And Lawrence was sent flying down the hallway, like he'd been hit by a semi truck.

I didn't smile — mind you, I wanted to, but I didn't. Man, did that feel good. I mean, I was *proud.*

"Oh my God, John, what was that?" Carrie said, not knowing what to think or do. She seemed... concerned. Impressed? Maybe sort of? But also concerned. Then *concerned* won out and *impressed* disappeared.

My pride fizzled, a firework fading to black in the night sky. "Nothing, Carrie. Um... Sorry — it was an accident. I didn't mean to hit him so hard." I tried a sheepish smile. It felt like a snarl.

"Whoa..." Carrie said, scrunching up her face, taking in the scene. Then she looked at me, a lot like that time in her room, where we kept those fish we killed. *Shit, I've done it again. Carrie just thinks of me as a freak. Again.* I wondered if I could use *double-jointed* as an excuse a second time. It didn't seem likely.

"What exactly is going on here?" a stern voice called out.

Oh crap. I'd been back in school approximately two hours, and I'd already become the focus of administrative attention. And that meant possible detention. Or expulsion. I turned to head to my next class, hoping to fade into the crowd.

"He was just defending me," Carrie said, loudly.

No, Carrie. Shhhh. No need to say any more.

"What? Who?" the stern voice asked. I saw her out of the corner of my eye. Mrs. Rice. Chemistry. She wasn't someone to trifle with. I tried to flee, willing Carrie to be quiet.

"John," Carrie said, even louder. "John Black. He was just standing up for me, really."

I felt a warmth on my back. The kind of warmth that signals the presence of a high-school teacher. The kind of warmth that doesn't soothe or calm. The kind of warmth that isn't really warm, but more like a precursor to heat. The feeling you get just at the moment you realize you've been in the sun too long, but no amount of shade or sunscreen can help. Mrs. Rice's eyes were on me and there was no longer anything I could do. "John, come here," she said in a tone that left no room for debate.

"Yes, ma'am?" I said.

Mrs. Rice looked toward Lawrence, sprawled out on the hallway floor. You know, they buffed those floors, probably nightly, but did that make them clean? I doubted it. Buffed filth, sure. Maybe he landed in a slightly clean spot. But *really* clean? No way. That thought made me happy.

"Did you punch this boy?"

Boy? Lawrence was large, adult-sized. He was 50 pounds or more heavier than me. A boy? That was a joke. "Well. Um..." The mix of emotions over what I'd done was strange. First pride, especially having defended Carrie. Then a bit of shame, embarrassment. Then...

For good measure, Lawrence rolled in toward the lockers, making it look like the effect of my punch was even more severe. *Clever, jerk*, I thought. Looking at him, I got angry again.

"John?" Mrs. Rice asked.

I said nothing. Seething.

"John?" Mrs. Rice asked.

The fire. I felt like it could overcome me. It did.

In a low voice, I said, "Yeah. But if I'd been *trying*, Lawrence would be in the hospital right now."

"John?" Carrie said, confused.

"John!" Mrs. Rice said. "I heard that! Come with me."

So there. In just about two hours, I went from "welcome back" to "the principal will see you now." This day was going great.

You can probably guess the rest. The long wait in the office, the serious conversation with the principal, who warned me about "going down the wrong path." Inside, I laughed. *Wrong path? You wouldn't believe the path I've taken, buddy.*

I was suspended for three days. Mom came to pick me up. She did the mom thing, angry and embarrassed and apologetic to the school staff. But in the car, her tone changed. "You should have thought of this when we *needed* an excuse to get you out of school."

I looked over, but she wouldn't meet my eye. Still, was she making a joke? Was that a little smile I saw?

8

Once again, my family became TV-news junkies. Not targets — thankfully — but junkies. Even Holly this time. Previously, when I couldn't communicate with her, I assumed she'd rather we change the channel. Now, with our mostly mental connection, Holly told me she wanted to know everything there was to know about the Gorgols and the man they called Ranger.

Of course, I told Holly and Mom that his real name was Jake Weissman, but it's hard not to start to refer to things the way everyone else does. When the talking heads on TV say *Ranger* every five minutes, your mind begins to think *Ranger*.

Which must have meant that people were calling me *Black Sword*. Did my own mother or sister start to think of me that way? I had to believe that, to them, Bobby and I were the same as we'd always been. Holly probably thought of Pip as Pip because of their past together. But Mom? I bet she thought of Pip as *Red Hope*. And so what? Why did labels make things so… strange? Probably because *we* didn't choose the labels. If the entire rest of the world started calling you Purple Wombat, you'd probably think it was odd. Right?

But then again, we didn't choose any of this, so maybe what people called us was the least of our worries. Maybe we needed to think about the future. Was it really possible to stay in hiding forever? If not, then what? What would change about us if the world knew who we were and everything we could do? For that matter, how would that change the world?

My head hurt.

So I just watched TV with my family. Not that it made things any better, once I heard the news.

"…Ranger appears to be guiding the Gorgols east, creating a nearly straight line of destruction across the country…"

Air strikes were called. Tanks deployed. Blockades set up. You can probably guess that they were ineffective. Sure, the Gorgols winced when they got hit, but they were tough, especially Alpha. She was a force of nature, and it's not nice to shoot rockets at Mother Nature. That may not be the original phrase, but it's applicable. Meanwhile, Sigma spent a lot of time zipping around in loopy circles, breaking through defense lines and hitting flanks. Alpha just stomped into the fray and destroyed everything.

When the going was particularly tough, Ranger disappeared. I wasn't surprised. Jake was like me, and I didn't think I could take a cruise missile to the forehead, so he stepped out of the way and let the Gorgols do their thing.

But *their thing* had changed. It had turned angry. This wasn't the random movement, the seemingly inadvertent trampling that Omicron and Sigma had done on the western shore. It was a willful destruction, particularly amid any cities they encountered. Buildings were collapsed for little to no reason, even ones out of their way. Either Alpha had a significantly more offensive agenda, or something was changing their behavior. No longer were human beings just ants, stepped on by accident. This was different. Alpha and Sigma destroyed with intent.

Why?

Was their true nature coming out? Or was something — or someone — changing them?

Jake.

Despite the fact that they were coming for my sister, I'd begun to feel like Jake was right about the monsters. That they weren't really monsters. That they could be reasoned with. Now, seeing him in action, I had to wonder if he was even sane. I mean, these were giant creatures of unknown origin, big fighting and killing machines. But Jake balanced on Alpha like she was nothing more than an oversized carnival ride.

So came the darkness of evening, and with one (partial) day of school under my belt, I was absolutely confused about what to do next. Thanks to the principal, I had a weekend to sit and think, then three more days to do the same. Five days free. Hmm.

I knew what I *really* wanted. I wanted to have nothing to do with all of this nonsense. Maybe just play video games and watch old TV shows.

Yeah, right. I knew the days of endlessly, aimlessly playing while staring at a screen were, well, if not over, darn close to it.

All of this is to say, sitting there that night, getting our news fix, we saw the line on the map. The line they drew between "where the Gorgols are now" and "where they were headed."

That line ran through a lot of things. Two or three larger cities. Countless smaller towns. A national wildlife refuge. (Maybe they were going to live there!) The blah-blah people on TV had a lot of opinions, none of which made any sense.

I looked at the line. How it extended across the country. Some news anchors wondered if the Gorgols were headed to the opposite ocean. But why? West-coast beaches not to their liking?

No, the line was purposeful. Only now it wasn't just Holly's words that explained it. It was right there on TV for us to see.

The line they followed led directly to us.

To my sister, still in jeopardy.

One side of me said, *Make peace*. The other said, *Make war*.

I got both of them ready.

9

Saturday. Late morning. Mom and Holly had gone out, so I was doing what you do when no one bothers you late morning on a Saturday. I was sleeping.

The phone rang.

At first I tried to ignore it, but after several rings, whoever was calling must have hung up and tried again. As it began to ring a second time, I went to the kitchen and answered. "Hello?"

"John Black, I assume."

Oh crap. I knew the voice. "Jake? How the hell did you get my number?" Jake knew how to reach me. He must know how to find me. *How did I screw up?* This was even worse than monsters 2,000 miles away, potentially coming toward my house. This was a direct connection to *me*. Not Black Sword, or some other silly attempt at anonymity. There were no more grey areas.

"Hello, John," he said. Just *hello*. Like we were friends. "My father used to tell me, *You learn something new every day*."

"Fascinating," I said. "So you somehow found my phone number, and you called to say that?"

"No, no, of course not." Jake chuckled, and an icy shiver went through me, toes first, then creeping upward. "I just mean that all of us — you, me — are capable of learning. I *learned* from you, John."

"Very sweet of you to say so, and thanks for calling, but if that's all, I'll just be going —"

"I read your dreams," Jake said.

No.

No way. That's what I do! I was in denial for just a moment, then immediately had to contradict myself. *Well, why not? How could that be only my thing? Still… read my dreams?* I took a moment to compose myself. "And what exactly did you learn?"

"Oh, many interesting things, John. The town where you live looks very nice. So does your house. Bobby's is a little fuzzier. But I got to see some of your… *friends*. The redheaded girl. Your mother. Your sister. Holly, I believe her name is?"

"Son of a *bitch*," I muttered.

"Sorry, John? Were you referring to me?"

"If the shoe fits. That's something *my* dad used to say." But there were more important things to do than throw barbs back and forth. I realized that it might be useful to know something about Jake, so I found a piece of paper and a pencil, and wrote down the number on caller ID. "Okay, so you know where I am. Just what do you plan to do about it, Jake?"

"Well, I have really good news there, John. We're coming to see you! You and Bobby."

"*We?*"

"Don't play dumb, John. You don't live in a cave. You know that I'm with the Gorgols now, and that we're traveling."

"Sure, right, I've heard some things."

"As have I." Suddenly, Jake spoke more deliberately, like he wanted to choose his words, his phrasings, in a special sort of way. "I understand that one of the larger questions people have about myself and the Gorgols is, *Where are they going?* And so now you get to be the very first to know."

"You're controlling them. With your mind," I said, spitting the words out. "And you talk about *nature*. What you're doing is unnatural."

"Well, yes, we do have a connection. A close one. After I last saw you, I was able to position myself close enough to start a… shall we say, *conversation*? Of course, they don't speak, or at least not in our language. But through our minds, I've found that we have mutual needs. And of course, in the interest of self-preservation, a few pushes — once I found the right place to push — were necessary."

"And now you're pushing them toward me!"

"Hardly, John. They *want* to find you."

"Me? Just me?" Now it was my turn to be coy. To see if Jake had any idea about Holly and her connection to the Gorgols.

"Just you, John? I should say yes. Aren't you *deserving* of their attention? I can't really understand all of their motivations, but a mother's revenge seems fairly likely." No mention of Holly. That was good. "John, do you know the poet Rainer Maria Rilke?"

Awkward silence.

"Do *I* know a *poet*?" I replied. "Um, no. Do you?"

"Yes, of course," Jake said. As if that really qualified as an appropriate use of the words *of course*.

"You're into poetry?" I asked.

Awkward silence.

"Your time is short, John Black, so I'll skip all this trivial bickering. Rilke, yes, a poet, said it best, I think. *Everything in Nature grows and defends itself any way it can*."

"And that means?"

"The Gorgols, John. They are nature's response to *us*. Well, at least to most of us. The humans who are actively destroying the natural world, every single day."

"You're telling me that 200-foot-tall monsters are here to teach us to be eco-friendly? Maybe recycle?"

I don't think Jake appreciated my humor. "Of course not! It's too late to make *amends*. They're here to *erase* the problem. *Nature tries to be itself at all costs and against all opposition*." Another quote, I assumed, based on Jake's tone.

"Let me get this straight," I said. "You were able to figure out where I live directly from my mind, from my dreams?"

"Yes, with a little bit of online research to fill in the gaps. Once I knew *where* you were, looking up your phone number was surprisingly easy."

"And so you're helping the Gorgols find me?"

"Yes."

"So they can come here and kill me because I killed Omicron?"

"Well, that's a little blunt. But I suppose I should give you at least the dignity of knowing. *Yes.*"

"And then the Gorgols will wipe out humanity — or at least a good portion of it — to even the scales between us and nature?"

"Something like that."

A silence hung between us for a moment. I wasn't sure there was much else to be said.

Until a thought — no, a belief — came to mind. "But, Jake?"

"Yes?"

"I have to tell you. I know I was wrong. Killing Omicron was wrong."

Another long silence. Then a sudden burst of laughter. "You know, John, it never ceases to amaze me the lengths that people will go to save their own skin. That's a clever ploy, but it won't work. The Gorgols will come, and they'll repay you for what you've done."

"I'm serious. This isn't a ploy. Come or don't come, that's up to you." I felt like I had to say it, get it off my chest, to someone who might understand. Even if that someone was trying to engineer my death. "But I mean it. Before I killed Omicron, I *felt* his mind. I know what you mean, that they don't speak the same language. But they have feelings, and I could sense things from him. Omicron was lost."

"He's lost forever now, thanks to you." Jake spat the words.

I couldn't disagree. "You're right about that. I killed Omicron. And now I regret it. But about the rest? You're wrong."

"How so, John?"

"The feelings I felt within Omicron. They had nothing to do with killing people, or revenge on behalf of nature. They were, I don't know, *personal*. Anger and fear, but also confusion. When I felt those things, I tried to stop. I tried to understand, but it was too late. He was dead."

"You're lying," Jake said, but his tone lacked conviction.

"No, I'm not. I felt those things, and I tried to stop. I don't want to fight the Gorgols, even if you come here. I don't want to kill them anymore. And I don't think they really want to fight me, or any of us people. They may have an agenda, but nature's revenge isn't it."

A huff on the line. A mutter. Jake said something, but he was shifting the phone and his voice was unclear. He seemed, for a moment, to be talking to himself. Finally, almost like he was waking up, he spoke again. "I need to think."

The line went dead.

10

I was still standing in the kitchen, holding the loudly complaining phone, when someone knocked on the front door.

My entire body tensed. *My God. He's here already.*

I peeked through the small kitchen window above our sink, expecting to see a giant Gorgol toe in my front yard, but of course there was none. Realizing they couldn't exactly sneak up on me like that, I let out a sigh of relief, and hung up the phone.

Then, once more, my breath caught as I noticed movement.

A man was standing at my front door.

I looked him up and down. Dark hair, short and stocky. Long pants and sneakers — a bit of a weird look for an adult, if you ask me. And something like a little pouch sat atop one shoe, interwoven into the shoelaces. I decided I didn't need to deal with some sort of door-to-door sales pitch, so I went to my room and pretended no one was home. The man knocked two or three more times before he gave up.

Well, he *sort of* gave up. Nearly ten minutes went by before he knocked again. *Seriously, dude?* Figuring the guy must be desperate and would keep coming back and knocking all day, I decided to answer the door and play the dumb kid. You know, *sorry my mom's not home right now. Come again never.* That sort of thing.

Just before I opened the door, I caught a glimpse of something through the side window. A flash of color. Curls of red hair tossed over a shoulder.

It wasn't the man this time. Carrie McGregor was standing on my front step.

She wore a black skirt and a green top, and looked like a dream. Hell, who am I kidding? Carrie McGregor could've worn used trash bags and I still would've thought she looked like a dream. I felt my hand slightly shake as I reached for the knob to open the door.

Then I froze. I was in my pajamas.

Or, more correctly, the clothes that I *used* for pajamas, which were a ratty t-shirt and shorts that I'd probably worn more nights in a row than I cared to remember. "Be right there!" I shouted, then raced to my bedroom and quickly changed. The end product? T-shirt and shorts, but less ratty, and I did stop to slap a little deodorant under the pits for good measure.

I ran back and flung the door open. At which point I realized that flinging the door open was decidedly uncool. So I leaned against the doorframe, trying to look at ease but coming off like a mannequin propped in a display window. "Carrie? Oh, uh, Carrie. Hi! I thought you were... um, my mom, uh, with the groceries. So I ran to help out." Making things up on the fly here, people.

"Oh. Well, that was nice of you," she said, smiling.

I smiled back. And seconds passed. Suddenly it became an awkward silence. *Oh crap*, I thought. *Say something.* "So, how are you?" *Excellent. Such banter.*

She looked at her shoes. "John, I wanted to apologize."

"For what?"

"Yesterday, in school. I got you in a lot of trouble."

Did she? Well, maybe. She did tell Mrs. Rice that I was the one who had punched Lawrence Blatnik. But she'd been *explaining*, not really turning me in. "Oh, don't worry about it." I smiled again, this time awkwardly. Carrie had walked all the way to my house to apologize to me. That fluttering, deep inside, kicked up a notch.

"But I *am* worried about it. You got suspended, and all you were trying to do was stick up for me."

"Well, sort of," I said.

"What do you mean?"

"I just mean, yeah, I was sticking up for you. But I have other reasons for wanting to punch Lawrence Blatnik." I shrugged, and smiled yet again, because what else was there to do?

And she returned the smile, batting her lashes.

My heart leapt. I know, that sort of thing was pretty much automatic. If she rang a bell, I guess I'd drool. Call me Pavlov. Or, wait. He was the scientist, right? Ah, crap, what was his dog's name? Sorry, I digress.

"I think a lot of people have a lot of reasons for wanting to punch Lawrence Blatnik. Me included," Carrie said. Then we both laughed out loud. When it passed, she did the most unexpected thing. *She* asked *me* out. "John, do you want to go to the coffee shop with me?"

I was flustered. Flabbergasted. Flummoxed. And other descriptive words beginning with *fl*. Flax-seeded? Flailing?

Probably those, too. "Um, sure, yeah. That would be nice, uh, whenever you want to do that. Sure." I tilted my head down so she wouldn't see exactly how red my cheeks were becoming.

"I mean now," she said.

"Oh," I said, raising my eyebrows.

And that's how I ended up at the coffee shop with Carrie McGregor around noon on Saturday.

Carrie was apparently quite familiar with the place, stepping right up to the counter and ordering a double macciamericanofrappalatte. I had no idea what that was, nor did I understand virtually any other word on the menu. I scanned it nonchalantly, trying to look like I belonged there. In the coffee shop. In Carrie's world.

"Know what you want, John? I'm buying." She waved a gift card and smiled.

Wow, not only was it our second date, it was a sort of *equalizer*, too. I did all the work for date one, she did everything for date two.

I realized at that moment how happy that made me. This wasn't about fictitious expectations. It wasn't about cool. It wasn't even about smart. And most importantly, it wasn't about power. I was so used to thinking about Sol and Jake and Pip and Bobby and even the Gorgols — which one of us could top the other? Who had more strength or power or ability? And this was just two people, treating each other equally.

I must have stood there, sappily smiling at Carrie, for too long.

"John?" She snapped her fingers twice in front of my eyes, not a rude gesture, but a silly one. Still, equals.

I came back to reality and focused again on the menu. Still, all those damn words. What did they mean? I ordered an *espresso macchiato*. How do I remember the name? Because once I took a sip, I vowed to never forget it.

I hated it that much.

When our order arrived, Carrie received a tall glass filled with swirls of whipped cream and sprinkled with something probably delicious on top. Mine came in a tiny glass, a dark bit of liquid topped with a small dab of something frothy.

Did I mention the glass was tiny?

I mean, I couldn't really figure out how I was supposed to hold the thing, much less start drinking it.

We got a small table, in a corner by the window. It was, well, it was kind of romantic, or at least what I thought romantic was supposed to be like. Carrie sat across from me, pulling the paper off a straw and slipping it into her drink. She leaned forward to take her first sip, her red hair falling around her face, framing it on both sides. "*Yummy*. I love this drink," she said, licking whipped cream from the corner of her mouth.

So that wasn't too distracting, right?

Then it was my turn.

I pinched the small glass handle between my thumb and index finger, raising and tilting it toward my mouth. Have you ever tried this particular move? It's basically impossible to do such a thing and *not* stick out your pinky like a froufrou snob.

Still, I sipped.

It was hot — that was the first thing I noticed. Thankfully, not *too* hot. I could only imagine the embarrassment if my powers had kicked in and my mouth tried to sluice around the hot coffee, making me dribble it all over the floor. So, small victory, I suppose. But the taste?

My face puckered. Involuntarily, I swear. It was so bitter and just flat out *awful*. Like I said, I hated it.

Quickly, I tried to smooth my features, pretend it was good.

Carrie chuckled. But it wasn't a derisive laugh, it was sweet. "Not your favorite?" she asked.

I couldn't help but smile back. "It's a little, um… bitter," I said.

She rolled her eyes. "Well, did you put any sweetener in it?"

"No?" It was a question. It meant that I didn't even know that was a thing you could do. My coffee-shop inexperience was showing.

Carrie got up, grabbed a packet of something from the counter, and came back. "Try it with this."

I did.

I still hated it.

Interlude

Opposites. Magnets. Attracting. The undeniable pull.
Getting closer. Getting stronger.

Changing.

Syncing.

Locked.

Coming together.

One side pulls harder than the other.

There are more.

11

"Johnny?" Holly asked as I popped into the kitchen.

Yeah, Hol? Mom, busy making our breakfast, still had time to roll her eyes. I forgot she might resent our mental conversation. "What's up, Holly?" Mom nodded in appreciation. I gave her a wink.

Holly was absent-mindedly scratching one arm, but her eyes were fixed on mine. *Johnny, the burn. I don't like it.*

You mean the sunburn feeling?

Uh huh.

Still getting worse?

I think so. She kept scratching at her arm, harder than before. So much I wondered if she would make herself bleed.

Suddenly noticing my stare, Holly dropped her hands into her lap. *Sorry. I can't help it.*

* * *

"High five!" Bobby said, one hand raised. I just gave him an annoyed look. "Come on, man, you're a hero!"

"What are you talking about, Bobby?"

"Johnny, look. Even back when *I* was the biggest jerk around, *I* didn't like Lawrence Blatnik. Everyone wanted to loosen a few of his teeth. You've done the community a great service." Bobby laughed at his own joke.

And I couldn't help but smile. "It did feel good."

"Of course it did! And, with any luck, Lawrence will fly under the radar for a little while."

Bobby was smiling, but his eyes told the truth. Something was bothering him. Still, teenage boys aren't known for their particular skill at sharing feelings. So when I asked him a question, I may have skated around what was really on his mind. "Do you want a sandwich or something?" See? Maybe that was changing the subject. Perhaps.

"Nah, I ate at home."

Four hours later, Bobby finally spoke up. It was a lazy Sunday afternoon, the kind of fall day when the weather is just right — cool with a little breeze, but enough sun to keep you warm and comfortable. The leaves were starting to turn, so the world was flush with color in places that were normally muted green or brown. From above our heads, the occasional red or yellow leaf would decide to go AWOL and jump to its imminent death.

Bobby and I didn't really have a place to hang out, not like the self-storage building or the warehouse. We pretty much stayed around my house, but even we couldn't avoid going outdoors when the day was so inviting. So we ended up aimlessly walking, making our way to Merrick Park, probably drawn by the *ding* of aluminum bats striking balls, the indistinct voices encouraging pitchers and batters and fielders alike, but mostly pitchers, as long as they weren't belly-itchers. Beside one of the ballparks, we found an empty set of risers and sat down, watching a bunch of 10-year-olds in red take the field while other kids in green and white came up to bat.

"I'm torn, Johnny," Bobby finally said.

"Go on."

"Well, you know I came back here with you, and that was my choice. I don't want you to think you forced me or something…"

"But?"

"But I'm torn. Pip is out there, by herself, tracking two Gorgols and Jake. I feel like I should help her."

"Then you should," I said.

Bobby nodded slowly. A boy in green and white made contact and sent the ball looping into left center field. Mass chaos ensued. I don't know if you've ever seen 10-year-olds play baseball, but it isn't the fluid game you might be familiar with from the pros. The runner advanced all the way to third before the red team got things under control. "I don't think we're looking at athletic-scholarship material here, Johnny," Bobby said with a laugh. "Anyway, I want you to know that I completely understand your point of view. Who are we to just decide to kill the Gorgols? And I respect you for thinking that, especially if they're coming toward Holly." Now it was my turn to nod, although I didn't say anything. "Lately, I've been following things pretty closely on the news. The creatures are really going to town in some places."

"Going to town when they go to town?"

"Right," Bobby said with a smile. "I mean they're really destroying things, any place they run into. And Pip is still tracking them. I've heard reports and seen her in some of the video clips. As for us..."

"I know."

"They think we either *died* from our wounds or just *gave up*." Bobby sighed. "I'm not sure which of those I like the least."

"We sort of did give up — well, *I* gave up. You chose to leave with me."

"Yeah."

"And now you regret it?"

"No, Johnny. Not really. But I do find myself wanting to help."

"Go, if that's what you need to do," I said. "But you know they're coming here."

Bobby thought about that for a moment. He scanned the area, taking it in. "I know. But... they'll destroy this place. They'll destroy *our hometown*."

"Probably, if we let them," I said.

He turned to me, a little too eager. "Then you'll fight?"

"I don't know. I don't think so. I don't want to kill anymore. Besides, I don't know how much Jake is pushing them."

"Well, then, I know one thing for sure."

"What's that?"

"We can't let them come here and destroy the place where we live. Where our friends live, our families. Even though my family sucks. I mean, I actually *like* your family."

We shared a laugh, the kind of laugh friends can share no matter what they're talking about. Life, death, anything from potato chips to terminal cancer — friends can find a laugh in any conversation. "But there's more," I said. "Jake thinks the Gorgols want to find us — well, *me*. For revenge, because I killed Omicron. And he actually thinks the Gorgols are here for revenge against all of humanity, for what we've done wrong to the world."

"That would be something, huh, Johnny? The world pumps out giant monsters when it wants to knock mankind down a peg."

"Yeah, but he doesn't know they might actually be coming for Holly."

"Okay, so they're coming to us, but we don't want them to, because we like this stupid place and all of its stupid people, and Jake thinks the Gorgols want to avenge their dead and then avenge the world."

"Correct," I said. "So… What do you suggest, Bobby?"

His face became serious. "We go to them. Meet up with them before they come here and destroy everything. I have no idea what we're going to do when we get there, but we have to go to them, so they don't come here and mess everything up. Or hurt Holly."

I'd like to say that I was altruistic and full of peace when I said, "You're right." But honestly, the bloodlust was there, too. Even I hardly noticed that one my hands was repeatedly balling itself into a fist.

Besides, I had a history of going to great lengths to protect my sister.

12

I was suspended, so no one thought twice when I didn't show up for school the next day. Bobby skipped, too, mind-pushing his mom to call him out sick again. There was no saying how much longer that thin guise would last.

We followed the beacon. The weird, fuzzy one that Jake — I mean, *Ranger* — put out.

And so there we were, once again, headed directly for trouble, facing down a man who may or may not have been crazy, and his two lapdogs. His two giant, deadly lapdog monsters.

I had to tell myself that this wasn't just a rehash. It wasn't the bravado and stupidity of us flying west to kill Omicron.

Jake had made it clear they were coming for me. And the Holly connection scared me.

Somehow, I had to reason with Jake. Or at least figure out clearly what the Gorgols wanted and try to resolve things without more killing, without letting them get to my sister. If Jake could tap into their minds, I figured I could, too. I just needed to do it a little more slowly and carefully, not like I had with Omicron.

Still, with all that running through my mind as we prepared to leave, there was something that stood out even more. Winner of The Most Insane Moment of the Day was this: Bobby stole his parents' car.

Stole is probably a harsh word. He borrowed it. He pushed his parents' minds so they wouldn't miss him or the car for a little while. And he was going to bring it back, assuming it didn't become Gorgol toe cheese or something. I reminded him we should park a safe distance away.

So, you might ask, how did Bobby know how to drive? That's the thing. He didn't. Neither did I. We were about the right age for driver's ed, but hadn't actually gotten there yet. So Bobby winged it.

Turn the car on. Put it in D for drive. Big turny-wheel makes it go left and right. Right pedal is gas, left is brake. It's not all that different from countless racing games we played. Bobby was good at those, and he was pretty good at real driving, too, after only a few minutes.

But the hat. My God, the hat.

Bobby figured that we'd get derailed pretty darn fast if some cop pulled us over thinking an underage kid was driving. So he also *borrowed* one of his dad's hats. It was like a fedora or bowler, or maybe a sombrero. You can see that I don't know hats. It was tan and roughly woven, with a bright blue satiny band in the middle. And a big white feather. An *actual* feather. What bird produced big white hat feathers? Condor. I'm going with condor.

"Shut up, Johnny," Bobby said when I hopped in the car, took one look at him, and started laughing.

I dramatically snapped to attention and saluted. "Aye aye, *mon capitan*! Should I cast off the lines?"

Bobby balled up a fist. "Don't make me pop you. I do *not* look like a pirate, Johnny."

My lip quivered with a coming wave of new guffaws. "Whatever ye say, cap'n!" The wave hit. I laughed.

"I'd punch you in the arm, but… you know." Then Bobby couldn't help it, and he laughed, too.

We sat like that in my driveway for a while.

Finally, wiping tears from my eyes, I asked, "I understand it's a disguise, but why did you pick *that* hat?"

"Because," Bobby said. "The old man never wears it. My grandma gave it to him, and he hates it. I figured he'd never miss it. And I figured it'd make me look older."

"Mission accomplished, admiral," I said.

"*Admiral*?" Bobby considered it, then nodded. "Admiral!" He smiled and tipped his hat. "Admiral…" And we set sail.

* * *

It wasn't even two hours before we hit a snag.

"Ah crap!" Bobby said, looking down.

"What?"

"The gas light just came on. Did you bring any money?"

"Maybe?" I said, starting to fumble in my pockets. I pulled out a few crumbled bills, one of which was a ten. So we could buy some gas, but enough to get to the Gorgols and, with luck, return? Not a chance. That meant doing it *our* way.

We started looking for road signs, and pretty quickly found that there was gas available at the next exit. Bobby had been firmly entrenched in the right lane since the moment we got on the highway, so he was already well primed to get off. What he didn't plan for was the people coming on.

A blue sedan attempted to merge directly beside us, and a comedy of errors ensued. Bobby slowed down, the other driver slowed down. Bobby sped up, the other driver sped up. The merge area was ending quickly, so something had to be done. Finally, Bobby just hit the brake, nearly stopping in the middle of the road. The last we saw of the other driver, he was careening left onto the highway and mouthing something at us through the window. I'm pretty sure he was saying, *What's with that hat?*

At the gas station, Bobby started filling up. It was my job to go inside and make a few mental suggestions to the attendant, to ensure he believed that we were never there and never stole a tank of gas. Above the cash register hung a little TV that the attendant must have used to pass the time. And on the TV was our goal, the Gorgols themselves.

The video showed Alpha and Sigma, pounding their way through some wooded area. I was struck once more by the size and sheer power of Alpha. She was like a giant reptilian gorilla, with an extended, hooded neck and a long tapering tail. And the scales — those massive, granite scales, just like Omicron had. I knew how powerful Sigma was, but standing beside her mother, Sigma looked small. Well, not small. But slighter, more lithe.

And, of course, up on one of Alpha's wide shoulders sat the khaki-covered form of Jake. *Ranger.*

The TV announcers spoke over the live footage.

"In an amazingly short period of time, the Gorgols have made it across most of the country."

"That's right, David. In another day or two, depending, they could reach the eastern seaboard."

The view changed to a map, showing the past progress and forward projection of the creatures' marathon.

"In fact, it seems the only thing that really slows them down is when they pause to destroy something."

"Correct — other than that, they've been relentless in following this line. The problem is that we still don't know exactly where this path will take them. It's endpoint, assuming the ocean is an endpoint, is an area of marshy, indistinct shoreline. Not much there but a couple of farmhouses and maybe a duck blind."

"Nevertheless, officials in populated areas along the route have begun initial evacuations."

I had a decent sense of geography, especially after my long walk to find Sol. It looked like very little land separated the Gorgols from where I was standing. We'd be upon them sooner than I realized.

I had to talk to Jake. Luckily, I'd remembered to bring the paper with his phone number on it. I just needed a phone of my own.

At 15, I really should have had one. So many of my friends already did. Bobby didn't, but that's because his parents sucked, as you likely recall. For me, with a single working mom who had run through her insurance money and still had to support a disabled daughter — well, me begging her for a phone seemed a little crappy.

Luckily, virtually everyone else on the planet had one, so after a little push, the gas-station attendant offered up his phone.

Jake answered after only one ring. "Yes?"

"Jake, it's me. John. We're coming to meet you. Think you can control your pets long enough for us to talk?"

"Of course, John. Of course."

13

"You have it, right?" I asked Bobby.

He looked confused. "Have what?"

I pulled out my black mask. "Right now, we're just another car on the road, but if we drive any closer to those things, we're going to be on TV." In the far distance, we could see the Gorgols heads rising above the trees. Around them, like flies on a turd, helicopters circled.

"Yeah, yeah, in the back."

"Then find a place to pull over, hopefully where your parents' car won't get stepped on."

He did, and from there, with masks on, we walked.

* * *

It didn't take long before we were spotted. One helicopter, branching off from the rest, zipped toward us, with its *thump thump thump* sound getting closer.

This time around, we had no swords, no weapons of any kind — well, truth be told, I wore my belt, but I told myself that was strictly to keep my pants from falling down.

The Gorgols, of course, weren't terribly hard to find. Second large monster to the right and straight on 'til morning. In an hour, we were close. In two, we could see the entire situation at hand.

Jake had *parked* the Gorgols in a wide field of corn, their massive feet and tails smashing who knows how many stalks. Some farmer was having a bad day. Or maybe not. My grandmother used to use corn meal in everything. Maybe the farmer could get creative and sell The Official Corn Meal of Gorgol Alpha. He could make a mint.

Jake himself waited for us outside a large wooden barn that looked like it had been painted red once in the preceding three or four decades. As always, Jake stood like a veiled threat.

Still, I couldn't help but stare. The Gorgols…

It was odd and unnatural and terrifying to see them so close while they were so docile. Or maybe it was natural for them. It made me believe there truly was something inside each of them besides just a smashing, destroying, killing machine.

Sigma stood almost lazily watching us approach, her strange, glowing amber eyes seemingly dimmed in the daylight, her posture at rest. Next to her, Alpha loomed, also at ease. Her diamond-like eyes burned a darker orange as they followed us, and she huffed loud — and, I presumed, stinky — clouds of breath far over our heads. Comparatively, Sigma snorted smaller puffs of air through her flaring nostrils. I was glad the prevailing winds were able to carry the stench away, because I'd experienced Gorgol breath up close and personal before, and I could do without a repeat. Besides, even without smelling their breath, the monsters reeked.

I'd never noticed the odor before, not while fighting them. Or at least I'd never attributed it to them. Perhaps it was the adrenaline, the heat of the moment. But this time… Do you know what old mud smells like? Not new mud. That's just water and dirt. Mostly, new mud doesn't smell at all. But old mud, the sort of greenish-greyish-brown, almost-slimy kind that's leftover from watery rot? From things that drowned in creeks and rivers, leaf and creature alike, bloating and decomposing? That kind of mud smells terrible. The Gorgols smelled like old mud times 10. Maybe it was all the smashing and smushing things into pulp, stuck between their toes. I didn't know, but I gave Bobby a sidelong glance, wrinkling my nose.

"Seriously," he said, nodding. "Somebody needs to light a match or something."

And the sounds they made, just breathing. Their slowly heaving chests creaked like the boards of an old-time sailing ship, punctuated by the hiss and puff of their expelled air. Occasionally they shifted, and the creaking increased, complemented by the clacking of their scales against each other, a sound somewhere between rattlesnake tail and pending avalanche.

All the while above us, three helicopters continued to *thump thump thump*, no doubt broadcasting us live for all the world to see. I wondered momentarily if Pip was somewhere near, keeping an eye on us, no doubt wondering what the hell we were doing talking to the man they called Ranger. The world at large probably wondered about that, too.

I was mesmerized, or something close to it, by Alpha's diamond eyes, Sigma's amber ones. What were these beasts thinking, seeing me again? The one who had taken their brother. I wished, not for the last time, that invisibility was one of my powers.

Keeping one eye on the massive creatures, we approached Jake, and he turned, gesturing for us to enter the barn behind him. I gave Bobby an *Are we sure about this?* look, but he just shrugged and went inside.

Just as I was about to follow, Sigma lurched, emitting a huge sound, a blast of noise directly at me.

I can tell you, I didn't just jump, I *leapt* into the air. My arms came up, a pointless fighting position, and I felt like every hair was on end. My heart was a hummingbird, flapping in my chest, so fast it might burst. Now came their move, I just knew it. I'd walked right into the trap. Now the Gorgols both would lunge at me.

Then Sigma settled back into her original position. Her nose twitched a little, side to side, as she resumed her normal breathing.

I hadn't even noticed him move, but Bobby was beside me, drawn back out by the sound and movement. "What the hell was *that*?" he asked.

I only stared at Sigma, meeting her glowing eyes. "I think... I think she sneezed."

Bobby goggled at me as I stepped past him. You know the old adage about frying pans and fires? We were walking out of the path of sneezing monsters and into a meeting with the man who had tried to cut off my head.

I'd take the frying pan or the fire instead.

14

Jake stood in the middle of a wide space, the large central aisle of the barn. In the privacy of the building, Bobby and I removed our masks as Jake spoke. It wasn't like he didn't know who we were already, anyway. "Let me make this clear, gentlemen," Jake said. "The Gorgols outside want to kill you. You're alive only because I'm holding them back. You attack me, they attack you. You don't give me a good enough reason to keep holding them back, they attack you. Your lives are currently a gift, from me. Have you read the Bible?" Bobby and I shared a quick, confused look. But Jake didn't wait for an answer. "James 1:17. *Every good gift and every perfect gift is from above, and cometh down from the Father of lights, with whom is no variableness, neither shadow of turning.*"

There was a pause. The pregnant kind.

"Um… 'Kay?" Bobby said.

Jake leaned toward us with a snarl on his face. "You give me so much as a *shadow of turning* and I will bring all hell down upon you. Nature's infinite fury." He spoke in a gruff, terse way, standing with shoulders hunched, like he was trying to loom over us as much as the giant creatures did. "Are we clear?"

"Crystal," Bobby said, returning Jake's bravado with a curl of his lip.

Suddenly Jake's tone changed, even his posture. Like he had changed skins. He was straighter, more polished, in stance and in word. "Excellent, my friends. Then you understand this isn't a game. If you've come to speak to me, to make me understand your position, I suggest you begin… now." He stood, waiting for us to answer. Physically, he didn't even seem to be the person he was only moments before, the one who had threatened us with the Bible. It was like there were two Jakes inside of one body.

"Before we say anything, I want you to explain, to Bobby," I said. "What are the Gorgols? Why are they here?"

I noticed just the slightest twitch at the corner of one eye, like a gnat was pestering him but he didn't want to acknowledge it. He twitched once, twice, a third time. I was reminded of Walter Ivory. The powers had made him go mad. Somehow I knew, at that very moment, that regardless of what Jake said, he was simply crazy. Something deep inside him was not right.

Who was I kidding? Something inside *me* wasn't right. The powers made me angry. Consumed me with rage, made me want to fight and destroy.

So, you know, the thorns in our cells should have come with some kind of side-effect warning. Ask your doctor if you're healthy enough for superpowers.

Still, the calm and polished Jake spoke. "Very well. John. Bobby. Do you understand the importance of fear?"

"The *importance* of it?" I replied, grimacing.

"Allow me to explain." Jake began to leisurely pace the floor of the barn. "In the natural world, fear can be an incredibly important regulator. Do you know what happens when any single population grows too large and overwhelms the available food supply?"

We didn't answer. In fact, Bobby and I pretty much just listened silently, keeping an eye on him. We heard Jake's questions, but we could tell they were questions he planned on answering himself, so we kept our mouths shut.

Confirming our suspicions, he continued. "You end up with an unnatural distribution. I'll give you an example. Along the northwest coast, there's a small island. Once upon a time, many snails lived on the salty rocks of the shore, and a healthy population of red crabs fed on those snails. In turn, there were raccoons that wandered the shore and ate the crabs. But at the top of the food chain, there were wolves. Not many, just enough to keep the raccoon population in check. Any guess what happened next on this island?"

Again, we were silent.

"Man arrived," Jake said, locking eyes with me. "And you and I both know what that means. Man always needs to *control* his environment. This is a remote island, so food was a concern. The first settlers began to grow crops, raise livestock. Presented with these new… *opportunities*, the wolves did the only natural thing. They attacked and ate livestock, whenever possible. After all, the raccoons were smaller, wild and harder to catch, but the chickens were kept in a pen. It was far too easy a meal to ignore. And humans, being human, gathered together and decided something had to be done about the wolves. So they killed them. All of them. And that changed everything."

"How so?" Bobby said, surprising me by suddenly speaking.

"Because, Bobby, without wolves — without the *fear* of wolves, the fear for their lives — the raccoon population exploded. But that's not all. The raccoons decimated the crabs, leaving very few to eat the snails. So, in turn, the snail population also grew. In the end, the island was inhabited by just a few humans, and an extremely unhealthy number of raccoons and snails. Which, ironically, was also a nuisance to the people, but much harder to eradicate than the wolves. The snails were simply everywhere. The raccoons were much craftier and could hide better than the wolves. And they, too, began to turn to the people's livestock and crops for food. So, you see, living in an unnatural way, taking away the critical components of the food chain, didn't solve people's problems, it increased them tenfold."

"But what does that have to do with fear? And us?" I asked.

"Excellent question, John, my old friend." Jake was doing what my grandmother used to call *soapboxing*. Speaking like he was a big deal, standing in front of everyone like he was up on a soapbox. I guess that was a thing in grandma's day. Personally, I'd never purchased soap by the box.

Something about the way he spoke gave me pause. Why did he call me *old friend*? I barely knew him, and I certainly wasn't his friend. But it seemed to fit the polished Jake, to speak like that. "Some humans, some sensible ones, attempted a test. To see if the *fear* of a predator is sufficient to change behavior. So they set up loudspeakers on the island — this is of course many, many years after the first settlers, who didn't even have electricity — and, randomly, they would play the sounds of wolves calling. And they found that *only that* — only the *sound* of the wolves, the *fear* that there *might* be wolves — was sufficient to thwart the raccoons' unfettered access to the beach and the crabs. In time, the raccoon population, afraid of these new and completely fabricated predators, stopped eating so many crabs, and diminished. The red crab population increased, snails were consumed back to healthy levels. In other words, *fear* brought *balance*."

"And that's what you think the Gorgols are here for?" I said.

Jake smiled a broad smile. "Yes, absolutely. Well, that and to kill you. You see, there are only a few Gorgols — only two, thanks to you, John — but that's enough for *fear*. Human beings have been living out of control for the last hundred years, maybe even longer. Nature is finally giving us something to be afraid of. To rein us back in, at last."

"You know," Bobby said, in a tone I knew immediately to be sarcasm, "that all makes perfect sense. And wherever the Gorgols aren't living, we can pump the sounds of Gorgols through loudspeakers. So people won't eat all the crabs. Or something like that." I stifled a laugh.

"Very well, Bobby. It's your turn. And remember what I said about *giving me any reason at all*. Why are you here?"

Bobby looked to me to answer. But I froze. I had no idea what to say, other than what I'd already told Jake. I didn't want to fight. I wasn't sure what the Gorgols were, where they came from, but I didn't believe they came to destroy humanity. Or to be our *fear*. Human beings could destroy everything, the environment, the ice caps, animal and plant populations, the weather, even each other, and the Earth was still going to be here, spinning around the Sun, oblivious. Maybe it would remember us like it remembered the dinosaurs, just by the crap we left behind. Maybe not. But I didn't think the Earth operated by sending three big bullies to do its dirty work.

The Gorgols had been brought to Earth by my sister, and now they were seeking her out. Jake's theory about balance was wrong. If the creatures could be dealt with, reasoned with, then it could only be because they were from somewhere else and wanted to go back. Because they were lost.

Jake twitched again, deeper and longer this time, and I knew that if I didn't speak, our moment would be over and he would unleash the Gorgols. But what did I want from this conversation? What could I say that could possibly make this all go away? I needed to make him see that his agenda was not the creatures' agenda.

"Jake," I started. "I… think I know what the Gorgols really want."

"Of course, John," he said with a chuckle. "So do I. I've just explained that. Other than their macro intent, they want to kill you."

"No. Well, *maybe*, but I think there's something else. Something more important to them. And it isn't what you think."

Jake scoffed, and something about him pulsed, like a spotty signal suddenly giving off a shock of static. Not a bright light, but a bright*ness*, inside, throbbing. "Really, John? This should be quite entertaining. Please tell me what it is the Gorgols want, and I do hope you have some sort of evidence, not just wild ideas to waste my time." Jake started to chuckle again, but suddenly froze.

And I was immediately off the hook from providing any real evidence, because the evidence suddenly presented itself.

Outside, the Gorgols were walking away.

15

Jake felt them leaving. We all could *hear* them leaving, but he *felt* it. "What have you done?" he spat, running from the barn.

Bobby and I exchanged glances, neither of us knowing what was going on. And just as Jake left the building, someone else arrived, coming in from the other end and pulling off her red mask.

"Pip!" Bobby shouted, rushing to greet her.

"So, the hounds return," she said, giving us a stern look. At first, I couldn't tell if she was mad. After all, not only had I abandoned her pretty abruptly, I had somehow convinced Bobby to join me.

"Uh, Pip, listen…" I started.

"Shut up, John," she said, tucking her mask into a small pouch at her side. A long metal sword was slung over her back. "Don't take everything so seriously." Then she smiled, and I knew it was okay. I laughed, and they both followed my lead. After a moment, Pip broke up the party. "Listen, I don't mean to fart in the henhouse, but the Gorgols are inexplicably leaving and Jake is out there doing who knows what. His next move might be to try to control them again and bring them back here, toward us."

"*Fart in the henhouse?*" Bobby repeated, laughing.

"No, he's not," I said.

"No? And how do you know what Jake's going to do?"

"Not Jake, the Gorgols. I know where they're going. And we need to do something about it." I started for the door, pulling the black mask back over my head.

"And just where are they going, John?" Pip called from behind me.

I paused between the large barn doors, turning back. "They're going to my house. They're finally done messing around, and now they're headed for Holly."

"Oh, shit," Pip said.

* * *

We never had the full conversation, but it was clear. Pip actually cared about Holly. She hadn't just *taken care* of her, back when Sol had abducted my sister. She liked Holly. I could also tell she felt guilty about the whole thing.

It came down to one story, something Pip had told me at her secret underground lair. (Don't tell her I called it that.) Despite our intense focus on training, it simply wasn't possible to practice fighting all day, every day. After a long afternoon, we sat in the front room, the same place Jake broke into when he tried to kill me. And Pip said something to me out of the blue.

"How is she?"

"Huh?" I replied, stifling a yawn. Long days of physical exertion were rather new for me.

Pip wouldn't meet my eye. Somehow, that told me this meant something to her. "Your sister. How is she?"

"Fine," I said. I was tired. I didn't want to deal with the conversation if it was just going to be lip service. My tone made that clear.

"No, I mean really."

I turned my head in Pip's direction, expecting to find sass and maybe a teasing expression. Instead, she seemed earnest. "Uh. Fine. Really." It took me a second to compose myself. "Well, I assume when you knew her she was pretty unresponsive. She was that way for us, too, for years. But after the business with Sol, things changed."

"Really? How?" she asked. Again, she seemed sincere. But it was hard to trust her. This was my sister we were talking about, and Pip had been with Sol then.

I shrugged. "I don't know. I mean, you know what we all can do, mentally." Pip nodded. "And you know Holly has power, too?"

"I didn't, originally. Sol was so blind to the fact that this little girl in a wheelchair might have strength, even more than he did himself. And that must have rubbed off on me, because I didn't see it either. It wasn't until the very end, when I thought I was going to die in that sandstorm, that I realized it was her. So much *power*. But nothing there to regulate it."

"Right. That was her. But, like I said, things changed."

"Can she control it now?"

"That's a good question," I said. "I think so. Well, I think she can keep herself from lashing out like she did before. But she can't really make her powers work the way she wants, except..." I laughed.

"Except what?"

"One time she made a quarter jump up and spin around. Pretty amazing. Something she could never do with her hand, but she can do it with her mind."

"Does she talk?"

"Not the way you mean. Out loud, she only says a few words. But I can reach her mind. We can talk. Bobby, too, though he usually doesn't."

Bobby perked up at the mention of his name. "Doesn't seem respectful, me popping into her mind whenever I feel like saying something."

I could understand that. It certainly was strange. "Yeah. But I do it all the time. It's just how my family works now."

Pip smiled. A true, warm smile. "I'm glad to hear that you can talk to her now, even if it's just with your mind. I…" She paused. "I really liked Holly."

Despite the fact I was in Pip's house and she was training me, I got mad. "Gimme a break. You kept her from me. From my mom. You *abducted* her."

"I know. And I just want to say how sorry I am for that. I was under Sol's influence, following him. Even then, though, I knew I had to do something, especially when everyone else left." I don't know if she meant to, but she glanced at Bobby. The implication was clear. Bobby left, the others left. What else could she do, being the last person between Holly and Sol?

"Don't forget whose idea it was," Bobby said in a quiet, sad voice.

I just nodded. Bobby's idea. To take my own sister.

If I could forgive that, maybe I could forgive Pip, too.

"I remember one time," Pip began, "Holly was restless. Just Sol's presence would get her thrashing around sometimes. I was scared for her, and wanted to calm her down. She likes cereal, a *lot*." Pip laughed, and I nodded. "But this time, her cereal just sat there, untouched. She kept staring at me. At first, I couldn't figure it out, but then I moved my arm and saw her eyes flicker with the movement. It wasn't *me* she was interested in, it was the banana I was peeling, getting ready to eat. I tried moving the banana to one side again, and her eyes followed it. So I finished peeling it, cut it up, and dropped the pieces into her cereal. She devoured it like she hadn't eaten in days, smiling at me the whole time."

Then it was my turn to laugh.

"But Sol..." she continued. My laugh shriveled up and died. "He didn't really like Holly to be happy. I mean, he never abused her, like, he never hit her or anything — which is good, because I *definitely* wouldn't have stood for that. Not with what I've been through. I mean, if Sol had hit her, I probably would have hit him, and I have no idea what would have happened after that. But if she seemed the least bit happy, his mood darkened. Two different times that I remember, Holly and I were eating after a long day on the road. She wasn't happy about any of it, I could tell, but in the moment, you have ups and downs. Both times, she was feeling up. And Sol didn't like that. He yelled at us to get back into the van and off we went, driving well into the night for no good reason."

"Yeah, he was a prick," Bobby added. Three heads nodded.

Pip continued. "After that first time with the banana, and even though I knew Sol wouldn't like it, I made a point of grabbing a couple bananas each time we stopped for food." She looked up, and I met her eyes with mine. "I just told him they were for me."

* * *

So I believed her. Pip cared for Holly, as did I, as did Bobby.

Outside, the sounds of the monsters diminished. We needed to go.

But first… "I need to ask you guys a question," I said. "Okay, maybe two."

"Ready, fire, aim, Johnny. Ask away," Bobby said.

It took me a second to figure out how to put it. "Do you all *feel* the things inside you changing you? Making you different?"

Pip spoke. "I'd say we're all pretty different."

I shook my head. "No, I mean specifically. Like, the thorns, the things that make us have these abilities, they also made Walter Ivory crazy, made Sol power-hungry..."

"And...?" Bobby said.

"And they make me angry," I said. "So angry, I can't always control myself."

They waited silently, until Bobby finally broke the spell. "Do I feel something like that happening to me? No. Pip?" She shook her head.

"So then why me?" I asked, but of course, no one had an answer to that.

Or maybe they did. "Maybe you're just a jerk." Bobby. Breaking the sour mood.

"Maybe," I said.

"But for now," Pip said, stepping toward us, "we need to go. And besides, if we need to get into it right now, with Jake, with those Gorgols... a little anger might be helpful."

I smirked. *It is what it is, I guess.*

Together, we bolted out the door, after Jake, after the Gorgols. With no idea how to keep them from my sister.

I didn't know what we would do, but at least we were back together, a team. And that was exactly what I needed. Me, Bobby, and Pip. Three people with one goal: Get those monsters to leave my sister the hell alone.

16

Jake was running, as fast as he could. He had to. Even though the monsters' pace seemed casual, they were huge, with an enormous stride. The Gorgols would soon be out of sight. It was comical, actually, watching Jake. This little speck of a person running to catch up with these giant things.

Alpha was closer, a little behind Sigma, who seemed exuberant in her release, similar to how she had seemed on the beach, calling Alpha to her. Sigma not only raced ahead, she weaved and snaked her way back and forth, eager to be on the move. But Alpha walked in a straight line, deliberate in her progress.

I'll admit that Jake impressed me, knowing he was trying to reach their minds while sprinting across the newly flattened terrain. So many times I'd tried to use my powers under duress, only to find them eluding me. As if the best way to work the thorns within me was simply to sit back and go along for the ride. Actively forcing them to do something was notably harder, especially if your mind and body lacked clarity. If you tried to walk and chew bubblegum at the same time, as they say.

Or maybe that was just me.

To keep up, Pip, Bobby, and I ran as well. That was comical, too. From the vantage of the helicopters, especially, I imagine. I didn't know whether to laugh or be embarrassed that the world was watching the most absurd little parade, monsters and superhumans. The Gorgols took the vanguard, Jake ran after the Gorgols, and we pursued them all, some distance behind. At least we'd had the smarts to put our masks back on as we left the barn.

We reached a wide grassy area, possibly the front lawn of the same unlucky farmer whose corn had been uniformly trampled by the Gorgols. A two-story white house stood beside a solitary old oak, with a separate two-car garage nearby. At the center point of the triangle created by the house, tree, and garage was a small pond. But the thing that caught my eye was the decoration right in front of the pond. It was a short, white pedestal, like a birdbath, and on it was perched a metallic, reflective sphere. I think people call them *gazing balls*. The name alone was worth a chuckle. No one in my town had one, as far as I knew, but out in the country, you'd see them from time to time, where some homeowner decided to get all fancy. Even from a distance, the sight of Gorgol Alpha and Gorgol Sigma, two towering beasts of destruction, mirrored funhouse-style in the curved reflection of the gazing ball, was laughable.

Suddenly, Jake pulled up, panting as he stood on the lush green lawn. Well behind him, at the fringe of the open space, we did the same. Was he letting the Gorgols get away? Was he giving up? And if he was, could I?

I knew the answer. No. The Gorgols were now on track to pay a visit to Holly, probably trampling my house in the process, so there was no way I could sit back and do nothing. I shook off my static entropy and began to run again, just as Alpha stopped in her tracks. I skidded once more to a halt.

Two hundred feet up, her head turned, her large diamond eyes glittering and glowing in the daylight. As she shifted, it seemed like every muscle individually decided to turn, like cascades in a tiered waterfall. One by one, her huge stony scales pivoted, and her head came around. To face Jake.

With malice.

For just a moment, I thought of class pictures. Where the photographer invariably has some ridiculous way he wants each kid to stand, ostensibly to get a good picture. But I knew better. I think those photographers are just looking for one thing — one thing — in each photo to entertain themselves, get them through another boring day of a dull and repetitive job. They say things like, "You, on the left. Turn your body away. Okay, good. Now turn your head to face me. No! Just your head." And the kid would try to comply, coming off like a contorted pretzel twist. Which of course made the photographer shout, "Yes! Perfect!" Alpha was the pretzel.

Seeing her turn, my fire was stoked. If Alpha wanted to tilt down and devour Jake, I would sit and watch. Hell, he deserved it. A part of me was looking forward to it. The angry part. The part that didn't shy from killing.

But if she came for me… that same part of me suddenly itched to fight.

Alpha pivoted sideways until she was fully aimed at Jake. They stood face to face, the world's most lopsided set of gunslingers, a nuclear bomb facing off against a cap gun.

This must have made for some riveting TV.

Invariably, commentators around the world, in every language, were pontificating on the impending doom of *Ranger*. The helicopters shuffled for the best angles.

And Alpha reared up for an attack.

If you can could call it that. Alpha was angry, but she also seemed to be held back by something, some sort of fear. But fear of what? Jake? His control? Probably… But, regardless of Alpha's mindset, in this David and Goliath confrontation, it looked like David was about to get squashed.

Alpha bellowed a deafening roar, head tilted skyward, with a voice so strong it seemed the clouds above her dissipated just hearing it. Of course, given Gorgol breath, it was entirely possible those clouds simply withered and died from the smell.

Her call shivered the branches of the old oak before us. Jake visibly staggered back a half step, but he didn't turn away. If anything, his body leaned toward her, like he was focusing his will in Alpha's direction.

Even Sigma paused.

The big serpent twisted and slithered around in a wide arc, coming back to face her mother... assuming Alpha really was her mother.

Alpha finished her long call, letting it fade away, echoing into the distance. Then she shuffled her feet like a sumo wrestler getting into a ready stance. The ground shook with each powerful step, clouds of dust bursting up from her giant feet.

For that moment, I was seeing me. The me that had faced down Omicron, trying desperately to reach his mind in the millisecond before he swallowed me whole. Yet I couldn't.

The effort took time, which I didn't have. The same time Jake now didn't have with Alpha.

She lurched forward, her giant mouth agape, spiked with jagged teeth poised to tear him apart. Yet Jake stood his ground.

"Good," I muttered under my breath, my bloodlust nearly turning my vision red, wanting to see red. I could feel Bobby's eyes on me, Pip's as well. I could feel their judgment. *Don't you dare judge me*, the angry part of me thought.

Alpha's body bent and her arms spread wide, a giant and deadly hug for Jake as she leaned in to devour him.

Then the world froze.

Alpha froze. The snarl on her face slowly shifted from active to passive. Her mouth hung open, a giant flycatcher. Her eyes dulled.

"Oh my God," Pip said from behind me.

Then Alpha's eyes flickered, in what I suppose was her version of a blink. She tried to shake her head.

"She's fighting it!" Bobby yelled.

Alpha started to straighten her back, stand up tall.

But Jake fought as well. Alpha's eyes dulled again, and her body became motionless. On the ground before her, Jake relaxed his posture.

"Damn." I shook my head. "He's won. He's got her back under control."

Alpha slowly returned to a neutral position as Jake strolled toward her.

And that's when Sigma shrieked. Writhing behind Alpha, Sigma barked and bellowed, furious. And why not? A human — me — had killed her brother. Another human had taken over her mind, and Alpha's as well. And just when it appeared they had broken free and Alpha was about to destroy at least one of those two pesky humans, the human won again.

Sigma slithered around her mother. She was going to finish what Alpha had started, but not in the slow, deliberate way of the larger monster. Sigma raced toward Jake, a full sprinting attack.

Even from behind, we could sense Jake's fear, his alarm. He'd just barely gained control of Alpha before she swallowed him whole. How could he possibly hold her and subdue Sigma in time? But clearly he had to try something.

Jake held out his left hand, palm toward Alpha, still. I knew the gesture had no effect, but it served as a mental placeholder for Jake: *This one stays here*. His right hand raised to point a karate-like edge toward the onrushing Sigma.

There's no way, I thought. *No way he can take over her mind in time. She's too big, too fast.*

Sigma lunged at Jake, and I knew in my heart that, even if he could somehow control her mind, nothing could stop her body, already in motion.

Jake was a dead man, standing before us.

Which, I suppose, he must have realized as well. Because he never even tried to control her, not completely at least.

With the blade of his right hand, Jake chopped the air toward Sigma, all the while keeping his left hand still. As his right hand swooped through the air, Sigma diverted, just enough. The hand continued its arc, and I watched it, mesmerized. *He's actually doing it*, I thought. *Doing just enough to redirect her!* That right hand swung around, over his left, and came to rest with fingertips pointed toward me.

Toward me.

I blinked out of my daze, shifting my gaze away from Jake, tilting my head up to focus on Sigma instead. The monster who was suddenly, viciously, and rapidly moving in my direction, coming for me instead.

17

I had time.

Time enough to wonder. *Did he damage her mind?*

Or can I reach it?

I had to try.

I *pushed.* Hard. Too hard, probably.

Added to the pushing Jake had done to Sigma, I realized fleetingly that this could be a very bad idea. Would I break Sigma? Burn her hollow like I'd done to Petrus? Did I want to? No. I pulled back a bit, like a firefighter trying to control the hose.

A 20-story, serpent-like creature from Planet X (or The Land Before Time, or whatever) was formidable enough. Remove any rational thought from the beast, and things might get really bad.

Dicey, my grandmother used to say. The situation was definitely dicey.

But there was no time for consideration. Blunt-force attack, direct to the mind. I had to stop Sigma, or start planning for my next eventuality, which was, at the very least, a great deal of Gorgol-induced pain.

STOP!

She didn't.

But she did divert, again. No, I wasn't lucky enough or quick-thinking enough to route her right back toward Jake. I was just able to knock her aside, sending her into a wide, looping arc that only seemed to delay the inevitable.

Pip and Bobby ran up on either side. "She's coming back!" Pip shouted.

Sigma circled around Alpha. I noticed Jake climbing one of Alpha's legs, no doubt seeking his roost on her shoulder. He paused, high on one side, looking down at us. "Prepare yourselves, for your time is nigh!"

I gave Bobby a sidelong look, and he rolled his eyes in response. *Your time is nigh?* Was Jake quoting something again, or just tapping some artsy-fartsy muse? Either way, who talks like that?

"John," Bobby said in a voice low enough that only we could hear him. "We can worry about the drama queen later. We've got a more immediate problem." He pointed.

Sigma was bearing down, nearly on us.

At that moment, Jake must have reached his perch, because Alpha began to slowly retreat, like a cement truck backing up, giving Sigma space for her onrushing attack.

"Deflect her!" I yelled to Bobby and Pip. "Just make her turn aside!" I raised my hands, preparing.

"What good is that? She'll just come back again," Bobby said.

I nodded. He was right. But we needed time to think, to come up with a better plan. "I know, but I'm not sure what else to do!"

Sigma raced toward us, and we all raised our hands in what appeared to be a futile, minuscule gesture before the huge beast.

"Now!" I yelled. And we each pushed at her mind.

The three of us, all at once.

Oops.

Sigma's head recoiled like a boxer in a movie, on the receiving end of not a quick jab but a roundhouse to the face. She uttered a short, guttural shriek of pain. And her body spun away from us at a sharp angle. *Too much*, I thought, just as her long scaly tail whipped around.

Directly into the three of us.

From above, from the helicopters, it must have been hilarious. A pro bowler knocking down the pins. *Strike! Put an X on the board!* Bobby, Pip, and I went flying in different directions. Each of our bodies tried to sluice out of the way, but Sigma's tail was massive and thick, and the blow fell so quickly there was little we could do.

So, for the second time, I went airborne courtesy of a Gorgol. *We have reached our cruising altitude of 30 feet, so the pilot has turned off the "fasten seat belt" signs. You are free to be dashed to pieces violently. Thank you for flying Gorgol Air.*

Thankfully, it was her tail. When Omicron had slashed at me with a hand — claw? paw? hoof? — it had torn into my body even as it threw me like a rag doll. This was blessedly simpler. A bat hitting a home run. I landed, aching, far back in the yard, but my body quickly pulled itself back together. Go Alien Thorns™!

But the blow also stirred up my anger. As I stood, my hand
instinctively went to my belt, like an abusive father about
to lay down a seriously old-fashioned whooping. And just
like such a father *should* feel, I was ashamed. I lowered my
hand as I noticed motion once again in my direction.

Sigma curled through another wide arc, rearing back to
attack. I looked left and right, not seeing either Bobby or
Pip. My hand started to go for the belt buckle again, my
body wanting to turn the cheap leather into a sharp weapon
of death again.

No.

There has to be a better way, I thought. *Jake can reach
these creatures. Why can't I?* But I was pretty sure I knew
the answer: time. I needed more time, in closer proximity to
the beasts, to figure out the lock that kept their minds
closed to me.

I needed Sigma to slow down. To *freeze.*

Of course.

As she approached, I raised one hand, imagining my task. I
pulled at the heat within Sigma's massive body as she
catapulted toward me.

And she slowed.

Not stopped, but reduced speed, movement. Something was happening. I pulled harder, seeing Sigma's writhing, snakelike body gradually slow. Her scaly skin took on a frosted sheen, the water in her body chilling to ice as I pulled more and more heat from inside.

Like I'd done to Sol before, I started from the ground up, letting the energy seep out of her and into the grass and dirt. She slowed, but still came on, getting ever closer to me. With a growing fire inside me, I pulled still harder.

Come on! Come on! Work, dammit!

A feeling overcame me. A rage. A strength. A certainty.

And Sigma came to a reluctant halt just feet before me, her body crackling into a frozen statue of a giant monster. Even her arms had stilled, unable to break my spell.

High above me, her long neck and head remained free. Her wide hood flared in renewed anger, unaware of why her lower body no longer responded. Why she couldn't move.

As I continued to suck the heat from her, moving ever upward, I sent a mental tendril toward her brain. *Let me in.* I searched for her mind's invisible doorway.

LET ME IN!

Sigma had other plans. She pulled back the parts of her upper body that could still move, then quickly lurched forward, preparing to bite at me, devour the thing that had caused her so much pain and strife.

Unconsciously, my right hand pulled at my belt, sliding it free. Although my rational mind was too occupied with freezing her body and searching her brain, something primitive inside me — inside my cells, maybe — reacted with foaming anger.

I didn't feel the fire coming over me, not directly. But if a mirror had been put in front of me, I wouldn't have recognized my own face, twisted in hate. The belt came up, now rigid. It changed texture and density, becoming hard metal, then morphing to a point. Grimacing like a crazed clown, all teeth, I awaited Sigma's attack.

Two John Blacks existed in one body. One methodically sapped the heat from Sigma while trying to find a gateway to communicate with her mind. *Let me in, Sigma.*

The other John Black raged. I would do to her what I had done to Omicron, stab into the soft tissue inside her mouth and kill her.

Kill her.

Kill…

So. How was your day?

18

The world became slow motion as I almost gleefully awaited my chance to destroy Sigma.

And then something unexpected happened. Sigma's head was knocked sideways by an object flying through the air. A *yellow* object, coming in from the left.

Bobby.

In that instant, I sensed the split inside myself, the two of me. Simultaneously, I thought, *Bobby!* and *No!*

He slammed into the side of her head, a battering ram sending her attack off course. Away from me.

"No! I've got this! She's mine!" I shouted. It was irrational and pointless, but it was how I felt. At that moment, I *wanted* Sigma's attack. *Wanted* to take her down. I knew I could.

And as the angry side of me won over, the other side's work, trying to freeze and control Sigma, slowly waned.

Shifting to my right, I tried to regain the monster's focus. "Come on!" I said, waving my free hand. In the other hand, the pointed, elongated sword-spear that used to be my belt grew even longer. It seemed to hum with energy, the energy I was pumping into it.

Bobby fell away from Sigma, dropping to the ground near me just as the creature shook her head. I want to say that I knew he was fine, that as a friend, I checked to be sure. But I didn't. I ignored Bobby, whatever his state might be, and focused on Sigma.

Bobby's blow must have stung or at least annoyed her, but other than his body itself, Bobby was weaponless, so his attack was nothing more than blunt trauma. Something we had witnessed the Gorgols overcome countless times. She turned her neck and head toward him, her lower body still frozen in place, but thawing.

"No! Look at me!" I yelled, barely intelligible.

Sigma leaned toward Bobby as he backpedaled on his hands and feet.

Both verbally and mentally, I screamed at the creature. *"NO! ME!"*

She reacted, her glowing amber eyes pulsing as she shifted to look directly at me.

My mental push found something to hold on to. *You.* She didn't think the actual word, but I sensed the concept. Recognition. Sigma reared for another lunge, and I stood ready.

I was exhilarated. I would stab into the monster's brain with my sword, and she would die!

I felt sickened by the rage…

A rictus grin came over my face.

Nausea swelled within me…

My whole body thrummed with excitement.

The nausea didn't dissipate so much as it was contained. Like the cap on a soda bottle quickly tightened before the fizzing drink can explode, something in me clamped down on the revulsion, making it instantly stop.

All that was left was the glee and the rage and the ready.

There was something about this creature, all of the Gorgols — creatures of anger and fear — that brought out those feelings in me, too. Like it was too familiar. Like it was contagious.

No, it was too easy to put the blame on something else. The thorns had changed me, and I embraced it. The worst part of me came forward.

Sigma's open maw lunged for me, an onrushing train of saliva and teeth.

And again, something came from the side, slamming into Sigma's head, this time red.

Seriously?

Pip.

She leapt at the beast, sword stretched out deadly before her. It wasn't technically the murder stroke, but it might as well have been called that. Driving down from her arcing jump, Pip drove her sword into one of Sigma's glowing amber eyes, piercing it as she fell, pressing the weapon deep into the socket.

"*NO!*" I screamed again. "*MINE!*"

Sigma reacted instantly, blind in one eye, blinded by pain. Her upper body, the only part that could move, twisted and writhed insanely, violently, causing the thaw to accelerate.

How long until she would be free once more? I was sure Pip would be shaken off, tossed aside, but somehow she held on, her hands glued to the hilt of the sword that now protruded from the Gorgol's missing eye.

I didn't know if the blow was fatal — how could I? All I knew was rage. And that rage suddenly shifted.

Just who the hell did Pip she think she was, taking something from me? Taking *this* from *me*?

Somewhere, far, far in the back of my mind, an echo of the nausea roiled, just a bubble from a dying boil, popping and then gone. Resistance to the bloodlust within me died with it.

Reaching down into my powers, pulling into myself both mentally and physically, I prepared.

And then, screaming, I jumped up, flying into the air, sword-spear raised and ready, toward my target.

Toward Pip.

19

Navigating the landing was a challenge. Sigma tossed about like a firehose blasting water with no one holding on. Still, I gave it no thought whatsoever. For I didn't think at all, not of anything. I was all action.

Somehow I shifted and reoriented in midair. Did the thorns in my cells release little blasts of propulsion like thrusters on a spaceship? Of course not, but it felt sort of like that.

I landed on top of Pip, reaching for her sword, wanting to pull it free. Sigma was my prize, and Pip wouldn't take her from me.

As you can imagine, Pip was stunned. It's safe to say that if I had leapt onto Sigma's head and done a vaudeville tap dance, Pip probably would have been *less* surprised. The last thing she ever thought was that I would attack her. Try to *stop* her.

It was almost enough to make her let go of the sword. But not quite. She held on for life and death and victory, and because she probably didn't know what else to do. I grabbed at the sword, both of us now clinging to the face of a 20-story beast as it shook and twisted, wanting nothing more than for us to be gone, for the pain to stop.

"What the hell are you doing, John?" Pip screamed.

In response, I shoved into her wordlessly with my shoulder, trying to dislodge her grip.

"Have you lost your *freaking* mind?" she yelled. She couldn't believe what I was doing, and I don't blame her. She caught a glimpse of my eyes, and that must have been enough to convince her that something was deeply wrong with me. She threw an elbow, knocking me away from the sword, then pushed with all her weight, driving the weapon in deeper. Sigma shrieked, still writhing.

I tried to pull the sword free. "Sigma is mine! You have no right!"

"No right?" she yelled. "What are you *talking* about?"

My grimace grew even more pained as I pulled at the sword. "You don't belong here! Sigma is mine!"

313

"*Mine?*" she echoed. "Mine for what?"

For just a moment, my motions ceased. I looked Pip in the eye and could see what she thought of me. *She thinks I'm crazy. She's probably right.*

"Mine to kill," I said, barely audible. With one hand I tightened my grip on Pip's sword, and with the other holding my own sword aloft. Then I lurched into Pip, head-butting her and slamming my body into her shoulders, driving her off the Gorgol.

But Pip kept hold of her sword. It must have been something in her training, or maybe just her pure, stubborn desire, but she wouldn't let the damn thing go.

What choice did I have?

I raised my sword-spear high, as Pip dangled from Sigma's flopping head. She saw it coming, the thorns within her must have felt it. But how do you sluice out of the way of a falling sword when you're hanging on for dear life by one hand?

One suddenly severed hand.

Her arm stretched, trying its best to bend around the blow, but it was impossible. I sliced through Pip's arm, cutting midway between elbow and wrist.

I will never forget the look on her face as she fell away toward the ground. It was familiar. I had seen it, seen Pip herself look this way before. In the mirror. In the dream. The look she gave her own father, as smoke curled around his head in the small yellow bathroom. A look of trust lost. Of betrayal.

A part of me cared. Almost wept for what it was seeing.

But most of me didn't. Most of me didn't give it a second thought.

I turned, easily pulling Pip's sword free now that her powers no longer strengthened it, and tossed the weapon and severed hand after her falling body. I nearly fell away myself, but quickly jabbed my sword-spear deep into the creature's eye socket to renew my hold.

"I get to do this, not you." The voice that rasped from my lips was almost unrecognizable.

Sigma shrieked again, stronger yet weaker, like it was the last thing she could muster. Her neck and head tossed, but in longer, slower arcs.

Death throes.

I drove my sword deeper. *Yes. Mine.*

There was nothing in the world that could speak to me, pull me back from the insanity that was my desire to kill.

Sigma's head turned, and, saddled to it like a bull rider at a rodeo, I went with it. The Gorgol sought something, then found it, steadying her gaze as best she could with one eye, in such pain.

She looked at Alpha, finally stilling her twisting neck.

Mother.

The idea came through me, through my arms, through the sword.

Again.

The engine of rage that I had become shattered. A wrecking ball smashed through me, destroying the wall of anger, hate, and viciousness that some part of me had erected. My rational self reemerged.

What have I done? How have I done this again?

Sigma faded. She started to fall.

I held onto the sword simply to avoid being flung to one side, but my energies dissipated and it began to shift back to normal. My mental push into Sigma's brain shut down, and the few remaining tendrils of power I used to pull the heat from her body flittered away in the breeze like autumn leaves.

She fell, and I held on.

Again?

I could no longer trust myself. How could I? How could anyone? Certainly Pip wouldn't.

Sigma dropped onto her side, with me on top still holding the sword protruding from her eye. Gorgol Sigma's last act was to crush anything in her path of descent, landing with a deep bass note that echoed into the distance. Dust and dirt billowed in huge clouds.

As the air slowly cleared, I stood, and my sword melted back into a crappy leather belt. I let it hang, almost forgotten by my side, as I stood atop the creature I had killed.

Sigma, like Omicron before her, looked lonely and pathetic and sad in death. No strength, no life force. Nothing but an energy gone, the doors of many possibilities now closed.

Like Sigma's fire, my rage was gone, with no hint remaining, almost as if it had never been there. Just as it had with Omicron, the anger died away with the beast.

And I cried.

As the tears slid down my cheeks, some touched my lips. In the salt, I could taste guilt. It tasted familiar.

The ground shook and the sound of rumbling footsteps approached as a shadow fell over me.

Slowly looking up, I saw Gorgol Alpha, and I welcomed the vengeance the mother no doubt was about to lay upon me.

I really won't fight this time. I can't. I deserve to die.

20

Jake sat high on one of Alpha's shoulders.

The look on the Gorgol mother's face was almost worse than what I had seen on Pip's. Anger. Loss. Betrayal. Fear. And, more than anything, an emptiness. Was that from Jake, because he'd taken over her mind? Or was Alpha now left empty? I thought both. But mostly, I thought she was hollow because of me.

"There he is, the very embodiment of the word *liar*," Jake called from above. Behind him, the shifting forms of several helicopters hovered, jockeying for the best camera angles. Apart from their distant thumping, the only sound was Jake's shouting voice.

I had no answer. What answer could I give? I'd told Jake I didn't want to fight. Didn't want to kill the Gorgols. And yet, there I stood, over the body of the second Gorgol I'd slain.

"You think you're more important than they are, don't you? That your wants and needs and desires are bigger, more special. More powerful."

I shook my head. I didn't think I was all that important, not usually, and definitely not at that moment. Rather, I felt like about the lowest piece of scum possible. I realized that, with my black mask still on, Jake couldn't see my face, my tears, couldn't read my expressions. "No," I said with a wavering voice. "I don't think that." I doubted it was loud enough for him to hear from so far above, but maybe Jake had enhanced his hearing or reached out with his mind. Because he definitely heard me.

"*Liar*. Just still your tongue. You've done enough with your actions for a lifetime of words. You're true self is clear to me."

"No," I repeated, weakly.

"You are a perfect example of the human race, did you know that? This…" Jake looked around, exasperated. "This world of people is at direct odds with the natural world. But I'll give you this. Humans have an almost limitless ability to destroy. It would truly be impressive, if it weren't so damned horrible. You flatter yourselves about your creations, your civilization, your accomplishments, but you sweep the true nature of humanity under the rug."

"What?"

"Don't pretend not to understand. Human civilization is a parasite living off the natural world. And the Gorgols came to eradicate the problem, to pluck the parasite from its host. But you..." Jake glowered at me. "You come along and step in the way. Because you think you're special."

"I didn't mean to..."

"Enough of your lies, now. I see who you really are. I know your soul now. I feel like I've known it for too long, more than a lifetime. I can feel it, like your treachery is a part of me."

What was Jake talking about? *I* was a perfect example of the human race? My treachery was a part of him? A flash appeared in my mind. Were our minds connected? I saw a horse, rearing up. Just for a moment, then it was gone. What. The. Hell?

Still, what counterargument could I muster? It wasn't like I *hadn't* just killed Gorgol number two. But I had to say something. "Jake," I called up to him. "I know how this looks. But it's not me." He scoffed but let me continue. "Or at least it's not who I want to be. These powers..." I looked at my hands like they belonged to someone else. "They do things. I don't just mean they *can* do things, but they do things *to* you. To me. I did something just now that I'm not proud of, that isn't me. I can't explain it, but it isn't me. And, Jake, you know we both have these powers. We're alike."

Jake couldn't control his disdain. "*Alike*? Hardly." He held out one hand, touching the stony scales of Alpha's shoulder. The Gorgol — the last Gorgol — stood motionless, but I felt her tension, like a shudder, stemming from the touch. She was a wire, pulled to the snapping point. I didn't know if Jake could truly control her much longer. "You and I couldn't be more different. *I* fight for the mothers. For the Gorgols and the world."

That was enough to raise something out of me, at last. "For them? Don't kid yourself, Jake. You control Alpha against her will. You don't fight for her. You enslave her."

Jake's face reddened. Even from such a distance, I could see it. Then, taking a moment, he calmed himself. "I like the mask you wear. That you all wear."

I was suddenly aware that Bobby and Pip were there, standing to each side. Near enough to make a combined front, but notably separate. We were three, and we opposed Jake, but we weren't a team. Not anymore. Not after what I'd done.

I mean, Pip's right arm ended in a stump just below her elbow. Healing powers or not, that's gonna piss a person off.

"Masks are an interesting thing, are they not? Sometimes we all wear masks." Jake began pontificating again. It seemed out of place and random, like his personality had shifted again. "We all use masks of one kind or another, hiding who we are. But why? Is it because we do not feel sufficient in ourselves to reveal who we really are?" He looked to us each in turn. "Or perhaps we use them to hide not our self, but those around us. Those dear to us." Then Jake looked only at me. "As you can see, I wear no mask whatsoever. Who I am is plain to see before you. I am no mystery. But you all…? Perhaps the people watching us from above —" Jake gestured toward the hovering helicopters "— would like to know who you *really* are, all of you. Know your *names*." He let the threat linger.

Did it matter? Was there a normal life to go back to? Our world was peppered with strange powers and stranger creatures. Did I care if the evening news knew that *Black Sword* was really John Black?

Yes. Yes, somehow I did.

Because I think that was the only thing that made everything worthwhile, the idea that maybe when we were done, we could go back to a normal life. In fact, if anything, the powers made me appreciate my normal life so much more. Before I had power, I longed for something more, a bigger life. With them, I longed for something… I don't know. Less? Not less, in terms of less interesting or

less fun or less quality or less important. But less...
complicated.

I thought of my mom, laughing at a joke as she cooked
breakfast. Of Holly and I, touching foreheads to say hello.
Of sipping awful coffee drinks with Carrie McGregor.

I suddenly realized how important those things were to me.
And remembering the hell of the paparazzi that we'd
already experienced once, how they caused Holly pain on a
daily basis. I didn't want to go back to that. I didn't want
the other things taken away from me. Didn't want to lose
my normal.

But what could I do? Launch an attack on Jake? Kill Alpha,
too?

Death was an anchor, tied to my neck, and I had already
been swimming a long, long time.

No, I thought. *Something simpler.* I reached out gently with
my mind, toward Jake.

I only wanted to nudge him. End the confrontation. I could
think of an actual plan to deal with Jake and Alpha later. I
just needed time. Armed with my new knowledge of what
really mattered to me, this time, I thought I could come up
with something that would work. Because an idea — or at
least the nugget of an idea — was born in my head. I
thought I knew what to do about Gorgol Alpha.

With Jake in control, though, we were at an impasse. I tried to gently push him to stand down.

Slowly and carefully, my mind reached into his. I felt his anger, and a healthy amount of fear. Fear of me, and Bobby, and Pip, all arrayed below him.

Still, I tried not to explore Jake's mind. I just needed to plant an idea.

This is not the time. Alpha is ready to snap. You need to change that.

I knew Alpha was close to her breaking point, and wanted Jake to use his influence over her to pull back.

Change Alpha.

At first, nothing happened, and I feared I would be unsuccessful. To each side, I could feel Bobby and Pip tense for more fighting.

The image came into my mind again, through the connection with Jake. The horse. Motionless, amid the chaos of a city.

Then, words came, too. Deep, resonant words I heard silently in my head.

Yes, change.

From high above, Jake's voice called out again. "No, I think I will leave you as I found you, this time at least. It's time for a change." Under Jake's control, Alpha's lumbering body began to turn away.

Bobby, Pip, and I just stood and watched as they left.

Looking back, Jake called out, one last time. "Because change is good."

Keith Soares

1

Pip jumped, and at first I thought she meant to follow after them, chasing down Jake and the last Gorgol. But after a moment she stopped and bent down to retrieve something from the rubble surrounding Sigma's body.

Her hand.

Then she turned back toward me with a face as dark as the most powerful sandstorm, blacking out the sun.

"What the funky hall was that?" Pip said, turning toward me with her hand in her hand. You know, literally.

And, by the way, she didn't say *funky hall*.

"I don't know," I said, shaking my head. "I —"

"That's it? *I don't know?*" I got the distinct impression that if she hadn't needed to use one hand to hold the other, she would have been pointing her sword at me. Somehow, she'd already recovered the weapon, and its hilt was poking up from the scabbard on her back.

Bobby felt the obvious tension. "Come on, guys. Relax. Let's talk about this."

Pip turned on him. "Relax? *Relax?* Did you see what he did to me?" As if Bobby hadn't noticed, Pip gesticulated with her hand. The detached one. And as she did, the hand started to… melt. At the same time, the stump of her slashed forearm stretched outward, growing. Pip just stared, baffled and stunned by what her body was doing.

"Put them together!" I offered. She took a moment to comprehend, but complied. No argument there. Pip didn't want to be a one-armed bandit for the rest of her life.

Like a clay sculpture that could make and unmake itself, the two parts of Pip's arm rejoined, melting back together. At first, the form was loose and inhuman, but after a few moments the normal shape asserted itself. She wiggled her fingers, right as rain.

"So, everything's fine now, right?" Bobby offered with a weak smile.

Pip's newly rejoined hand balled into a fist. "No, Bobby. Not right at all. Look at him," she said, nodding toward me. "He stands there and apologizes, but what's changed? He's not sorry."

"Come on, Pip —" Bobby started.

"No. No way. I'm not being played for a fool by *him* anymore. Even if he is sorry, what does it matter?" The old Pip was back, the one who didn't like me one bit. "I don't trust you, *Black Sword*." She spat the name at me. "I never have. And now I know why." Despite her words, she hadn't ratted out my true identity to the listening helicopters above. I should have appreciated that. Somehow, though, it fueled my fire. "You're too strong," Pip said. "Too strong for even yourself to deal with. And when you let the power out, who knows what's going to happen. That's why I don't trust you. Because you can't even trust yourself."

Don't trust me? Fine.

Won't even say my name? Fine.

Once the fire was lit, I didn't know how to put it out. No, that wasn't quite right. Once the fire was lit, I didn't know how to stop pouring gasoline on it. "Either you're with me, or you're against me," I muttered.

"What did you say?" Pip asked.

"You need to leave. Now," I said, louder.

"Hey, Johnny...?" Bobby whispered, trying to interrupt the full-blown fight he saw coming. He moved to put a hand on my shoulder, but I sloughed it off.

Pip scoffed. "*I* need to go? Who exactly do you think you are?" Still she wouldn't say my name. I knew it was the respectful thing to do, but damn, it pissed me off.

"I'm someone who's telling you to go. For your own sake. And *now*." I puffed up, full of myself. Where was this anger coming from? From me. But why? It was as if I was standing in a cloud of toxic gas and there was no way to get a breath of clean air.

Pip pulled back, eyes wide, and Bobby mirrored her surprise. "Yo! Calm down, buddy," he said, looking toward my right hand.

The hand that held my belt. Well, the thing that was sometimes my belt and sometimes stretched into a weapon. Just as it was in the process of doing at that particular moment.

I knew I was doing it again, but I couldn't stop myself. The bloodlust had taken me, once more. Standing there next to the still-warm body of Gorgol Sigma, something was deeply wrong with me. Something I couldn't control.

Rather than back down, I let it happen. Hell, maybe I even encouraged it. My belt completed its transformation back into the sword-spear, but at least I had the consideration to keep it low by my side. I don't know what might have happened if I'd raised it, but I suspect there would have been no going back, ever.

Pip stood ready to fight. And I think I was ready, too. I think I would have fought Pip, right then and there. How far? I don't know. There was a dead Gorgol at our feet, many times Pip's size. Let's just say that self-control wasn't my strong suit, not then. Picturing Pip lying dead next to Sigma wasn't hard to do.

I might have done it. Except for Bobby.

Even through the haze — no, the complete whiteout — of my anger, Bobby was my friend. And at that very moment, he turned on me.

By choosing sides.

Well, by choosing *a* side.

A side that wasn't mine.

Bobby silently moved to stand next to Pip, striking a ready pose that echoed hers. I couldn't see his face through the mask, but his eyes told me enough. His deadly serious eyes. "Enough, Johnny," he said.

"You, too?" I was livid. Probably someone in your life has told you not to make important decisions when you're angry. My dad had told me that countless times. I guess I was sometimes a hothead as a little kid, too. I mean, who isn't? What kid doesn't raise Cain whenever they don't get their way? But this was different. I was too old for tantrums and irrational decisions, like *Fine, if asparagus is for dinner, then I'll never eat dinner again! EVER!* Nonetheless, I made an irrational decision.

I pointed at them, one at a time, with my free hand. "So be it," I said. "You go your way and I go mine." As simply as that, I started to walk away. But, of course, my lunatic self thought that one last parting shot was required. "And don't bother following me!" Like Bobby or Pip were desperate to hang out with me after such a display of pompous stupidity.

So, with that, I set off on my own.

This sounds symbolic, perhaps even romantic, as if our intrepid hero must venture into the wild to face his demons alone, only to come out stronger and better for it.

Not so.

Leaving the farmyard, I found the road, turned right, and kept going. My belt was once again just a belt, so I threaded it back around my waist, a pseudo-scabbard for my pseudo-sword. I didn't even know what direction I was heading. There was no pathway of personal trials ahead, no clearly defined process to become a better me. Just walking. It dawned on me some minutes later that I was essentially lost. Where the hell was I going, and what the hell was I going to do?

I figured the smartest thing was just to go home, but the easiest way to do that was in Bobby's parents' car. Any guesses whether Bobby was willing to give me a lift at that time? Yeah, no.

Damn.

"Don't decide when you're angry," I heard my father's voice say in my head.

Now you tell me. Just be quiet, Dad.

Frustrated, I spied a large rock by the side of the road and used my mental powers to send it flying. It randomly careened into a hapless, innocent mailbox, crumpling the metal and knocking it from its wooden post. I was one of the most powerful humans on Earth, and here I was, reduced to mailbox baseball. *Oh, he got all of that one, folks! It's going, going, gone!* Far from impressing myself or providing any solace, the hurtling mailbox just made me feel more like an idiot.

An idiot alone.

"*Black Sword, can we talk?*" A woman's voice, slightly distorted, came at me from an amplified speaker.

No, no. I was worse than an idiot alone. I was an idiot on display. The *thump-thump-thump* of the helicopters had become so familiar that I'd simply ignored it, forgotten they were even there, despite the fact that they weren't ignoring me. I turned around, my mask blessedly hiding the flushed, chagrined look on my face.

Good lord, they're calling me Black Sword. *And I just answered to it.*

They must have been surprised that I would stop at their call. Or maybe they were just terrified. After all, they had just become the focus of a seriously dangerous and unstable person. The kind of person who severs his friend's hand and kills giant monsters. With a belt. Black Sword. Me.

There was a pause, and I almost walked away once again, until the speaker crackled and the woman spoke again. "This is Meg Branson, Daily 8 News. The world would like to hear from you, Black Sword. Can we land and ask you a few questions?"

"Can we land?" Did I now dictate where and when aircraft could land? Of course, they'd seen me defeat two giant monsters. I suppose manners were in order. No need to piss me off, right? I was simultaneously smug with self-importance and embarrassed at the stupidity of it all.

But if I sat for their questions, they'd just ask who I was and what I was doing. Of those two questions, I only knew the answer to one. And it was the one I wouldn't, couldn't, answer.

An image sprang to life in my mind, the recollection of Holly fading out, overwhelmed by the paparazzi.

And the image of my mother's bloody nose.

What would happen if I brought all that down on my family again?

Whether I let Holly be crushed by a Gorgol or permanently incapacitated by exposure to cameras and shouting jerks, was there a difference?

As Meg Branson called out several more times, I just turned and continued down my own personal road to nowhere.

2

After about 30 minutes, I came to truly respect Daily 8 News reporter Meg Branson. Why? Because she had about a million percent more scruples than her counterparts at the less reputable media outlets.

The helicopters swirled. Soon there were, by my offhand count, five.

Dwayne Pidgeon from ZZT TV made the first cash offer for an exclusive interview. And yes, I thought it was hilarious that a guy named Pidgeon was flying behind me. He also said his offer was for "a limited time," like I was buying steak knives from the shopping channel.

Other offers came, blasted toward me from trailing choppers. I tried to ignore them, but all of a sudden I realized that I had something more than just superpower.

I had earning potential.

I could be a made man.

So how would that feel, selling myself to the highest bidder? Was there any future in paid interviews? I suspected not. Once the tabloids' attention shifted to something new, my bank account would be as empty as my street the day the paparazzi up and left.

As I mulled this, not actually considering the offers but considering how unreal it all was, there came another voice from behind me.

"Black Sword, this is Mark Simeon from Banner Productions." I knew the name, and suspected what was coming. "We know you have a lot of offers for interviews, and we know many of them are offering to pay you quite a bit of money." The loudspeaker crackled off for a moment, and there was only the competing *thump-thump-thump*s of the helicopters. "This is what Banner can offer you: respect for your privacy — no questions about your identity. In fact, no questions at all. We only ask to follow you around, to shadow you, 24/7, for a period of no less than three weeks. You'll star in your own reality show, and you can even name it, pending approval from our lawyers and marketing team." Inside my mask, I rolled my eyes and kept walking. Respect for my privacy that involved being on camera every waking moment? Right. "We know it's an imposition, Black Sword, so we're prepared to offer you zabba glabba glab."

I froze.

No, of course he didn't say *zabba glabba glab*. But he did say a *really* large number.

Holy shit, that's a lot of money. Like, never-work-in-my-life, take-care-of-Holly, let-Mom-quit-her-job money.

I stood there.

"I see that I have your attention. Good. Shall I come down there so we can discuss the details? Iron out a contract and start working together?"

It was the voice. Something about Mark Simeon's voice was just too excited. Too *greedy*.

"If something seems too good to be true…" Once again, my dead father's voice spoke inside my head.

"It probably is," I said out loud. And my feet decided for me. I started walking again.

The offers kept coming, but none as lucrative as the one from Mark Simeon and Banner Productions. It was a struggle not to go back and giddily accept their money, and maybe I was the world's biggest fool, but that's what I did. Or didn't do.

I shunned the possibility of becoming the world's richest, most famous freak. But it wasn't as simple as just me selling me. I would be selling my family, too.

Really hoping I wasn't making a big mistake, I realized I somehow had to ditch the helicopters, or else I knew I'd cave. If night came and I was still wandering aimlessly, I'd probably sign with the first offer of a place to sleep.

How does one elude five helicopters simultaneously? I was alone and walking down a country road with alternating bands of cornfields and pine forests. Obviously the forests were the better option, but it wasn't like I could just duck in and they would give up. I needed a better plan.

So I stopped walking and turned around. "All right, everyone!" I yelled. "I'll consider your offers, but on my terms. I need you all to land, so we can discuss things face-to-face!" Realizing I was in a mask, I sheepishly added, "Well, sort of."

It didn't take long for them to comply. They were too eager, too ready to cash in. The helicopters slowly jockeyed for position, then landed, spaced out along the flat, straight road. From each one, a person or two jumped out and began to approach me. Some wore the professional attire of the real news media, others the more casual look of producers or celebrity journalists.

It wasn't enough. I needed *everyone.*

"Wait!" I held up a hand and, to a person, they all froze. In their way, each one was afraid of me. That's who I'd become. Someone the world feared. I lowered my hand and tried to look peaceful, to the degree that a monster-killing superhuman in a black mask can. "Wait. I need *everyone* out of the helicopters. Pilots, too. And power them down." That was enough to rouse plenty of suspicion. But what choice did they have? For the pros, it was the story of a lifetime. For the others, a heck of a lot of money. After a bit of hedging, they all did as I asked.

In the end, nearly 20 people approached me. Pilots, reporters, camera operators, and some others, maybe producers or interns or who knows what?

I waited. They walked toward me in a loose semicircle. I knew exactly what I had to do. The people with the cameras were first.

Switch off. I pushed the idea into their minds, and one by one they complied, lowering their cameras. For a moment, the others were baffled. As quickly as possible, I sent the message to every man and woman before me. A message not unlike the one Petrus must have sent throughout that police station when he found me.

Sleep.

And they did.

In their nice suits and their casual jeans, they sat down gently — I didn't make them fall over like Petrus had done with the cops — and curled themselves up for sleep.

Within two minutes, my world was finally silent and I was free to do what I wanted. Giving each person a last nudge to ensure they wouldn't wake up for some time, I turned and stepped between the nearest pines, leaving the road, and heading for who knows where.

There's no way that will ever work again. Fool me once, I thought.

The smell of pine sap filled each breath, and the only sound was my feet whooshing through the carpet of brown needles. Still, I knew the forest wasn't endless, wasn't someplace for me to hide forever. I knew I had to change my appearance, so I could somehow melt back into society.

The first thing to go was the damned mask.

3

As I walked alone through farmland many miles from home, I discovered something unexpected but awfully useful: Some of these fine people still used clotheslines.

I found a t-shirt roughly my size and swapped. Yes, I left my own shirt behind, so it wasn't technically stealing, it was trading, a grey one for a red one. Besides, it was plausible that someone might put two and two together and realize my crappy old grey tee was actually the same shirt seen on the infamous Black Sword as he killed the Gorgol Sigma, so maybe they could get some money out of it. Plus, it probably had Gorgol-blood stains on it. I didn't really check. Hell, there were probably blood stains on it from *Pip...*

Come to think of it, I hoped no one ever put two and two together.

Walking mask-free and with a new shirt — enough change that I felt I was probably anonymous — I entered a small town, a place most likely named Wayneston. I say that based on the First Bank of Wayneston and Wayneston Auto Repair Shop signs that cropped up as I emerged from the surrounding woods.

The hard part was actually entering town. How do you just walk into a town, without looking conspicuous? I'm not sure I did it right, but anyway, there I was. I was on the lookout for minds to push, to pave the way for my silent arrival, but if anyone was watching, they were indoors and not obvious to me. Catching myself eyeing darkened windows, I wondered if I should add paranoia to my growing set of bizarre attributes.

I paused at the intersection of Route 38 and Main Street — yes, their main street was really called Main Street — and that's when my head exploded.

Imagine the rumbling bass tone of pushing a heavy crate along a wooden floor — bone-jarring and teeth-chattering — combined with the shrill, pseudo-human call of a young girl's scream. Then take those two sounds and process them through an evil computer that wants you to die, using the ear-splitting sensibilities of your average bass-dropping DJ. That's what it sounded like. Or felt like. Both.

The pain was a metal rod thrust through my head, connecting my ears. I felt like I'd had my brain pierced.

Yet the world seemed still. Farther down the street, I saw a woman pumping gas like the only sounds she heard were the tweet of birds, the whoosh of fluid passing into her car's tank, and the mechanical ticking of the old-time pump. Lucky her.

About to collapse from the pain and sheer unrelenting force of the sound in my head, I pushed back with my mind.

HOLLY! STOP!

My sister was trying to reach me.

Not surprisingly, there was no reply. Holly was nowhere in sight, not close enough for us to mentally converse. But she was clearly trying to get my attention.

No.

She was trying to guide me. To her.

Bring me home.

Despite the pain, the corner of my mouth turned up in a smile. *Good idea, sis.*

I turned right on Main Street, following the blinding sound.

* * *

As I walked, I repeated in my mind the same phrase, beaming it outward.

Holly, please stop.

I could tell I was getting closer, but all that was doing was making the pain worse. I just kept repeating the same words.

And then they worked. The sound was gone.

Johnny? Where are you?

I looked up. I'd been walking with my head down, just making progress but otherwise ignoring the world around me. *Um. Somewhere on a small road.* I scanned left and right. Trees. Grass. A red house in the distance. More cornfields.

I don't know where that is, Johnny, she said.

Sorry, Hol. Why don't you tell me where you are, and we can try to figure it out?

Sure. We're in a driveway on the side of the road. In Mom's car.

Much as my description didn't help Holly, hers was useless to me. Then I had an idea. *Can you have Mom blow the horn?*

I had no idea how Holly would manage that, with her limited vocabulary. It was weird with her. Sometimes she could make Mom understand the most complex things with just a tone or gesture, and sometimes no matter what she did or said, Mom was in the dark. This time, it must have worked. In the distance somewhere in front of me, a horn started blaring.

Good job, Hol. I'm coming!

* * *

Minutes later I was sitting in my mom's van. And it was *awkward*. Without more than five words spoken, she started the engine and headed home.

We drove in silence for a while. In the back seat, I could tell Holly was bristling with energy. Why not? From her perspective, she'd accomplished something no one else could do — locate me and bring me home. But my mother had no doubt watched me on TV, killing Sigma, attacking Pip. The vibe I got from her was… complicated.

I don't know what the stages of response are for the silent treatment, but I assume they go something like this.

First: *Oh crap, she knows something's wrong.*

Then: *What do I do? Oh crap, oh crap, oh crap.*

Next: *Maybe I can make it up to her.*

Finally: *You know what? Hell with it! Who does she think she is, sitting there not saying anything? I'm sick and tired of this!*

It didn't take me long to work through the steps. We sat, three little islands in the car, one happy, one concerned, and one getting pissed off.

"Glad we found you," Mom offered half-heartedly.

"Really?" I asked, far too snide. As soon as it came out, I felt bad. But it was out.

Mom just looked over at me, only for a second. "When we get home, I think you and I should talk."

Oh crap.

4

The kitchen table is a multipurpose space. Sure, on the surface (get it?), it's where you set your food while you eat. But in a family setting, it's so much more. The place where you plan vacations, play games, read, maybe watch TV, joke, relax, whatever. Though it's not all fun and games. The kitchen table is also where talks happen. Not just any talks, but *talks*.

My mom and I were having a *talk*.

Well, technically. I mean, technically we weren't. Because she wasn't talking.

It was maddening.

But I knew what she'd say. What any mom would say. That I'd gone too far, had to reel myself back in. I was ready for her scorn, her disapproval of what I'd done, and the way that I'd done it.

"John…," she started.

Here we go, I thought. I crossed my arms and pushed my chair back a couple of inches from the table. If you want to see how I looked, there's a picture in the dictionary under "someone who's not listening to you."

"Don't bother," I said, briefly waving one palm at her. In retrospect, I'm lucky to be alive. Have you ever told a parent to "talk to the hand?" It's a bad idea.

So I shouldn't have been surprised when my mother echoed my pose, pushing back and crossing her arms. She cocked an eye at me, but didn't say a word.

What now? I thought. She'd spoken, I'd spoken, we both crossed our arms… was that the end of the conversation?

Finally, Mom cleared her throat. "Are you ready to talk about the killing now?" she said.

The words were simple and yet profound. And yet my reaction was complicated. At once, I found my crossed arms tightening defensively. "Killing" was precisely what I didn't want to talk about. But I was also disarmed, the way only a quiet word from a mother can do.

I didn't know what to say. I was responsible for too many deaths. My mother was innocent, kind. How could she possibly understand? "Have you ever thought about killing someone?" I asked.

"Yes." Her face was unreadable.

"Really?" I loosened the vice of my arms, letting them fall to my lap. Mom nodded. "Who?" I figured it was probably someone I didn't know, maybe some childhood archrival.

"Walter Ivory," she said, her eyes locked on mine. Did she know the truth? We'd never discussed it. The surprise must have shown on my face. "You remember him."

It wasn't a question. Then it was my turn to nod. "But, why?"

Mom leaned toward me, elbows on the table. "It's irrational, and there's no proof, but he was there. The day Holly had her first seizure. Do you remember that?" I nodded again. "Walter Ivory was looking for trouble with your dad, trying to start a fight. Walter was always looking for trouble. But that one time, trouble found us instead. Holly…" Mom didn't finish the thought. She didn't need to. I'd been there, that day, and every day since. Every day of Holly's changed life. "But it's irrational. I blame Walter Ivory in my heart, but in my mind, I know it could have happened any time. Holly and I could have been reading a book or at the grocery store…"

"But you weren't."

"No, we weren't."

"And so…?"

"And so, I've wished many times that I could kill Walter Ivory."

How could I respond? Would she think that what I had to say was good news? Or ghastly? No other way to find out than just telling her.

"I killed Walter Ivory," I said.

Again, she nodded. "Good."

That was too easy. "Wait… You believe me?"

Mom's expression was wry. "John, you can control minds, bend and twist your body like you're made of water, and you've killed two giant monsters on live TV. You think I don't believe you killed that son of a bitch?" See? Everyone thought Walter Ivory was a son of a bitch. I wasn't kidding.

"Don't you want to know how it happened?"

Mom gave a little one-sided shrug. "Well, I know how he died already — heard that he was killed in a fall over at the self-storage place. Now I know you were responsible."

Responsible. It was the kind of word you don't hold in the palm of your hand, you have to throw it over your back and hunker down to carry. Still, why was Mom so *calm* about the whole thing? "You... you're not upset?"

"At what? The fact that you were probably in danger, and never told me? Sure, a bit. But angry about Walter? Not at all. Good riddance." She made an offhand gesture, like throwing away a piece of trash.

I didn't know what to think. My mom wasn't callous. She didn't have a mean bone in her body. "But, why?"

"Because you're my son. No one — I mean, *no one* — better mess with my family. I can take a lot of crap about a lot of things, but not that. I won't let anyone hurt you. Or Holly." Her eyes fell to the table. "Or your dad."

Dad. Suddenly the story of Walter Ivory was forgotten. Anything I'd done to Walter just pushed him further into the insanity where he already existed. But Dad? That was all me, and Mom didn't know. "Mom, I..."

"John, I know you've had to do some terrible things. Like Sol. I know why you killed him — to save your sister. And, I'm sorry to say if this sounds terrible, but I'm glad you did. There are terrible people in the world, and I'm willing to let them be if they let me be. But if they don't..."

"I haven't only killed terrible people, Mom." My palms were flat on the table and starting to sweat. There was no turning back.

"What are you talking about?"

I swallowed hard. "I killed Dad."

In that instant, my mother aged a decade. The color drained from her face. "*No.*"

"Yes, I did."

"No, John. Your father died in an accident." But I could hear the shift in tone already. She doubted what she was saying, was worried that what I said was true.

"I caused that accident," I said, like air rushing from a balloon, something that needed to get out.

"Why?"

I could only shrug.

Mom started to shake her head, slightly at first, then gaining momentum. I had a vision of her shaking and shaking until her head flew off, like a broken doll. "Why, John? What did you have against your father?"

"Nothing!" I shouted the answer, and reached for my mother's hands, but she pulled back, unsure. "I loved Dad — I *love* him. It was an accident. But I did it. I didn't mean for him to be involved."

"You need to tell me exactly what happened," she said, her eyes cementing the urgency. So I told her everything. Bobby and the gun, in the warehouse. Me leaving and running into Roger Steele and his friends. The way they humiliated me, especially Lawrence Blatnik, and how I'd lashed out. How I tried to get them in trouble with that passing police officer, only to end up with their car stopped in the middle of the road. Then Dad came along in his car, and before there was time for him to do anything — for *me* to do anything — it was too late. The accident happened, and he died. And I realized, my anger, my reaction... even back then, it must have been the bloodlust. The thorns were already changing me.

I told my mother all of it. The thorns. The changes. How I didn't know what I would do myself, at any moment.

She listened, intently, analyzing.

Everyone has bad memories, some worse than others. This particular memory, the memory of my father's death — something that I'd witnessed directly, and that Mom had no doubt recreated in her mind countless times based on what she'd heard — was the worst we had, both of us. Separately and together, we had shed countless tears over this memory, and now it was all out. I was guilty, and Mom finally knew it.

"It's not your fault," she said quietly.

I had heard the same thing from Bobby, even tried convince myself. But it didn't change the fact that it *was* my fault. "You're wrong—"

"No, son, *you* are wrong." Mom reached forward and took both of my hands in hers. "What you just told me is the saddest thing I've ever heard in my life, and as much as I don't know exactly how to process it, how to live with it, I see one thing clearly. My pain over what happened must be nothing compared to yours." The empathy in her eyes turned me into a blubbering mess, instantly. As if the tears had been behind a dam, and my mother had just torn it down. This was forgiveness. Besides life itself, this was the greatest gift my mother could ever give me. "Every day, you've been telling yourself you killed your father, but you *didn't*. It was an *accident*. An accident. It really was. It's not some manufactured bloodlust or anything else. It was just you, and an accident. That's all. And I can't imagine how hard it's been on you, John. But I want you to know that I'm here. Don't hide these things from me, because when you do, I can't help. This was a terrible burden you didn't need to carry. You've told me that you never asked for your powers, not the good things or the bad things that come with them. Let go of this one." She squeezed my hands. "Please."

Through blurry vision, I tried to smile at her. Tried to make her see how much her words meant to me, how much she meant to me. We sat that way for several minutes until she finally spoke.

"John?"

"Uh huh?"

"What do the Gorgols want?"

Just by mentioning the name, I realized how arrogant I'd been only minutes before, how I thought she would scold me about the Gorgols, I would argue, and then we'd go our separate ways. How wrong I'd been. "I'm not totally sure," I said.

"But you have an idea?" she asked.

I nodded. "I think they want Holly. Well, I think Alpha wants Holly. But Jake — *Ranger* — wants revenge for the Earth or something weird like that, and Alpha's mostly under his control."

She let out a breath that told me she'd already anticipated the answer. "Why does Alpha want Holly, John?"

"Because she brought them here. I don't know where they were before, but when we were in the desert, Holly opened a window to… *somewhere*. And they came here through that window. Now I think Alpha wants Holly to make another window. To go home. But I don't think she can. And if they come to her and she can't do what they want, I think they mean to kill her."

"Then we need to do two things, son."

"What's that, Mom?" I could see the churning of her brain, ideas forming into plans.

"I need to take Holly away. Keep her safe."

"Alpha will just keep following."

"I understand, but I have to try. That's where you come in." Mom tightened her grip on my hands.

"Okay, what do I do, Mom?"

Unwavering, she spoke in a voice full of pent-up anxiety. Every word rang with maternal instinct, with rage, and bitterness. Mom had lived so many years with her anger at Walter Ivory, with the loss of my father. Now she held nothing back. All the words she seemed to have wanted to say for so long came tumbling out at once. "You need to *kill* Gorgol Alpha. Protect your sister again, John. Kill that monster."

I hesitated. Killing a Gorgol was at least something I was familiar with. But what about Jake? He was a wild card. "What about him — Ranger? To be honest, Mom, I worry that I've just been lucky so far. I really have no idea how to fight."

She thought, and I could almost see the light bulb go off in her mind. "Do you remember Marcos? He always comes to the family reunions."

The name was familiar, though maybe I was thinking of Uncle Howard. Or Uncle Bob. Still, I nodded.

"Marcos is a black belt. I was talking to him about it at the last reunion. I think he said he was fourth dan. I can't say I know exactly what that means, but it's way up there. I can call him. He can help you learn to fight."

She was earnest. But the whole thing was just weird. Plus, since I couldn't even quite recall this Uncle Marcos character, I wasn't terribly keen on revealing what I could do to him. Who knew if the lure of Banner Productions' money would be too much for him? "No, Mom. No way. This is my problem to work out. I just need to figure out what to do about Jake."

Again, she paused in thought. "If he has some other agenda, let him be," she said, giving me a hard look. "But if he threatens you or our family, don't hold back, John. You have power for a reason. Use it."

"You're really okay with that?"

She blinked, and for a moment, I thought she'd back down from what she'd been saying. But no. She squeezed my hand. "If Ranger comes for you, you kill him, too."

5

Not surprisingly, Alpha's change in direction took the media by storm. Where was she going? Why? It gave them something to talk about, and boy did they.

Of course, a lot of the speculation was around Black Sword. Would he chase down the last remaining Gorgol? And was he losing his mind? It was interesting to see how positive the pundits were in their baseless prognostication. Especially since they disagreed so completely. And especially since they were talking about me, when even I wasn't sure what I should do next.

I was glad for the extra time. Because the conversation with my mom had cemented an idea I already knew to be true but didn't want to deal with. A reckoning was coming, between me and Alpha. Holly couldn't send the big beast back to where she came. And me? I didn't even know where she came from, so for me to even try to send her somewhere was pointless. Besides, I had no idea how Holly did those things. I tried to picture the best-case scenario, one that didn't involve any more death. Maybe Alpha would let us move her to a deserted island, where she could live out her days in peace. And maybe Jake would see reason.

Yeah. I know, I know. A reckoning was coming.

I'll be honest, I was a little rudderless. I went to school Monday morning like nothing was happening. Like I wasn't *that* guy. To my surprise, Bobby was at school, too. Not to my surprise, we didn't talk, although I'm sure he saw me. He walked right past me as I dug through my locker for the fat red book labeled *Chemistry*.

"Hey, John," a female voice called. *Carrie*. My heart raced as I turned around, closing the metal door with a harsh *clang*.

"Hey, Carrie."

"Where have you been, stranger?" She smiled as she asked, but something about it seemed strained.

I realized immediately that I must have entered a new situation with Carrie, one where communication was no longer optional. Disappear for a few days, and it was a bad sign. A sign, perhaps, that I no longer liked her. In other words, not the sign I wanted to give her.

"Sorry, Carrie. I was crazy busy at home, you know, with, uh, my mom, and sister." I'm pretty sure that sounded like bullshit, but I hadn't prepared any better story. I made a mental note for the future. If I had to disappear playing hero, I was going to need to be better at coming up with alibis. It was with a strange sense of irony that I realized while I wouldn't let myself push Carrie's mind, I had no problem lying to her. Well, I had a problem with it, but I could make peace with the need. Besides, was I lying? I just wasn't telling her the whole truth.

Oh, shut up. I know that's lying, too.

"You wanna get together, maybe after school?" she asked with a hopeful gleam in her eye.

For a moment, I didn't respond. I stood there staring at her like a deer stares at an oncoming pickup. What had I done to deserve this? How could it be possible that Carrie liked me?

She frowned. Not a sad frown, a silly frown, and she snapped her fingers in front of my eyes dramatically. "You in there, John Black?" With a mock-serious tone, she called out to no one in particular. "I'm going to need 10ccs of reality, stat. This kid needs to snap back to life." She laughed at her own joke.

And then I unfroze and laughed, too. *That* was why it was possible that she liked me. Because Carrie was real. Not the cardboard cutout of a girl that some of the others pretended to be. Just a person. With a sense of humor.

She pushed a curl of red hair behind one ear.

Of course, it didn't hurt that she was so beautiful.

"Yeah, definitely," I finally said.

"Oh, we have a pulse," she said, laughing again. "Okay, John. I have some homework, but why don't we meet up at, say, five? Coffee shop?"

I made a face before I had time to think. *Coffee? Ew.*

"Fine. You pick the place then," she said, rolling her eyes.

I'll meet you next to the dead body of Gorgol Sigma. We can have a picnic and watch the flies cover her body.

You can imagine that would have been a terrible response, right? Of course. That's why I didn't say it, even though that image sprang to mind. Thankfully, I had a more conventional idea, too.

"How about the pizza shop, Bernie's? We don't need to get pizza, if you don't want, though. They have other stuff to eat there." I started to extol the virtues of Bernie's menu, pages three through six, when she interrupted me.

"Bernie's is fine. See you later."

* * *

After school, I rushed home to do my homework, so I'd be free and clear in time to meet Carrie.

Okay, fine, I also may have brushed my hair and teeth. Sue me.

I must have had some extra energy, or maybe not enough homework, because in no time I was done, and there were still nearly 45 minutes to go before my date.

I turned on the TV, figuring it couldn't hurt to get an update on Alpha's whereabouts. Good thing, too.

"…And we remind you that the footage is quite graphic."

Oh, well, that got my attention.

And they weren't wrong.

Since my little stunt with the helicopters — you know, their mandatory nap session — the media had apparently been rather conservative in how closely they would approach their targets. Of course, anyone with sense had been giving the Gorgols a wide berth since the beginning. But not everyone had sense.

The most outrageous, most dangerous shots earned big money. And big money was enough to make some people do crazy things, even if it meant risking their lives.

As the clip started, a nondescript green-and-white helicopter approached what appeared to be a dozing Gorgol Alpha. That seemed completely out of character for Alpha, so immediately my hackles went up. Within moments, the chopper was well within the reach of the creature, and I could tell already what I was about to watch — the demise of some fool pilot and cameraman.

But no, that was too simple.

"The chopper you see approaching Gorgol Alpha is piloted by Guy Mariana, and riding next to him is freelance cameraman Kurt Allen."

It wasn't Alpha that attacked, it was Jake. The helicopter wasn't only close enough to reach with monster claws, it was close enough for Jake to make a mental connection. That's when I realized he must have put Alpha into a type of sleep just so he'd be able to use his mental powers on something else without losing his grip on her.

Or maybe Alpha was hibernating. Going through some important period of her life. Maybe.

The chopper turned abruptly, heading away from Alpha and Jake. Once the idea was firmly planted in the pilot's mind, distance wasn't an issue. Jake didn't even have to try to maintain a connection, he could just sit back and watch, like the way I'd sent Margrethe off to live her life, blissfully unaware that I ever existed. Only the two lives in the helicopter were doubtful to have a lot of time left.

There was a period in the video where no camera was following the action. Why should they? The money was on filming Alpha, not some odd pilot who might be running back to fill up on fuel or grab a sandwich. No one knew where the green-and-white chopper was headed until it was too late.

Of course, the military had done their best to evacuate the immediate surroundings of the Gorgol and her expected path, but they couldn't evacuate everyone. Where would they put them all? And helicopters can cover a lot of ground very quickly.

"At this point, cameraman William Delaney in the C-News helicopter began to get suspicious," the voiceover intoned as the footage suddenly blurred and shook. "When asked later, Delaney told us that he and Allen were old friends, having had lunch together earlier in the afternoon, and having left from the same airfield within 90 minutes of each other. When Delaney saw Allen's helicopter speed off, he felt something was wrong."

A muffled voice could be heard asking "Do you see that? Can you follow him?" Another voice, no doubt the pilot, sounded doubtful, but the cameraman — Delaney — was adamant. Soon the view changed to follow Allen and

Mariana's helicopter as it raced away from the hectic scene around Alpha.

The footage showed them flying oddly low, very close to the tree line, approaching a suburb with medium-sized office buildings arranged in a tight group.

It was calculated. Jake must have planted the idea to look for a sensitive target. The chopper circled and paused before making its move.

Then it dove straight into a five-story building, igniting a fireball that could be seen for miles around. They had many different angles of that.

In the end, 23 people died. How many did that total for the three Gorgols together? I had no idea. But this was all Jake.

Fourteen men, including the pilot and cameraman, six women, and three kids. *Kids*.

Furious, I punched at the TV, ostensibly to turn the damn thing off, but instead smashing it to pieces.

Well, that was going to need an explanation when Mom got home.

6

Sweeping up took a while. I didn't try to hide it. Why bother? It isn't like my mom wouldn't notice that the TV was missing. But clean-up made me leave the house later than I'd wanted to, with not a lot of time before I was supposed to meet Carrie. So I ran.

I was filled with conflicting emotions. Anger at Jake and his stupid random violence. Concern about what I'd have to do about him, and about Gorgol Alpha. And yet, there was also excitement to see Carrie, mixed with fear of what I would say to her.

So it shouldn't surprise you that I never saw it coming until it was too late.

Rounding a corner, two hands grabbed at my clothes. Sure, my *body* was excellent at sluicing away from attack, but my clothes were a different story. I'll be blunt. My clothes were too stupid to get out of the way of a punch. There, I said it.

The rest of me was immediately on guard. A fist came up, I ducked. Another. I slid to the side. Then I threw a punch of my own. There were blurs, all around. It only lasted a few seconds.

"Are we really doing this in public, Bobby?" I asked.

He stopped.

"You're a dick, you know?"

I thought about how I'd spoken to him, to Pip. What I'd *done* to Pip. How I'd walked off. "Yeah, I know. Sorry." I tried to look sheepish. After all, I actually did feel bad about it.

Despite the fact that I knew I might do it again.

In any event, Bobby rolled his eyes. And that was that. I figured I might never make it up to Pip, but with Bobby, it was already over. "Where are you headed in such a hurry?" he asked.

"I'm meeting Carrie, and I'm going to be late." I began walking quickly and Bobby picked up a backpack and slung it over one shoulder as he paced me silently. "Are you... are you coming along?" I asked, not sure how pleased I'd be to have a third wheel on my date.

Bobby shook his head. "Nah. But I've got something for you." The way he looked at me got me suspicious. "It's from Pip." From the backpack, Bobby pulled out a box, about half the size of a shoebox. I noticed the outside was stained on one side.

Oh crap. What's this? I expected the top to spring off and snakes to fly out. Not those springy fake snakes that lame comedians use to scare people. I mean live, deadly snakes. Or maybe scorpions. Or both.

Bobby held out the box, and I took it.

"What is it?"

"Not my place to say," he said. "Not my present."

"*Present?* Pip got me a present? After...?"

"After you cut off her hand?" Bobby offered, and I nodded, turning a little red. "Yeah, no. She definitely is not in the gift-buying mood with you after that. She must've bought this before."

I turned the box in my hands. "Why is it so... dirty?"

"Because she threw it away."

I stopped. "Pip bought me a present, and then threw it away."

Bobby grinned at me. "Congratulations, Johnny. You understand English."

"But why?"

"Why, what? Why'd she throw it away? Didn't I just mention that you were a dick? Don't think she didn't notice that, too."

"Then...," I started.

"Then why did she buy it in the first place? Who knows? Maybe she likes you. Or did." Bobby looked away, his expression unreadable. Then he started walking again, and I hurried to catch up. "Anyway, open it."

So I did.

At first, I had no idea what I was looking at. Because I had never seen anything like it before. It wasn't fancy. More like a novelty.

Inside the box was a belt. Well, actually, two belts, sort of interconnected. Each one was about half the width of my normal belt, and they slid together in opposite directions, clasping each other in the middle. "Um... thanks?"

"Don't thank me, Johnny. I didn't get it for you."

"But what am I supposed to do with it?"

"You're not firing on all cylinders today, huh, buddy? It's a belt, actually two belts. Pip figured you kicked so much ass with one belt, that with two you'd be out of control. The two belts work in opposite directions, meaning you can pull both out at the same time, one in each hand. Put it on, try it."

I twisted my mouth up, turning the belt over in my hands, considering.

Handing the dirty box back to Bobby, I slid off my old belt as we walked, trading it for the new double-belt. It was awkward to feed the two parts in opposite directions, but once it was in place, the buckle clicked with a satisfyingly solid sound.

"See? When you wear it, it just looks like one belt."

We were minutes away from the parking lot for Bernie's. I looked at the box and old belt in Bobby's hands, and the concern must have been apparent on my face. Or maybe it was just that friends read each other's minds. "Go on. I'll hold this stuff for you and bring it back to your house later."

"Thanks," I said, taking another look down at the new double-belt. Bobby waved and peeled off, headed who knows where, leaving me to ponder the strangeness of it all. "Thanks, Bobby!" I called out, meaning much more than just gratitude for the present. He waved without turning back.

I crossed the half-empty parking lot and walked up to the single-story pizza joint. In the window, signs promised food that probably looked delicious a decade or two back, before their color had faded to mostly different degrees of blue. The smiling face of a blue-tinted woman posed with a slice of blue-pepperoni. The poor woman had to sit like that for eternity, so close to her goal and yet never able to take a bite of that wonderfully blue pizza. Pity.

And prominently, near the door, a handwritten sign read "To Hell With The Monsters, We're Open!" Below the words, someone had scrawled a drawing that looked more like three fat ducks than Gorgols. I had heard about the trend on TV – businesses posting signs like these, staying open. Maybe it was altruistic, serving the public, but I figured a good part of it was simply the fact that mom-and-pop shops needed the money to stay afloat.

A thought rolled around in my head. *Pip likes me — or liked me — enough to get me a present.*

It was a really awkward thing to think at the moment I was opening the door to Bernie's and waving to my date.

* * *

Turns out, we ruined our dinners.

Isn't that what parents say when you eat before you're supposed to eat? But what sense does that make? If you eat, you eat, right? How did I *ruin* dinner, if pizza *became* my dinner. I don't think we ruined anything. We had a really great time.

Until the end, that is.

I collected the change after paying for the pizza that ruined our dinner, and we headed for the door to leave. Pip trailed behind me.

"New belt?"

Huh? I thought. It was a belt, not like I was wearing a new purple feather boa. What I'm saying is, it was easy to forget, once you put it on. "Oh, um. Yeah." I nodded. Instantly, I was nervous.

We walked outside, and I blinked at the still-bright afternoon. The smell of grease might have have diminished if it hadn't completely permeated my nostrils.

"Where'd you get it?"

It was an innocent-enough question, with an innocent-enough answer. But I couldn't just mention Pip's name. Carrie had no idea who Pip was. "A girl gave it to me," I said with a shrug. *Smooth.*

"Really? Who?" Carrie stopped. She wasn't angry. Maybe not even concerned. But there was a twinge to her voice that was… different.

I heard the change and freaked out. I knew immediately that I had to cover up this whole new-belt thing. Make it a non-issue. "Oh, nobody. It's just a belt. No big deal."

Do you want to know how you make something into a big deal? Say that it's no big deal.

Carrie crossed her arms, and the edges of her mouth dipped downward. Not quite a frown, yet. But working on it. "You don't want to tell me who gave it to you?"

"It was…" My weak little fool of a mind spun and twisted. *Who?* "My mom!" I said it way too forcefully.

"Your mom?" Carrie said, clearly not buying it. Her crossed arms had tightened and her face was a full-on frown. Still, I nodded. Might as well double-down on the lie, right? "You said *a girl* gave it to you." I nodded again, beginning to look more like a bobblehead giveaway than a real person. "You call your mom *a girl?*" I continued nodding.

She gave me a moment to come clean, but I didn't. I stood there nervously grinning at her. I tried to look confident. To put off an air that it really was no big deal. And that I hadn't just lied. It didn't work.

"Whatever." Carrie huffed and headed for home.

Great. Just great.

7

"John, can you come here?" Mom called out as I lounged in my room later that day. Basically, I holed up there in self-pity. Carrie was pissed at me, and I had no idea what to do about it.

"Okay, Mom," I said, slowly rolling out of bed and padding to the door in my sock feet.

Coming into the kitchen, I slid to a stop on the tile floor.

There was a man sitting at the table.

Well, not just any man. It was Uncle Marcos. I'd only seen him a handful of times in my life, always at big family get-togethers on my mom's side. My first thought when I saw him was *I can't believe my mom called him here without my okay.* Other than that, the only thing that came to mind when I saw him was that he carried matches in his shoes.

I know, right?

"Hi, Uncle Marcos, good to see you," I said in that flat way people talk when it may not be really all that good to see you.

"John." He nodded at me with a sort of reverie about him. Weird.

Without thinking, I looked at his shoes, and sure enough there was a little pouch intertwined within the laces. I had no doubt whatsoever that there were matches in the pouch. And then I realized something. Uncle Marcos was the guy knocking at my front door, the guy I ignored. *Oops.* I hoped my face didn't turn too red. "What brings you by?" I asked, nonchalantly.

Uncle Marcos was quiet, looking toward my mother.

"I thought you two should talk," she said.

As I suspected. I tried to play it cool. "About what?"

Mom took on a strange appearance, a large, toothy smile. "John…" she began, far too pleasantly. "I just thought you'd been having so much trouble with… *bullies* that you might want a little advice." She smiled and nodded toward Uncle Marcos.

Dear God. Did she tell him? No, no way. But she thought I could learn something nonetheless.

I couldn't hide my embarrassment, mixed with a healthy amount of annoyance. "That's okay, Mom. I'm good," I said, turning to head back to my room.

"John?" Uncle Marcos's voice was deep and resonant, holding an inherent sense of peace. I don't know if anyone could resist such a voice. I couldn't. I turned around. "John, I don't want to tell you what to do. You're almost a fully grown man, now. I just had a question for you. One. And if you don't want to answer it, that's fine, too. I'll leave you in peace."

Do you see what I mean? Uncle Marcos had a way. *One* question. That's it. How could I be such a jerk to turn down a single question? Despite wanting nothing more than to go back to my room and bury myself under my pillow, I responded. "Okay, that's fine. What's your question, Uncle Marcos?"

He smirked. "*Uncle*? Funny how you say that. I think maybe *cousin* is more accurate. I'm definitely not your uncle." He looked at my mother and shared a smile, not lording it over anyone, but an inclusive smile. *We're all in on this little joke*, it said.

I liked him. I'd never really thought about it one way or the other. But, yeah, Uncle Marcos — sorry, cousin Marcos, or maybe just Marcos… he seemed pretty cool. Still, I didn't want him preaching to me.

"Sorry, Unc — Marcos. What's your question?"

He smiled again. I realized immediately that I'd let him win, in whatever game we were playing, and yet it didn't feel like I'd lost. Marcos was interesting.

"John, what's the thing that scares you most?" he asked.

How could I answer that? There were too many candidates. Gorgol Alpha. Jake. Carrie's rejection. Pip's scorn. Even the memory of Sol. But, no. None of those took the prize. The winner was something I simply wouldn't say to him.

Me.

I was afraid of me.

So I shrugged. "I don't know."

Marcos looked at me without expression. His eyes held mine, in a way that I completely understood. For the second time that day, I could *feel* someone seeing through one of my lies. He knew me. Maybe better than I knew myself. But how?

Or maybe he didn't. Maybe he simply was at home with himself, to such a degree that he was also at home with me. After all, technically he was.

"Mom…" I started. I was about to politely excuse myself.

"I'm sorry, John," Mom said. "Sorry if I said something you didn't want me to say. But your cousin knows a lot about how to fight, and more importantly, how *not* to fight. How to, I don't know… *present* yourself, so you don't have to fight. And with all those bullies at school…" She didn't quite wink at me as she said it. She could be really subtle, too. "Marcos is a black belt, fourth dan." She said the words, though I knew they meant about as much to her as they did to me.

Did she really think that *not fighting* would work with Jake, after all this time? Hell, maybe it would. But Alpha? No way. I scoffed before I could catch myself.

"You think this is ridiculous, don't you, John?" Marcos asked.

I managed not to laugh, but nodded.

"You think you understand how to handle your own situation better than anyone else, yes?"

Again, I nodded. "No offense, but —"

"But you don't need my help?"

I stiffened at the interruption. But Marcos's question was accurate. "Yeah, I guess not. Sorry."

He thought for a short while, quietly. "No need to apologize, John. Every man — and woman — must walk their own path. I can't walk it for you. I'll only offer you a word of advice."

My left eyebrow raised, the skepticism obvious on my face.

"Know your enemy," Marcos said. "There's no way to defeat your enemy without knowing what you're fighting."

He sat there, not necessarily smug, but that's what I envisioned. *Know your enemy?* Marcos didn't even really know *me*, despite how it felt, so how the hell could he talk to me about my enemy? Besides, after defeating Omicron and Sigma, I hardly feared Alpha anymore. But Jake... He was like me. He could fight like me, move like me. And he seemed crazy. He was the something I wasn't sure about.

A self-satisfied expression dawned on my face. "What if my enemy was water? What if my enemy moved and flowed like water? How could I defeat *that* enemy?"

I didn't expect an answer, but Marcos mused over what I'd said, until he finally spoke.

"If my enemy could move and flow like water, then I should study water," he said. "Water is only a thing, and all things may be understood with study. How does water react? If I push *here*, where does it react?"

"You don't understand," I said. "It's impossible to hit someone who flows like water."

Marcos looked at me with grave seriousness. "No, John, it isn't. All you have to do is understand water. Don't strike where the water *is*, strike where the water *will be*."

8

I went for a walk. Alone.

What a load of crap. "Where the water will be."

Easy to say, wasn't it?

I found myself at the fence surrounding the self-storage building. Mount Trashmore. Technically, I was at the hole in the fence. Maybe someone had tried to improve security in the wake of Walter Ivory's death, but time had passed and people get lazy. It was still easy to duck through the hole. The back door was as unlocked as it had ever been, the whole place just as deserted. I soon found myself alone on the roof.

It was weird to stand on that roof. The last time I'd been there, Walter had tried to kill me and Bobby, and we broke his mind. I felt strange, almost dirty, being there, but so much had happened. It was hard to remember the kid who only thought of his power as a novelty.

I considered what would happen if Walter Ivory suddenly appeared again and tried to hurt me.

And I imagined what I would do to him. Not the timid, old me, trying to figure out my power. The new me, the one who killed monsters.

Walter Ivory wouldn't stand a chance.

I'd been harboring an idea, but the longer it sat in the back of my mind, the more foolish I realized it was. To make peace with the Gorgol. And with Jake.

Peace with Jake was out of the question. What he'd done to that helicopter, to those people. When he tried to cut my head off. Jake wasn't a good guy. Which meant he was a bad guy. Bad guys had to be dealt with.

And Alpha? What would Alpha do when she finally got to Holly, and Holly couldn't help her? I had seen the Gorgols' rage. I imagined my sister as the target of that rage.

And I got mad.

I heard a buzzing in my ear and felt a tickle on my neck. Instinctively, I swatted at the mosquito, but there was no point. I couldn't willfully penetrate my own skin to draw blood, to try to analyze the thorns in my cells. So how could a pathetic mosquito hope to bite me? It would have more luck biting into the surrounding brick wall.

I was alone on the roof with the forklift, the one Mr. Gerald apparently still kept there despite the accident, and a few storage pods full of people's possessions. Things so treasured that they couldn't be given away, even though storing them in a metal crate on some distant roof was perfectly acceptable.

Where the water will be.

Wordlessly, I fell into a fighting stance. No one could see me. I could do whatever I wanted.

What did cousin Marcos know about me, about fighting? He said he was something called *fourth dan*. It represented his commitment, something I couldn't suddenly recreate. But I could try to flow like him.

I threw punches, lashed out, leapt and twirled just the way I remembered so many martial artists from so many movies. It was a comical scene. I was terrible.

Until…

I caught my stride.

Somewhere along the line, I went from a child play-acting to a blur. A blur so fast that it was no longer a joke. Maybe I had no specific moves, or years of martial-arts discipline, but I could do things. Raw force, raw moves, a raw display that no one saw.

Like water, I flowed.

Where the water will be.

I spun and struck at the air.

I spun again, throwing a punch at nothing.

I spun once more, and damn if I didn't run right into the forklift.

For a guy who couldn't be harmed by any normal attack, I still had at least one weakness — speed. I was so fast, my own body couldn't react in time.

I punched and my fist hit the tines of the forklift, and I bled.

Not a lot, but enough.

A couple of droplets fell to the white surface of the roof.

I stopped, amazed.

And, of course, the cut immediately healed. Like nothing had happened.

But the blood… it pooled on the smooth roof, gleaming like polished steel, until it was disturbed. By a mosquito, maybe the same one that had buzzed in my ear.

As if watching a movie, I saw the bug suck up my blood. Such a small amount, but to the mosquito it must have been like doubling its body weight. I stared.

And then the blood was gone. The insect sat, satiated, for some time. Maybe it was five seconds. It felt like five years.

Until the mosquito went to fly away. And I thought, *That's my blood you're running off with.* Was it arrogance? The anger in me? Not really. Just the way we always behave, we self-important humans, when we're confronted by bugs. *You are nothing, I am something.*

I slammed a fist down to crush the mosquito.

And it *sluiced* out of the way.

My eyes went wide. What the hell was this? My powers? In a damn bug?

The mosquito lifted off, trying to get out of reach, and I swatted at it. It sluiced again. I hadn't imagined it. The bug had my powers.

My blood.

I'd given the mosquito my abilities by accident, from my stupidity. It was the tale of so many superheroes, but in reverse. *Insect gains powers from radioactive teenager. Full story at 11.*

The mosquito flew higher. Desperate, I jumped for it.

I have no idea what would have happened if I'd missed.

But I didn't. The bug tried to evade me, but I'd been using these powers for much longer.

As the mosquito flowed like water to one side, I remembered something important.

I remembered where to go.

Where the water will be.

And I caught the bug, squashing it to death in my grasp.

Huffing, I looked at the little stain of red and black in my hand.

Damn, that was close.

9

"I'm sorry about that, John."

I didn't look up from my cereal. I knew what she meant, but I was pissed.

"I should have talked to you about it first."

I kept eating.

"John?"

Nothing. I kept quiet.

"John?"

Still I kept quiet.

And then Holly decided to join the conversation, and my mind felt like it would split in two. Her beacon blasted on and off quickly, like someone blowing an air horn in my brain.

Ow! What?

Johnny, talk to Mommy. Why are you being such a turd?

There you have it.

I was a turd.

But Holly was right.

Rubbing my head, I finally answered. "Fine, yes. Mom, look. I would have appreciated a heads-up about Marcos. You know, it was a nice idea and all, but it just came out of nowhere. If you think I need help, it'd be good for you to, I don't know, maybe tell me first."

"You're right, John. I was wrong to ask Marcos to come here without your approval. I'm sorry." Her face told me she meant it.

My chest puffed up in righteous vindication. But that immediately felt wrong. Despite the fact that I was in the right, Holly was staring at me. And that was enough.

Holly could make me feel like the tiniest ant. It was a superpower of hers, but it wasn't from her power, if you know what I mean. My sister simply owned me in that way.

All of a sudden, I felt like *I* had done something wrong.

How does that happen?

"It's fine. It's done. And besides," I said, mumbling through munched cereal, "maybe he can teach me a thing or two, after all."

Mom smiled. "Good, John. Glad to hear that." She turned toward Holly and frowned. "Holly? What's wrong, honey?"

Probably a casual observer wouldn't even have noticed, but we were family, and, given Holly's lack of vocabulary, we had become quite adept at picking up on gestures and smaller things.

Holly was scratching her arm. Not drawing blood or anything crazy, but not just lightly relieving an itch, either. I reached out to her mind again. *Okay, sis?*

Yeah, Johnny. It just stings.

The sunburn feeling?

Yes.

Is it getting worse again? Getting worse meant Gorgol Alpha was getting closer. And that was something we had to keep tabs on.

She nodded.

"It's the feeling she gets, from the Gorgol," I told Mom. "It's getting stronger."

"How strong?" Mom asked.

Is it changing quickly, Hol?

Yeah, I think. Maybe I'm just used to it by now, but I don't remember even feeling it when I woke up this morning. Now, it's really itchy. Really...

She searched for the word, so I offered a few. *Painful?* She shook her head. *Hot?* Holly just screwed up her face in a way I knew meant *No*. What other word could it be?

Intense. Having found the word, she rocked a bit in her chair, satisfied.

That settled it. Alpha was coming, finally. "Mom, I need to show you something." I went to my room, and Mom and Holly followed.

Using my computer, it wasn't hard to get a general sense of where Alpha was, how far away she was and what direction she was heading. She was definitely coming for us. For

Holly. "I need you to take Holly and leave town," I said. Mom didn't argue. We'd been through enough that she trusted me on this. Besides, she'd been the one to tell me to kill if need be. "Look." I pointed to the spot on the map where Alpha was, drew a line to us, then kept drawing that line past our town. "Go this way, directly away from Alpha. I don't want her to realize you're getting away, so try to go as straight as you can. If she feels that sunburn thing, too, it'll get lighter for her, but I think that will be gradual, so maybe she won't really notice until it's too late."

Pointing out the obvious flaw in my plan, Mom's eyes slid to the right on the map, until brown ended and blue began. "What do we do when we get to the ocean? We can't keep going straight."

No idea. That's what I thought, but I couldn't say it. I realized that I was suddenly taking on a role my dad might have fulfilled in the past — the planner. It reminded me of the last vacation he ever planned. "Playa Beach."

"Huh? Head north to Playa Beach?"

Sure, why not? It was either north or south, and at least if she went to Playa Beach, I'd know where to find her. "Yeah, Playa Beach. If you reach the ocean and haven't heard from me, go north to Playa Beach. I'll come find you there."

Mom turned Holly's chair toward the hallway. "Come on, young lady. We need to pack."

"Wait. One more thing," I said.

Mom turned back. "What is it, John?"

I looked past her. "Not you. Holly."

Yeah, Johnny?

Hol, I need you to try something, as hard as you can.

Try what, Johnny?

I spoke out loud so Mom would hear it, too. "Try as hard as you can to break the connection. The way you can turn on and off your beacon? Try to turn off your connection to Alpha."

10

"Isn't this the part where there should be a montage?"

"Showing what? It's not like we're building a sand pit or wiring a bomb. We're just waiting here." It was the truth. I had killed two Gorgols, and honestly I wasn't all that afraid of the third. The hardest part would be getting up to the sensitive parts — her eyes, mouth, or maybe even her ears or nostrils. I winced. The idea of acting as a giant earwax swab or nose-picker wasn't all that appealing.

There was, of course, one major difference in this fight: Jake. I really didn't know what to expect from the Jake-plus-Alpha combo attack.

But I still wasn't worried.

When the time came, I knew I would get mad. And then I knew what would happen to Jake and Alpha. My anger was deadly.

I'd resigned myself. Alpha wasn't going to stop coming for Holly, and Jake apparently wasn't going to stop coming for me. Mom, Bobby, probably Pip, too — wherever she was — all agreed. It was time. Maybe with them gone I could figure out the anger boiling inside me. Maybe.

Still, I didn't want to do anything stupid. Bobby and I waited on the roof of a building just west of town, one that housed a bunch of doctors' offices. It was the tallest building we could find, clocking in at 12 stories — 50 percent taller than old Mount Trashmore. That meant it was a bit more than half of Alpha's full height. The idea was to attack quickly: draw the beast close and then launch myself from the rooftop. We figured that would take less time than jumping from the ground, giving her as little time as possible to react. Or Jake to tell her to react. Or both.

Bored, I sat down on the flat roof with my back to the low perimeter wall, dropping my black mask to one side.

"Did you call her?"

Bobby nodded, sitting beside me. "Yeah, but... I wouldn't get your hopes up, Johnny. Pip's not going to forgive you any time soon." He scuffed his shoes on the white rubbery surface of the roof. "Do you like her, Johnny?"

"Yeah, Bobby, of course. I really am sorry about what I did."

"No, I mean, do you *like* her? You told me before she was your dream girl."

"Well, there was a time when the only way I knew her was from dreams…"

Bobby pursed his lips, thinking. "Which technically was from *my* dreams, right?"

"I suppose so, yeah. You actually knew her. I got the vision of her from your mind."

Bobby nodded and made sort of satisfied little grunt.

"Why are you asking all this, Bobby?"

"Passing time, waiting for a monster to show up," he said, grinning.

But he wasn't just passing time. I knew Bobby too well to believe that. He was prodding for information, and sounded smug about what he'd found out. The whole issue boiled down to one thing, which was clear in teenage-boy parlance. Bobby wanted me to step aside. He was interested in Pip. And why not? She was beautiful, albeit in a sort of beautifully dangerous kind of way. She was smart. Fierce. Plus she was what my grandmother used to call "full of piss and vinegar," which was basically a strange way to say she did what she wanted and said what she meant. Not sure which one of those things was the piss and which was the vinegar. Remind me to ask my grandmother some time.

Of course, I thought. *Those* were *Bobby's dreams. So when it seemed like Pip was my dream girl, she was really…*

Yellow Fury had a thing for Red Hope? *What a tangled superhero web we weave.* Of course, the fact was he could literally be himself with Pip. No secrets about powers or where he went off to in the night, fighting Gorgols and evil villains. No lying about belts and being double-jointed.

I think it also explained the whole business with Bobby delivering the belt. She had gotten *me* a present. In a way, him giving it to me showed he was jealous.

Idly, I fiddled with the buckle of the new double-belt. "Did Pip get you anything?"

Bobby smirked and shook his head. "Nope."

Bobby's dream girl. Suddenly, remembering our times together, I felt like the world's worst third wheel. And then I realized something.

I bet that's how Bobby has felt the whole time.

11

"Oh shit," I said, peering over the edge of the roof. "Wait here!" I ran for the door that led back to the elevator, then turned quickly back to Bobby and shoved my black mask into his hands. "And hold this!"

Inside, I pushed the only button there was — down — and waited. An interminable amount of time. Finally the elevator arrived, but even just the sliding of the doors — slowly opening, then after a healthy pause, slowly closing again — seemed to take forever.

I watched the number above the door blink on and off, counting down, at a pace that would have made a turtle tap its foot with agitation. Anticipating when "L" would light up and the lazy doors would open, I tensed. The moment the doors began to move, I took a quick glance into the lobby, saw no one, and willed my body to sluice through the thin gap.

This is what I had become. A guy who used amazing physical powers to get out of an elevator faster. Please, try to stifle your applause.

Sure, I could've just floated down from the rooftop. That would have been quicker. But someone might have seen *that*. Most likely the someone I was hurrying to catch: Carrie.

I called out to her. In the time it had taken me to get from the rooftop to the ground floor, she'd passed the building and was already a block and a half away. I called again, and she turned, giving me a little wave. There was an awkward moment. Would she turn back and walk to me? Should I walk to her? *No, stupid, you need to go to her. You're the one chasing her down. Besides, she was ticked off about the belt thing. Go to her.* So I did.

"Hey, Carrie. What are you doing around here?"

"Dentist appointment. Just finished." That's all she said. Rather curt. She didn't even smile to show off her professionally cleaned teeth.

"Your dentist took appointments today?"

She nodded. "Yeah, he says it's impossible to be closed all the time just because something *might* happen. I mean, what are the odds, right?"

Pretty good, today, I thought. I looked around and didn't see anyone else. "And you walked? Alone?"

"Yeah, my dad's office is just around the corner. He'll drive me home." She looked like she was ready to leave, darting her eyes to one side.

"Carrie, I..." I swallowed hard. "I'm sorry. I lied to you. This belt... It's not from my mom."

She rolled her eyes. My heart fluttered. A bit. It was distracting. "Well, duh."

"I don't know why I said that. It's just a gift, from a friend, who is a girl. Not a *girlfriend*."

"Maybe she thinks she's your girlfriend."

I had no answer to that. Maybe she did, but if so, my cutting off her hand probably put an end to that. Although I couldn't exactly explain it that way to Carrie. "Well, I don't think that. I have a girlfriend. Or at least, I hope so."

Carrie was silent, raising both eyebrows. Waiting.

"Will you be my girlfriend?" Wow, that sounded official. It also sounded incredibly lame and awkward. But she smiled.

And, you know, her teeth did look whiter than I recalled. Dazzling, even. Nice work, Mr. Dentist.

"Isn't that what we've been doing for a while now, John?"

"Yeah, I guess so." We shared that sort of sappy young-hearts look that is horrible and silly for anyone watching, but pretty awesome for the people doing it.

And then Bobby spoke in my mind. *Johnny. It's go time. Gonna need you back here, pronto.*

Crap.

I must have looked distracted. "Something wrong, John?" Carrie asked. The look she'd been giving me disappeared.

"Um, hey. Are you leaving this area soon?"

She furrowed her brow.

Yeah, that was a horrible way to ask. "Sorry, I mean, is your dad taking you home soon?"

"He was supposed to drive us home as soon as I got to his office."

"Oh, good. Then, you should go." Again, she gave me a strange look. "I mean, I don't mean to keep you."

"*Keep me?* Why are you suddenly being weird, John?"

A helicopter zoomed overhead. In the distance, there were popping sounds and a low rumble.

Need you back here, partner. Coming in hot.

Just a second! I shot back to Bobby.

"Is something going on?" Carrie said.

"Yeah, maybe. I think it would be safest for you to get home, Carrie."

A second helicopter flew over. Not the light, rounded news-chopper style, but the heavy, angular military kind, guns hanging off each side.

"Oh, my God, is that monster *here*?"

"I think so."

Johnny! Where are you?

Carrie shivered. "John, I'm scared. You need to come with me to my dad's office. We can take you home, too."

John!

Another set of popping sounds, closer this time.

And then she roared. Alpha let out a shriek of rage that echoed off the nearby buildings. Carrie instinctively hunkered up her shoulders. "Come on, John!" She reached for my hand, turning to guide me away.

But I pulled out of her grasp.

"I can't."

"What are you talking about? We've *got* to get out of here!"

Okay, I guess I'm flying solo, Johnny. Please at least tell me you'll bring flowers to my funeral.

I rolled my eyes. At Bobby, but Carrie didn't know that. *Shut up, Bobby. I'm on the way.*

Carrie reached for my hand again. "You're scaring me, John. Come on."

I took her hand in both of mine, not letting her lead me away, but holding on for a moment. "I can't. You know my friend, Bobby Graden?" She nodded. "Well, he's back there somewhere. I need to go find him. You go to your dad, quick. Get home. Bobby and I will get out of here as soon as I find him."

It was a lie, but there were truthful bits in it. Like putting candy sprinkles on a dog turd. But it was the best I had.

"I—" Carrie started, but I had to interrupt.

"Go! I'll call you later!" I released her hand and began to leave.

And in the split second before I turned away, I saw a look of confusion on her face. Maybe disappointment.

I thought that would be the thing that hurt me more than anything else that day. And it was, emotionally.

Physical hurt is another story.

Interlude

The burn does not cease.

Yet...

Where there was silence, there is noise. A new sound.

Something is wrong.

12

"Oh, well, welcome back, your highness," Bobby wisecracked as the elevator door slowly slid open.

Slinking over to where he sat against the wall, I scanned the horizon, immediately noticing the swirl of activity around Alpha as she lumbered toward town.

"Ready?" I asked.

"I'm both as ready and as unprepared as I will ever be," Bobby said. "You?"

"Same." If I was going to do what I had in mind, I needed my fire. But could I control it? I searched inside myself for a scrap of anger, something to fuel my fight. And I found nothing. Did I need my anger to fight, or was I just grasping at straws, knowing that one way or the other, Alpha would be in front of me soon? "Bobby?"

"Yeah, Johnny?"

"I think we've got this. They're two, but we're two. I know Alpha is a giant creature, but other than being huge and strong, we have powers she doesn't. And Jake, even though he has powers like ours, he seems new to them. Like he hasn't had enough time to practice, you know?"

Bobby smiled. "Not unlike a couple of kids I know who used to hang out at the self-storage building."

"Exactly." It was almost time. We knew our powers had distance limits, so we were going to start out old school. By yelling our heads off.

I slipped on my mask and stoop up. Bobby did the same. Coming closer, Alpha and her entourage were a strange sight.

It reminded me of the diagram of an atom — a central hub surrounded by orbiting dots. Here, the nucleus was Alpha, and if I strained, I could see a speck on her shoulder that I assumed was Jake. Around them flew the first orbit of electrons — two gunmetal-black, heavily armed military helicopters. Circling farther out were the media, with their red, green, white, and other colorful choppers.

No one was really doing anything. They looked like they were escorting Alpha into town.

Below us, at street level, dull green jeeps zigzagged through the streets, blaring messages to evacuate. By now, these rolling evacuations had been well-covered by the press, with varying opinions on their success and usefulness. In the military's defense, they had set up a 24-hour Gorgol tracker online, and pleaded for people located even remotely near Alpha to keep tabs on it.

But since Alpha had deviated from her original course, they were at a loss for how to pre-warn the populace. It appeared like they were scrambling to make up for it. I was pretty sure Carrie's dentist would have been postponing appointments if there had been prior knowledge that Alpha was coming to town.

But *we* knew. Because we knew where she *had* to go. Toward Holly. "Just like we did it in rehearsal, right... Yellow Fury?"

"Sure thing, Black Sword. But I think I missed rehearsal."

We started jumping and yelling. And it had almost zero effect. Until finally, a single news helicopter spotted us and broke from the pack. That must have been enough.

Jake or Alpha, or maybe both of them, saw us, and they turned.

"All right, Black Sword, now or never, right?" Bobby's eyes twinkled, the sign of someone who is either 100-percent percent certain of victory or has completely lost his mind. I didn't dwell on which.

Above, the helicopters rearranged to fit us within their orbits As Alpha neared, she let out another deafening roar, and all I could think was *Did Carrie make it out of here?* I hoped so.

The plan was simple. Bobby went first, flying off the rooftop to the ground below, making a feint toward Alpha's lower left side while also reaching out to do whatever he could to mess with Jake's mind.

Then I would follow, going high and to Alpha's right. Aim for the soft tissues. End it quickly. Humanely, if that was possible. But definitively, no matter what. The Earth and the Gorgol just couldn't coexist.

We didn't have much in the way of a plan for Jake. We figured we'd deal with him after the fact. But Jake had another idea, I guess.

Alpha roared again, standing right in front of us, nearly blowing us backward with her foul-smelling wind.

Giving me a confident nod, Bobby was off. He jumped up and over the rooftop wall, making his feint, controlling his fall to the street below. Or trying to, until Jake decided turnabout was fair play and pushed hard at Bobby's mind and body all at once.

According to our plan, Bobby was supposed to yell something to let me know when I should attack. He never told me exactly what, saying he'd figure it out on the spur of the moment. I expected it to be something clever like *Underpants Bok Choi!* or *Excelsior Flamethrower!* Instead, all I heard was a loud *Oof!* Not having more specific instructions, I assumed this was the cue.

In those last milliseconds of waiting, my fire returned. Something about Alpha being so near. Like it was uncontrollable in her presence. The switch had been flipped. Adrenaline mixed with whatever the hell was wrong inside of me, becoming a near-toxic stew of bloodlust. I wanted to kill Alpha.

With one motion, I pulled out my double belts and jumped.

And immediately saw that the plan had failed.

Alpha was glaring right at me, waiting.

Here's the thing. I had an *oh shit* moment, sure. But I wasn't afraid. If anything, I thought it was funny. My anger had come back, and I was completely smug, flying toward Alpha with a sword-spear in each hand like some weird downtown, building-leaping samurai. I was grinning ear to ear underneath my mask, laughing at myself for the botched plan but knowing I would win anyway.

Knowing I would kill Alpha.

Gritting my teeth, I doubled down, willing myself higher, past Alpha's middle section, toward her shoulder.

That's when I got a clear view of Jake. He held on to one side of the monster's neck, using her big scales for grip.

I could tell right away that something was wrong. I mean, he was smiling at me, but that could have been because he had messed up Bobby's feint and was pleased with himself. But, no. There was something *different* about him.

If you've ever had sunburn — not the mystical kind Holly was experiencing, but actual scorched-pink flesh — you've probably found your skin peeling off a day or two later. Jake looked like someone after several bad sunburns in a row. His face looked, I don't know, *irregular*. But what had burned him? The Gorgol? Was being near the creature burning him up?

He'd been acting increasingly strange, almost schizophrenic. It was like the internal conflict within Jake was taking over his external body, too.

Unable to shake the idea that it was sunburn, I thought, *Dude, wear a hat next time*.

Still I flew upward, toward Alpha's face, and the giant beast leaning into my attack and bellowed, baring her massive teeth, giving me the perfect avenue — right into the soft tissue of her mouth.

Just like I had done to Omicron.

It was going to be too easy.

13

Up I flew, willing more energy into the swords, watching their points stretch like oversized, deadly needles in my hands.

Alpha roared on and on. For a moment, I wondered if she thought her breath alone was enough to dissuade me.

It almost was. Yes. It was that bad.

I was strong. At that moment, I felt like the most powerful creature alive, able to decimate any foe. I drove forward, two swords ready to slay the dragon.

Milliseconds from delivering a fatal blow. Until…

Everything blurred, a huge swath of motion.

And I found myself hurtling into the open air, looking at nothing but blue sky.

That was unexpected.

Johnny! Bobby yelled into my mind. *Behind you!*

What the hell was going on? Where did Alpha go?

I started to turn.

Johnny — Oh my God. The way she just moved! SHE HAS POWER, TOO!

What? What was Bobby yelling about?

Alpha's tail hit me in mid air like the best slugger in baseball swinging for the fences.

I didn't just hurt, I felt like every cell in my body would collapse, independently. *That'll get the thorns out!* I thought, but the weak attempt at humor definitely didn't make me feel any better.

The thorns.

If Alpha had power — *the* power — then she had the thorns in her cells, too. But I'd seen her attacking and being attacked many times. She was a giant beast and undeniably powerful, but *power*? I had never picked up on that before.

Alpha's first blow sent me spinning wildly through the air. Her second was straight down, smashing me to the pavement, face first. Ever see someone face-plant off their bike or skateboard, or just flat out fall on their face? It looks painful. It *is* painful. Now think about your entire human body being swatted like a fly. I don't recommend trying it at home.

I made a John Black-sized crater in the middle of the road, right in front of a dentist's office. Was it Carrie's dentist? I didn't have time to ask at the front desk. Besides, it looked dark and deserted, assumedly because the people had evacuated.

Which seemed like a pretty good idea right about then.

I had to get up, even though at that moment any semi-intelligent third-party observer might have advised me to stay down. Throw in the towel.

The belts were just belts again, dribbled like dead snakes next to the flattened blobs that were my hands. My arms. My body. All squashed and lumpy, a bag full of marbles and broken sticks. And damn, everything *hurt*.

I had to get up.

There was an earth-shaking thud that reverberated through my aching skull, but I could see the form returning to my left hand, and slowly I tightened the grip on that belt.

Get up.

The other hand started to form and tighten as a second thud hit the ground. She was coming. She roared.

Somewhere, glass was breaking. An alarm was blaring. Above, helicopter blades chopped circles in the air.

Get up, John, I told myself.

Get up, Johnny, Bobby echoed.

Working on it.

Listen, Johnny, I'm trying to get to you first, but it's gonna be close. And then...

I raised my head and could finally look around a bit. A large monster foot stomped toward me from not that far away, and another thud shook the ground. *And then what, Bobby?*

I think we need to bug the heck out.

My legs tightened and I pulled them beneath me, trying to centralize my energies. *You know, I like that plan better than our last one.*

You came up with the last one, Bobby said.

Are you trying to make me feel bad, Bobby? I pushed up, trying to stand but swaying on legs that quivered like spaghetti noodles.

"If you feel half as bad as you look, there's nothing I can say to make you feel worse," Bobby said, sliding to a stop in front of me. "Can you run?"

"I can barely stand."

"Okay, well, that's a little less than ideal." He looked over his shoulder as Alpha stomped toward us. "We've got, oh, I'd say a negative amount of minutes, but that wouldn't help things much, would it? Could you run in, say, 60 seconds?"

"I can try."

"All right, that's a start. *One... Two...*"

I held up a hand. "Were you thinking of counting off all 60 seconds?"

"Definitely not. We'll be embedded in this street in half that time."

"Then let's go now." I turned and my amoeba-like form over-corrected. But still, it was a bit like starting up on a bike. The wobble was just part of the deal. Work with it, let it work with you. I did. And with every passing second, every step forward, my body solidified. I was even able to push my will into the belts and turn them back into swords, little by little.

"Faster, please," Bobby urged as the ground shook again.

We hurried around a corner — well, Bobby hurried, I sort of shambled. Problem solved, right? Out of sight, out of mind.

Nope. Alpha smashed through the edge of the building at the corner, sending bricks and dust and who-knew-what-else flying.

Bobby put a hand on my shoulder, guiding me left, trying to use the maze of buildings at least as cover if not exactly a permanent solution.

I saw a blur on the periphery of my vision and Alpha's tail circled us, cutting off every avenue. She sluiced and swirled, impossible physical movements. Movements that required power. *Our* power.

There was nowhere to go. Well, one way to go. Back to Alpha.

Bobby and I slammed ourselves into a back-to-back stance, and I raised my sword-spears.

The sun was behind Alpha's head as she leaned forward, a giant-creature eclipse. Her shoulders hunched and she bent toward us.

The earth shuddered twice as her hands touched the ground. And like a bear sniffing its prey, Alpha lowered her massive, toothy face, so close.

Bobby and I tensed, breathing heavily, turning to see the face of our doom.

Slowed to a stop just inches away, I saw one of Gorgol Alpha's huge teeth, taller than me. Her entire mouth looked like a small apartment. Central heating, sleeps four, possibly forever. Slight odor problem.

She snorted, and my hair tossed in the breeze of her breath. I was going to need a shower. If I lived.

"Ready, Bobby?"

"For what? To become dinner? Not really."

I looked over my shoulder at him. "If this is it, then this is it, right? If we're going to die here, would you rather die running or die fighting? You know, with your boots on, and all." I gave him my best *Let's go get this!* look.

"Is *not dying* an option?"

I laughed. In the face of death or whatever we were facing, a creature more than 20 times our size, with the same powers we had, Bobby, my friend, made me laugh.

"I don't know. But let's find out." Instinctively, we tensed. Pulling inward, we prepared to jump, even though Alpha was only inches away.

And then Jake stepped forward. *"In the midst of chaos, there is also opportunity."* His voice shifted as he spoke, modulating and changing, word to word.

"Huh?" Bobby replied, cleverly.

Jake looked us over, his face covered in bumps and strange ridges. His weird sunburn, peeling. "Which do you prefer, boys? Chaos or opportunity?"

14

I couldn't help but stare. It was as if Jake's face had decided to take a holiday and jump off his skull for a while. Needless to say, it was disturbing. You know how some people say that skin can be *smooth as a baby's bottom*? Well, Jake's was nothing like that. Which, oddly, sounds like a compliment.

He eyed us. "What do you think?"

"I think you're a jerk and the only reason we haven't slapped that stupid look off your face yet is that you've got a really big dog," Bobby said, cheeks flushed. The bully Bobby was making an appearance. *Good*, I thought. *We might need a little brute force here.*

Jake scoffed. Above the helicopters must have been having a field day. *Showdown in Downtown!* I imagined the news-channel graphic artists were selecting dramatic fonts as we spoke.

Alpha hunched above us, looking down, her breath coming out in long pulls, a deep bass tone echoing everywhere, threateningly, with each exhale. Her tail wrapped around all three of us, almost like a protective mother. *MOTHER.*

I knew one thing. We were in deep doo-doo. I had to come up with something, and fast.

"You're so funny, Bobby," Jake said, shaking his head. "I mean, what do you think of my work?"

"You gave her power," I said, and Jake nodded with a smile. "You're out of your mind."

"Am I, John? Gorgol Alpha is here to save the world from humanity. All I did was make sure you two, and your red friend, can't mess that up."

"How are *you* any different?" I asked.

Idly, Jake scraped one hand along his cheek, and flecks of something I didn't want to think about fell away. "I don't know what you mean."

"You say Alpha will save the world from the mess people have made of it. But you're wrong. Alpha just wants to get home. Look inside her, you'll see it's true. My sister brought the Gorgols here, and Alpha thinks my sister is her ticket home." Jake flinched, his face contorted, not believing. "But here's the thing. Holly can't do it. She can't send them back. She doesn't know how she brought them here in the first place, and has no idea how to send them back. Alpha is here for good. But she isn't natural and doesn't belong here. And even if she *did*, what have you done? If you've given this monster your powers — our powers — then you've *corrupted* nature. You're as guilty as any of the humans you're busy condemning. Maybe more so."

Jake froze momentarily, then flicked his head dismissively and looked down. Something else was at play. I felt a shift that I couldn't see.

His eyes were dark as they slowly looked up at me from sockets that appeared burned. "John, my friend, you talk a good game. You have always been a deceiver." *Always? How long does he think we've known one another?* He was using our names out loud. Obviously Jake had no concern about our private identities. He was only feet away, speaking conversationally, not shouting. But if any of the helicopters above could hear his words… "As I am certain you're aware, for every action, there is an equal and opposite reaction. The collective actions of all of mankind have brought us to where we now find ourselves, with such a force of inevitability that no man could stand in the way. Then you, John…" Jake's eyes met mine again, and I shivered. "You made a mess of things. You killed the life

427

forces of the world, Omicron and Sigma. I don't know how
to explain such a thing other than to say you are evil. I saw
you in action. I saw your anger and brutality. You even
attacked your own friend, simply for the right to kill one of
these creatures. What makes you think, after all this, that
you're really on the side of *good*?"

His accusations floored me. Even if the Gorgols were from
somewhere else, weren't Jake's words true? Hadn't I been
angry and brutal? Was it possible that I was evil? *If he
threatens you or our family, don't hold back, John,* I heard
my mother say in my head. *Kill.*

My mind reeled. I'd chased down Sol, destroying the lives
of Petrus and Margrethe in the process, blowing Sol into a
billion tiny pieces. I did it to save my sister, but in the
grand scheme, was that an act of *good* or an act of supreme
selfishness? I remembered the near-glee I felt, driving my
weapon deep into the Gorgols, killing both of them.

I'm not who I think I am.

That very idea, the very concept, rising as a serious
possibility in my mind, staggered me.

"I see you admit the truth at last, John," Jake said. "And
now you know why I *had* to do what I did." I thought of the
mosquito. How my blood had changed it. How I had only
just barely stopped it from getting away. What would have
happened then? I'd heard of invasive species before, but
never considered that *I* might be the ultimate example.

I felt like I might faint or black out. Everything was wrong.

"Johnny, you okay?" Bobby said from my side.

I was dizzy. The blood rushed to my head, filling my ears with deafening noise.

"Johnny?" I could barely hear Bobby anymore.

"I gave of myself, so that Gorgol Alpha could be *more*. So that the likes of *you* could not stop her ever again." As I blinked stars from my eyes, Jake stood triumphant. "I have given nature the upper hand." He glared at me, and my focus blurred.

I was going to fall, but I knew that if I did, it was over. I would die, and so would Bobby. I had to do something.

Was I good or bad? In the end, do any of us truly know? The good you do, might it harm someone else? Does that make you evil? Or if you willfully commit evil, and that benefits someone, do you accidentally become good?

Perspective was all that mattered. Sometimes you stood above it all, looking down with the sun shining on you. And sometimes you got punched in the face and had to lie down in the dirt. How you felt about things differed based on where you were, how you looked at them. The black eye of the beholder.

Instinctively, I reached out a subtle tendril of my mind.
Jake hadn't noticed the last time I'd done it. I prayed he
wouldn't again. And inside Jake's mind I found static. A
phone call that wasn't quite right. I heard voices.
Something reminded me of flapping, leather wings.

"So now we come to the end of you," Jake said. "I would
offer you a choice, live in peace or die as enemies, but the
simple fact of the matter is that *I don't trust you.* You'll
plead for life and peace, and then work the rest of your
days to bring me down. To bring Alpha down. And I can't
let that happen."

Jake looked up at the creature above him, and like a
remote-controlled toy, Alpha fired up, inhaling and rising
to her full height. "So instead, you die here."

15

I felt the pulse of Jake's mind, as it wavered back and forth, between two sides I couldn't understand.

One side.

Then the other.

Not switching regularly, like a metronome. More like a fight. One side would get the upper hand, then the other would. And in the brief transitions, the connection went dead, like a disconnected phone. Not a dial tone, ready to make a call. Just that peculiar emptiness of a dead line.

I'd pushed a lot of minds in the time that I'd had my powers. None of them had felt like Jake. Then again, I'd never tried to connect to someone dealing with schizophrenia. But was that what I was dealing with? Was I peering into that sort of fractured mind? Knowing nothing but working off intuition, I thought it was something else entirely. Something unnatural.

Jake had given his powers to Alpha. Well, *given* wasn't the right word. *Shared* was more accurate. Then I remembered working my microscope, seeing the alien thorns in my cells.

No, he's infected *her with what we have. This disease.*

A disease without a cure.

How had he done it? I thought again of that little mosquito, slurping up my spilled blood, then sluicing away from me. My blood. Jake's blood. Sharing his blood, Jake could infect others, just as I had done to that bug. And the idea of Jake sharing blood with Alpha didn't seem all that far-fetched. I mean, Gorgol Alpha was a bloodletting machine.

I hadn't seen any human, any machine, that was able to stop me with my powers. Or Bobby, or Pip, or Sol, or Jake. And now, this giant animal, this Gorgol, had the same abilities.

And she wanted to reach my sister. What possibly could keep that from happening?

Good? Evil?

It didn't matter what I was. Alpha had to be stopped.

But how? She'd clearly taken to the physical aspects of the power quickly. No doubt Jake's control of her mind helped tremendously.

If I were facing her as an equal, normal human creature to normal Gorgol creature, I would lose. She was simply too much for me. Now I faced her as another equal, powered human to powered Gorgol. The outcome looked to be identical — that is, bad for me.

Unless…

Single point of failure. It was something my dad and I had talked about, once in a while. The place where everything, even something terribly large and complex, could fail if only one thing happened.

Jake controlled Alpha, but what controlled Jake?

The alternating battle inside Jake pulsed again. To the nothing. The nothingness in the middle.

The disconnected phone.

And I pushed, hard.

Like mirror images, the tiny figure of Jake and the massive figure of Alpha staggered backward. Alpha's tail slid through the air, uncoiling from around us.

"Run, Bobby!" I yelled, and he didn't argue. We ducked around a corner, down several streets, as fast as we could, putting ground between us and the dual threat of a powered Gorgol Alpha and Jake.

Of course, the monster was 200 feet tall, so for a long time, even though we ran, Alpha's shadow hovered over us. Still, she wavered. Like a computer rebooting, she seemed to be going through the motions, trying to come back to reality, but not quite there yet.

I must have hit Jake pretty damn hard. Or maybe it was just *when* I hit him. At the most vulnerable moment. Like Alpha, he looked like he was rebooting.

After a few turns, we figured distance was our only hope. We ran on, as directly away from the Alpha as possible. Our masks were still on, as were the mental silencers of our beacons. We were doing everything we could to disappear.

Did I mention I hate helicopters?

I mean, did they *want* us to get killed?

Several of them followed us, high enough up that they were out of physical or mental reach. See? I told you I'd only get to do that *put 'em to sleep* trick once.

But they might as well have been broadcasting *JOHN AND BOBBY ARE HERE!* and pointing down at us with giant neon arrows.

Behind us, Alpha roared, and I figured the reboot must be complete. There was a crashing, smashing sound as buildings seemed to tear themselves apart simply to make way for her.

A car flashed by, some straggler from the evacuation, rushing to get away from the destruction. *Is that Carrie?*

"I hope she got out," I whispered to myself. I wanted to find her, make sure she was okay. But at the moment, running from imminent death was my only option.

We turned down a narrow alley, passing the entrance to a parking garage, and for a moment the helicopters couldn't see us.

A female voice called out from inside the garage. "Lucky timing, boys. You better come with me."

My only thought was, *Oh, good. Does Pip want to help me or kill me?*

16

"Pip, I just have to say, I'm really sorry," I said. She was busy driving a stolen minivan, fast, through the bowels of the garage, looking for another exit, trying to throw everyone off our trail.

"At least you two idiots had the sense to turn off those noises we all make." That didn't exactly sound like *Apology accepted.*

"You mean our beacons?" Bobby asked, sounding kind of hurt. I assumed he didn't like being lumped in the same idiot category as me, for several reasons. He'd taken over the shotgun seat, I was in back. I don't know why I remember this, but there was a video screen dangling down just above my head. *I can watch a movie. Awesome.* Idly, I checked the seat pockets, trying to see what they had.

"Yeah, sure, that. But you've gotta lose those masks if we're going to blend in. I took the liberty of picking up a couple of plain black t-shirts. I figured you guys were going to need an anonymous getaway. They're in the back." She hitched a thumb over one shoulder, in my direction.

Our masks came off quickly and were tucked out of sight. I saw a plastic package on the floor, ripped it open, and pulled out two shirts, tossing one to Bobby. Then we each performed an awkward dance, like choreography for the world's worst classical music composition, *"Two Fools Change Clothes in a Moving Car, in D minor."*

"I guess you saw the bad news?" Bobby asked, as Pip slowed and slipped out onto a side street. Within a couple of turns, she had managed to merge into a stream of traffic that looked to be made up entirely of people trying to evacuate. I saw other minivans almost indistinguishable from our own, and realized, once again, that Pip was pretty darn clever.

"Oh, whatever do you mean?" Her tone was sharp, speaking to Bobby like she was as mad at him as she was at me. "The fact that there's now a giant monster with superpowers? That just seems dandy to me." Yep, she was clever, but also acerbic.

Bobby just turned toward the window.

I tried to help. "What are we going to do now? We've got to stop those two." It was stating the obvious, but I said it to take up space that otherwise was likely to fill with an unproductive toxic anger.

"Why don't you just jump on up there and kill Alpha, like you did the others?" Pip chided.

"That's sort of what we tried to do," Bobby said.

She sighed heavily. "All right, then. Are you ready to work *together*?" Pip looked at me in the rearview, and I nodded emphatically. "You sure about that? What if you decide to get pissed off again? It was bad enough having you go to work on my arm. I don't want to find a sword sticking out of my back."

I had to be honest, and that meant I really didn't know. "Pip, I really am sorry about what happened. And I do want to work together. The anger... I just don't know. I want to tell you that everything will be fine, that I'll never do it again, but... I'm not sure why it happens to me, so I don't want to lie to you. I don't *decide* to do it, it just happens."

There was silence, nothing but the hum and rattle of the road passing underneath us and the minivan doing its job.

Then Pip nodded. "Fine," she said. "At least I know where we stand. I'd rather have you shoot straight with me than give me a load of bullshit."

I don't think we ever talked about it again.

* * *

To see if Jake and Alpha were on our trail, Pip drove all over the place, north, south, east, west... I think she even made up some directions. We turned on the radio, finding a news channel that had all the audio quality you expect from radio news. From that, we heard that Alpha was, once again, following a straight path.

Either they didn't know where we were and hoped to stumble upon us, or they weren't looking for us at all anymore.

I figured the latter.

"Holly," I said.

"You think they're back on her trail?" Pip asked.

"I bet they are."

"Then we have to get to her," she said. "Where is she?"

"I don't know exactly. I sent them away, her and my mom."

Pip twisted up the side of her mouth, thinking. "Your mom has a phone, right? Call her and find out where they are. We're going to need to get to them."

"*She* has a phone, but *I* don't."

Pip looked at me funny in the rearview. "How is it you're 15 years old and you don't have a phone? You did grow up on Earth, right?"

"I don't have a job — *yet*." Who was I kidding? The way things were going, I might not live another week. There wasn't a lot of time to learn a vocation. "Anyway, what I mean is that I don't earn any money. My mom works, and there was some money from my dad's life insurance, but you know, we have Holly to take care of. A phone just always seemed superfluous to me. I know everyone else has one, though."

Pip looked down, eyes out of the rearview so I couldn't gauge her expression. Then she fumbled through a pocket and produced a phone, holding it back for me. "Call your mom."

17

"We turned north, John, once we came to the shore," Mom said. "We're only about a half hour from Playa Beach."

What was I going to say? *Keep running, forever?*

No.

Besides, I had no other plan. Drive this way or that, fine. It might buy a little time, but it didn't change the end game. And, like Mom had said, I had to protect my family.

"Once you get there, stay put. I'm coming." With that, the little fire was set alight within me, once again. The familiar fire.

Pip drove into the night, snaking through traffic, which seemed to be everywhere. Everyone wanted to get away from the oncoming Gorgol menace.

We made good progress, at first. I thought we'd beat Alpha to Playa Beach by a day or so. I was wrong.

At some point in the dark, we hit a traffic jam that seemed like a billion red lights receding into the never-never land of the distant horizon. Only the rare pair of white lights headed back the way we came. Who knows where those people were going?

We inched along, like everyone else. Funny how something so mundane as traffic equalizes the ordinary and the extraordinary alike. With nothing to do but sit quietly in the back seat, I couldn't keep my eyes open. I started to drift off.

"Did he doze off back there?" I heard Bobby say softly to Pip with a chuckle.

"Think so," she replied.

Bobby was silent again for a long while, and I almost fell completely asleep. "Hey, Pip?"

"Yeah?" We crept slowly in the traffic, the minivan making a monotonous hum all around me.

"I hope you're not mad at me for getting back with Johnny. He is my friend and all."

"Oh, shit!" Pip said, stopping abruptly.

There was a static noise that at first I thought was the radio acting up. Then I realized it wasn't a sound you could hear out loud, it was in my head. It was Jake. He was nearby.

I sat up quickly, scanning the windows for some sign. "Where?" I said. Pip pointed to our left.

It was nearly pitch dark and we were on a lonely stretch of highway, amid tall pine trees. Well, I would call it a lonely stretch except that we were there with 600,000 of our closest friends.

From above the trees to the left, a glow filled the sky as Alpha thudded into view, bathed in floodlights from the surrounding helicopters.

"Choices, gentlemen," Pip announced.

"Oh, now we're gentlemen," Bobby riffed.

I expected Pip to get mad, but she shot him a coy look instead. "Boys. We have three choices, as I see it. Fight our way toward Alpha and do this now. Push to get out of here. Or sit exactly where we are and do nothing."

"I vote for option three," Bobby said. When we both shot him a look, he rolled his eyes. "I'm *kidding*, you guys, come on!"

"John?" Pip asked.

I had to think. What was the best plan?

"Plan?" I said out loud.

"Huh?" Bobby replied.

And that was that. I realized our dilemma. "We don't have any plan. If we attack right now, we're no better off than we were in the fight we just ran away from." They both nodded. "So that leaves run or do nothing. I'm not really a fan of do nothing."

"So?" Pip asked, watching Alpha loom closer.

"Run!" Bobby said.

* * *

It was slow and awkward, getting to somewhere — anywhere — where we could get off the highway, but we did, eventually. You certainly couldn't call it *running*. I think our top speed was a snail's pace above zero. That is, until everyone started freaking out and all the rules of driving went out the window.

Cars went in every direction, not caring about white lines, yellow lines, median strips, forests, or anything else. We careened right, followed the highway through the mess, and eventually found an exit.

From there, we were on a rural two-lane road, with houses spaced out at maybe one per quarter mile. Not big fancy places, either. Squat little brick homes with barren yards. Most had too many cars, unless every bedroom in the house slept four people, which I suppose was possible but seemed doubtful. Many had some sort of overblown lawn ornament. Water wells to nowhere? Ornamental planters that could be seen from space? Completely unnecessary stone lions on equally unnecessary walls plopped down on the lawn? Check, check, and check. And more gazing balls. Go ahead and laugh. I'll wait.

We made some space between ourselves and Alpha, but could still see her illuminated in the ghostly spotlights from afar.

And then something happened.

Not that I would know, but it seemed that if you messed with the military long enough, they felt obligated to try to return the favor. All of a sudden, there was an eerie silence. And then three or four heavily armed helicopters were swarming Alpha, flooding her with light.

Without warning, they fired.

I had to admit, it wasn't the worst idea I'd ever seen — hit her from all sides at once. How could she evade everything at once?

Well, she did, and the missiles hit unexpected targets all around Gorgol Alpha, sending up flames and shockwaves in every direction. The creature slid and flowed like water, sidestepping every attempt to bring her down.

She was a blur, almost a figment of my imagination, a haze on the horizon. Streaks came from each of the firing choppers, and, as far as I could tell, not one shot came close to landing.

You know how, in video games, you can just keep firing forever? Well, that's not how it works in reality.

Soon, all of the helicopters ran out of missiles. And then they simply turned and flew away, pathetically.

"Okay, great," Bobby said, sliding down in his seat. "We're going to fight *that*."

18

"Halt! Who goes there?"

Okay, I lie. He didn't say that.

Ahead of us, shadowy in the blinding lights, the silhouette of a soldier raised one hand. Stop.

"*Masks*," Pip whispered to us, and we quickly obliged.

"Why? Just push their minds," I said.

"No, Pip's right," Bobby said. "If we're going to risk our necks, I'd at least like a little respect for it."

"Suit yourself," I said, pulling on my mask. Bobby followed, and Pip was last, pulling hers on with one hand still balanced on the steering wheel.

"Plus, I don't want to spend the energy here," Pip said. "We'll need it when we face Alpha and Jake. Pushing the minds of every person from here to Playa Beach sounds exhausting."

"Okay, sure," I said. "Except I think you two just like being recognized as superheroes."

Neither of them answered me, but in the rearview I thought I saw a twinkle in Pip's eye.

She rolled to a stop with the soldier just outside the window, and he twirled his hand in a gesture meaning *Window down.*

The name FELDMAN adorned a patch on the left side of the soldier's chest. "What have we got here? Bunch of jokers? I need you to take those masks off." A second soldier, ORLANDO, appeared on the passenger side, and the two exchanged amused smirks.

"We can't," Pip said.

"Oh, you can't? And why's that?" Feldman asked, still smirking.

"Um… It would reveal our secret identities?" Bobby offered from the passenger seat.

Feldman laughed. "Hey, Orly, the jokers here say they can't take off their masks because it will reveal their secret identities. What do you think of that?" They both laughed.

"Don't you know who we are?" Pip asked.

The smile faded from Feldman's face. "I know who you're *pretending* to be… *Red Hope. Yellow Fury. Black Sword.*" He pointed at us, one at a time, ending with me. "But I know one more thing. You're not really them, so *take off the masks*. Last warning." Feldman adjusted the strap of his semi-automatic rifle, a not-so-subtle gesture.

"Told you guys this was silly," I muttered. Bobby shushed me. Which made me understand something a little better. This was a chance for Bobby and Pip to do something I didn't like, even though it was minuscule and pointless. So I kept my mouth shut and played along.

"That's who we really are. And since we're the only ones who can do anything about Gorgol Alpha, I'd appreciate it if you'd go ahead and let us through. We're just here to help." Miraculously, Pip said all this in a relatively sweet tone. For a billionth of a second, I actually thought it would work.

Feldman paused. I doubt this was a scenario he'd considered prior to roadblock detail on that particular

evening. But he recovered quickly. "Out of the car. Now."
He stepped back, hands firmly on the gun.

And Pip, she just slowly opened the door, mask still in
place. Bobby did the same, and I slid open the back door to
the minivan, joining them. Orlando guided Bobby around
until the three of us stood shoulder to shoulder, facing the
soldiers and the bright lights behind them.

A voice called out. "Feldman, what's going on down
there?"

Feldman shouted back over one shoulder. "Sir, these folks
are wearing masks and don't want to take them off. Seem
to think they're those superheroes from TV, sir."

"Well, cuff 'em and let 'em think about it for a bit. And
move that car out of my road," the voice demanded.

"Yes, sir," Feldman replied, nodding to the other soldier
beside him. Orlando walked around behind us, pulling
handcuffs from his belt as he approached Bobby.

And that's when things went south fast. I didn't see it, but I
could guess what was happening. Orlando tried to cuff
Bobby, and Bobby's body sluiced out of the way. Orlando
made a little surprised sound and jumped back, which was
enough to make Feldman raise his weapon.

I was just trying to calm things down. I raised my hands,
too quickly, toward Feldman, in a way that was supposed to

communicate *Hey, let's talk this over*. He must have assumed my intent was much more threatening. And I guess Feldman and the others were probably a lot more jumpy than usual.

Because he shot me.

Well, you know. He tried to. His aim was true, dead into my gut, a bullet that would certainly have dropped me. If my body didn't just arc around the bullet and then reform.

Still, that was enough. Someone yelled from back where the bright lights were, and other shots rang out. Pip, Bobby, and I slid and sluiced like three marionettes in a crazy dance number.

And then it was over.

"Oh… my… God," Feldman said, staring at us in disbelief.

"No," Pip said, dusting off her outfit with one hand. "We're not hardly gods. But we *are* Red Hope, Yellow Fury, and Black Sword. And I'd appreciate if you'd let us pass now."

Mouth gaping, Feldman just nodded his head.

19

Playa Beach had the vaguely haunted appearance of a place that had been heavily populated until five minutes ago. This was even more pronounced along the boardwalk, where lights still flashed, arcade games still blared music and sound effects, and the detritus of the human race still blew in the wind.

But no one was there.

It *smelled* populated. You know how things just smell when people are there in great numbers? The natural ocean salt mixed with sweat and sunscreen and greasy food to make a sort of human cologne. But it was dissipating. The place was empty.

From the backseat, I was no longer lazing about, half asleep. Mom and Holly were near. I scanned for them in every direction.

It was weird. A place I had been so many times before, a place I associated with the simple idea of being crowded.

Nothing.

Finally, after another call to my mother, we arranged to meet on the north end of the boardwalk. The shops and wooden walkway ended there, and so did the beach. A steep, rocky hill took over, leading around a bend in the coastline. Of course, whenever you combine steep rocks and public beach, you get the obligatory and supposedly illegal jumping spot, a flattened section about 20 feet up the rock wall. I had never done it. When we first started coming to Playa Beach, I was too small. Later on, I was too chicken. And now, well, I had other things to do. Once or twice a year, you'd hear stories of teenagers sneaking up there to jump at dusk (usually not at dawn, because, really, who wants to get up at dawn?) and hurting themselves. I never heard of anyone dying from the jump, but that possibility always lingered.

Pip didn't so much park the minivan as she just stopped and got out. It seemed unlikely that we'd get a ticket, and besides, it wasn't even our car. Going to the back, Pip pulled out her sword and strapped it on. Bobby took a second blade. Then Pip looked at me, up and down.

"I see you got the belts."

"Thanks."

She shrugged.

Out on the boardwalk, the odd feeling of the empty city increased. Even the roller coaster performed its endless streaming of light, enticing us to ride, though none of its cars would run on this particular night.

In the moonlight, I saw Mom waiting with Holly in her chair, facing south toward us, a short distance from where beach turned to rock. I ran to give them both a hug. Thankfully, we could do all this sans masks. The helicopters — and therefore, Alpha — were some distance off, toward the southwest edge of town.

Holly was scratching her left arm, and I could see it was raw and irritated, nearly bleeding, probably only kept from doing so by her powers.

Bad, Hol?

Yeah, Johnny. The worst it's been. But I tried.

Tried what?

I tried to disconnect. Hide from it. Make it go away. I — I just couldn't, though. It's like the feeling is part of me.

I pressed my forehead against hers and smiled. *It's okay, Hol. We can't run anymore. There's nothing left to do but stand and fight, and then I think this feeling will go away.*

I hope so, Johnny. Thanks. She scratched her arm even more intensely.

"What should I do?" Mom asked, looking completely lost.

You know, that kind of question never stops being weird. Your own *parent* asking you for advice.

"Just stay with Holly. Keep her out of danger." I nodded to Bobby and Pip. "We'll go after Alpha. And Jake."

"No need, my friend," a voice said from behind us.

We turned to find Jake standing alone on the boardwalk, illuminated by the colorful flashing lights of the shops and rides.

Wordlessly, Pip, Bobby, and I arrayed ourselves around Mom and Holly, and each of us drew our weapons, my double sword-spears coming to urgent life in my hands.

"Such a welcome, so friendly." Jake chuckled, then coughed. He looked sick, like something was coming apart inside him. The idea that he was sunburned no longer seemed accurate. It was too far gone for that. He looked irradiated. Which, of course, made him seem all the more dangerous.

"Someone knows how to quiet his sound," Pip muttered. "What do you guys call it? His beacon."

Quiet. It was then that I realized things were too quiet. Something I'd been hearing so frequently for so long was missing.

The sound of helicopters.

If Jake was here, why weren't they? The likely answer to that question made me sick. Jake had sent one helicopter crashing to its doom, why not others? Why not all of them?

Suddenly, I was very afraid.

Not for me. For my friends, my sister, and more than any of them, for my mom. I realized, with a deep sadness, that of all the people standing on the boardwalk, only one of us didn't have powers.

My father was gone. My mother wasn't. And I wasn't ready to see that change, no matter what Jake had done to the Gorgol.

A fire started, within.

"Leave us alone, Jake, or else," I said.

The bastard clucked, dismissing me. "Really, John? *Or else* what?"

I took a step toward him. Bobby and Pip followed. "Or else it all ends for you, right here, right now."

Jake chuckled, and the hairs on the back of my neck stood up.

What is —?

"John Black, you're strong. And you're brave or you're foolish, the difference is immaterial. But more than anything, you're vicious. You've killed two Gorgols, Omicron and Sigma, and yet one remains. The most powerful one of all, made even more powerful. By me." Jake stood tall, but the appearance was deceptive.

From behind, I heard a faint sound. A rustling or shaking. I started to turn, but Bobby spoke. "Let's take him down, Johnny. One against three."

I nodded, and my sword-spears grew, looking more lethal than ever before. "Right now," I said, "it's just you and us." I began to walk toward Jake with confidence and purpose, Pip and Bobby trailing me.

Once more, Jake chuckled, but his voice cracked and the laughter turned into a cough. He hid his face in one hand as the coughing worsened, his back hunching.

Finally, the hacking stopped, and Jake slowly stood straight again, his head gradually turning back toward us again.

There was something. His eyes. I think it was his eyes.

The sound behind us grew louder, distracting, and for a moment I turned my head back. Holly was scratching furiously.

Holly?

Oh, Johnny, it burns so bad, she said, eyes pleading with me, scratching harder.

"Don't be foolish," Jake said. "I'm not alone."

Oh no.

We'd been looking in the wrong direction, it seemed.

The massive form of Gorgol Alpha, curled in on herself as her children had done when they first arrived, pushed through the water, creating a mountain of swell that looked like a tidal wave. As she hit land, the water frothed and sloshed in every direction, surging up the long white plain of sandy beach before us. Then Alpha rolled to a stop and stood, smashing shops and lengths of boardwalk as she unfolded, so close to us the smell was nearly overwhelming. She towered over the rides and attractions, striking a terrifying silhouette in front of the colorfully lit Ferris wheel spinning idly and empty in the distance.

Alpha roared, and a spray of water flew off her scales in every direction.

A giant monster just snuck up on us, I thought. *We suck.*

My fear and anger coalesced, fueling the fire within me. This was too close, too dangerous. Mom. Holly. I had to do something.

Jake had been in control of Alpha for so long, but now he hardly seemed in control of himself. Maybe if I timed it right… in that dead space between the pulses, between his two sides.

I closed my eyes.

And reached out my mind, to see if I could wrestle Gorgol Alpha away from the man they called Ranger.

20

It didn't work.

Whatever else Jake might have been, he was deeply connected to Alpha, like maintaining the bond for so long had only made it stronger.

I couldn't pull him away.

But now I could feel him fighting me, with his mind. I sensed all the energy he put into it, realizing that there was nothing I could do.

Unless…

While I kept fighting for Alpha's mind, I also sent a tendril into Jake's. Nothing much. Just gauging the pulse.

One. The other. One —

And I physically launched myself at him, not the lofty jump I'd done before, but a cannonball shot into his chest. His body sluiced but not enough, my speed was so great. He fell backward in a heap.

And his connection to Gorgol Alpha snapped.

The creature wailed, a forlorn sound. For Jake?

Behind me, Holly moaned, a sound that turned from a low bass note into a scream.

Gorgol Alpha smashed through more buildings, one massive foot destroying a huge section of the boardwalk.

And Jake stood.

I looked to Bobby, to Pip.

Bobby nodded toward Jake. "You take care of him." Then he looked up at Alpha. "We'll dance with this devil for a bit." With that, they leapt forward, swords out. I had to laugh. *"Dance with this devil."* He'd been practicing his *material.*

Two small blurs surrounded one giant one, as Bobby and Pip pestered Alpha, running around her in circles, slashing and jumping and diving away. She wasn't hurt — her body was too quick for that — but they kept her occupied.

I turned back to Jake.

"Why us?" I yelled. "I told you Holly can't do anything for Alpha. So why us?"

Jake, his face falling apart, smiled a hideous, rictus smile. "I did what you suggested. I looked into Alpha's mind. It's not quite what you think, John Black. Alpha, she wants Holly. She wants your sister."

"I don't understand," I said.

"In time," he said, his smile fading. "Gorgol Alpha doesn't wish to return to your sister for a way home. She thinks your sister *is* home."

"What? Why?"

"That, you would have to ask Gorgol Alpha."

I shook my head. It made no sense. "What about you?"

He paused, looking around as if he were pondering an interesting news article or listening to smooth jazz. "You, John Black. I came for you. Because I owe you something."

"What?"

"How many have you killed, John? Not just the Gorgols. People, too. *Your own father.*" Jake raised a mocking eyebrow. "How many more will you kill, John?"

I had no answer. And the fury rose in me. *How dare he?*

"That's the funniest thing about all of this. The funniest, saddest, most tragic thing."

"What?"

"It's that *you* still think *you're* the good guy."

I couldn't breathe. My vision began to collapse, pulling inward to a blackout.

Then Jake attacked.

He lashed out with a devastating blow, too fast for any power to stop. And at the same time, he drove his mind deep into mine. Scouring every part of my brain.

I tried to push back, but he was everywhere.

How can you fight everywhere?

The blackout tightened, and I knew it was over. I would succumb. Would Pip and Bobby defeat Alpha? Who knew? But I imagined blood. Bobby's. Pip's. Holly's. Mom's.

How can you fight everywhere?

There was nothing to do except one thing.

Try.

If these thorns in our cells were to blame, then they could help, too. I called for every cell to fight.

And the cells responded.

They were eager to fight.

They were the root of my fire.

No.

In that instant, I knew I was wrong.

The cells, the thorns were *not* the fire. That fire was my own. My own anger, my own grief, my own viciousness.

The thorns just enabled me to act on those things in ways that would otherwise be impossible. They were ready, always.

I knew I could do great things. And terrible things. The thorns were always ready, but they did not judge. They simply acted. *I was responsible.*

I alone.

Despite the grief, I had one more job to do.

I used each and every thorn in my cells at that moment to dispel Jake. Mentally and physically.

Maybe it was completely silent, maybe there was a riot of light and sound, an explosion. I don't know. But every single cell in my body — every thorn in every cell — blasted forth its energy.

Jake wasn't simply pushed back, he flew away from me like a bomb had gone off.

Me.

* * *

I turned back to see Holly and Mom, the center of all things and yet too vulnerable.

Why did I ask them to come here? I asked myself. But I knew. *Would it matter where I sent them? Is any place any different? This had to happen. Here. Wherever.*

Bobby and Pip swarmed around Alpha, and the giant monster circled and sluiced. An endless dance that nonetheless would end. Someone would slip up. Someone would tire. I figured I knew who.

And Jake was nowhere to be found.

Looking up, I saw the blinking lights of the roller coaster —where I'd first learned that Jose do Branco, Sol, was more than I'd assumed. It was a place with history for me. A fitting place to end.

To my family, I sent messages.

I love you, Mom. Maybe she could understand, maybe not.

I love you, Holly.

Holly twitched. The sunburn feeling, or something else. I don't know.

Then I slowly lifted myself toward the top of the roller coaster's biggest hill.

A fitting place to end.

21

I landed amid flashing lights, still dozens of feet below Alpha's height, but closer.

Close enough to call to her.

Screaming up at Gorgol Alpha, I let my two sword-spears hang to each side. "I'm here now. Come on."

The swords fell limp, nothing but the simple belts they'd always been. Then they dropped away, tumbling down between the wooden supports of the roller coaster's main incline.

Alpha still twisted and evaded Bobby and Pip, so I reached out.

Bobby, pull back. My turn.

Below, I didn't see so much as feel the two of them separate. I was certain they were exhausted.

Phew, yeah, Bobby said. *Okay, give us a breather, then we're back at it.*

I only need a minute.

It must have been something in the way I said it. Friends know each other. Friends read between the lines. Bobby did.

What are you doing?

I was silent. Yet he must have seen me, weaponless atop the garishly lit hill.

Johnny, no. Whatever it is you have in mind, cut it out. There's three of us *now. Work with me! We said we were a team!*

I shut him out. He said more, but it was like a muffled voice from a phone you hold away from your head. I could hear he was talking, but I wasn't listening.

A voice came nonetheless. Because I didn't expect her to speak. Because she'd never been able to start the conversation before.

Johnny. Stop.

I sighed. *I have to, Hol. For our family. For you, and Mom.*

I don't want you to die for me, Johnny. Neither does Mom. We need you. Just — I don't know — just do anything. Run away.

Holly, I have to. At last, my anger broke, and beyond it was emptiness. *I let myself turn bad, Hol. I used these powers and killed, and I can't just ignore that anymore. But Alpha is not from this world. You know that. You brought her here by accident. Despite what Jake says, the Earth and this creature can't live together. And I can't let her hurt you. I have to do this.*

There was a long pause, and I thought we had finished.

Johnny? Holly asked.

Yeah, Hol?

It's true that they aren't from Earth.

Holly, I know. You opened up that hole and they came through. And now maybe Alpha wants you to send her back, but you can't, right? Or maybe Alpha just wanted Holly, if I could believe what Jake had said.

No, I can't.

Then there's nothing else to talk about. I tensed. Without Bobby and Pip fighting, Alpha had turned toward me. Her eyes glowed and burned. She paused, maybe relishing the last moment, her chance to get revenge for the deaths of her children.

Holly spoke in my mind again. *I can't send her back, because she didn't come from anywhere.*

What? What does that mean, Holly?

Alpha is me, *Johnny. They all were me.*

Something shattered inside. Because it made sense? Maybe. Holly had shaken the world before my battle with Sol. She could do things I couldn't understand. *What do you mean?*

When you saved me before, from Sol, I was so angry. So angry and so afraid. I had to put that stuff somewhere or else I'd never be free.

I don't understand, Holly. What did you do?

I asked myself how to get rid of those things — the anger and fear — and all I could think of was throwing them out the window. And a window appeared.

The window in space, where the three things had fallen. Where the Gorgols had come through.

But Johnny, she said, *there's nothing on the other side of that window except me. I made the Gorgols. Me. They're my anger and... and my fear.*

My head spun. The monster lumbered toward me, raging, roaring eminent death. Holly *made* the Gorgols.

LOST. MOTHER. HOME.

Jake had told me the truth. The Gorgols weren't trying to get to Holly to find a way home. She *was* their home.

I couldn't focus. Alpha would be upon me in moments.

I had killed two parts of my own sister.

My heart fell and my stomach rolled. Staggering to one knee, I nearly threw up.

Johnny? Please come back, she said.

Holly, I — I don't know what to say. I killed Omicron. And Sigma. And they were you. *I have such a terrible anger inside me that I let myself do those things. I killed two parts of you!*

No, Johnny, no! They came from me, but they're just things I don't want back. I don't want to be angry or scared. And now I know why they're burning me. The Gorgols are like a poison I pushed out. And now my body is all itchy and weird because that poison has come back.

That still doesn't let me off the hook for the things I did.

Johnny, the Gorgols are my anger and fear. And you're my brother. Just being near them, I think, changes you.

It was all too much. I reeled. Could it be true? My own sister's anger had fueled *my* uncontrollable anger? Even if it was true, a question burned at me. *Why monsters? Why three monsters, Holly?*

That's the part I just figured out, Johnny. It was those movies we watched. The monster movies. Those monsters looked so angry to me. I thought that was what anger looked like.

Okay, fine. But why three?

I don't want to tell you, she said.

Alpha swooped close. *Please, Holly.*

Seeing my plight, that I might be destroyed by Alpha at any moment, she relented. *There are three… a mother, a brother, and a sister, because…*

Because they're us, I said.

Holly didn't respond, and Alpha was so near, I thought I'd never hear Holly's voice again.

Johnny, yes, but it's more than that… they've killed people. Something that I made killed people. Come back, so we can figure out how to stop it, together.

Finally, a thought arose, from the deepest black in my mind, beginning to clear my head. I slowly lifted off the roller coaster track, looking at the onrushing, toothy face of Alpha. *It doesn't change anything, Holly. Because I already know what to do.* I pulled into myself and readied.

No, Johnny, don't!

And I flew.

* * *

Reaching out with my mind, I began to feel every cell within Alpha. Something reverberated. The thorns, I assumed.

Tuned together, we fell together.

Sluicing wouldn't help her. Sluicing rearranges the cells to avoid attack, but I wasn't attacking with gross force. Not blunt force. Instead, I attacked every cell.

And the plan was simple.

Reach all of her cells, and do the one thing no living creature can overcome.

Blow it to pieces.

There was only one catch. An eye for an eye. A cell for a cell. The only way I could figure out how to make it work was for all of my cells to do it, like little magnets. To drag Alpha's cells apart with mine.

We had to die together.

I flew closer. She gaped at me, still roaring. I would finally fly down her throat, just as she wanted. Fly into the belly of the beast made of my own sister's anger. And fear.

Time crawled. I saw every detail. The spittle around Gorgol Alpha's giant mouth, the shine it put on her long, jagged teeth.

The smell. I felt like I was bathing in eau de monster merde.

I flew.

For a second time, I pulled in, lighting the fire within me, lighting each cell, a billion little flames. I must have looked like a comet, blazing a trail to Alpha through the night sky.

Something warbled in the air. Maybe the air itself. Gorgol Alpha's skin rippled and glowed.

I was almost there. Ready to explode. Every cell in me tingled, every cell in Alpha echoing.

And then, she was gone.

The world around the creature snapped open, sucking her in with impossible force. Then, just as quickly as it appeared, the rift collapsed like charged summer air after a lightning strike.

I was blasted away, sent flying toward the rocky outcropping.

As I tumbled through the sky, the night was quiet. Except for brash music and arcade sound effects. *I used to love the boardwalk.*

I landed face first on the rocks, looking down to the sea, too tired to move for a moment.

Finally, I twisted and looked back at my family. Mom was holding one hand over her chest like she was in danger of a heart attack, staggering to recover, a line of fresh blood trickling from her nose. Next to her, Holly slowly tilted upward, like she was coming back from a fade. Finally, her eyes locked on mine.

You sent her away?

Yes, Johnny. Even mentally, she sounded out of breath.

But where?

I don't know.

An idea came to me, a black and festering idea. *Not back into you, right?* She didn't answer for the longest time, so I pressed her. *You didn't send it back into you, did you, Holly?*

I don't know, Johnny.

Maybe I dreamed it, but I swear the earth trembled just a little, under my feet.

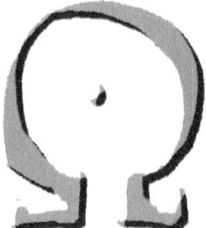

Keith Soares

Epilogue

There was a sound behind me, up on the rocks, but I didn't turn back. I was too tired.

"Hello, John."

That voice…

I didn't move. Didn't dare turn around. I didn't want to. "No. That's impossible."

"Any more impossible than your body shifting and healing itself, than your mind coercing others and moving things without touch? Than literally *anything* that just happened? I dare say no." He chuckled.

Damn that chuckle.

"Come on, John. The fact is that the impossible is something quite different than you or I have experienced in our previous lives. *There are more things in heaven and earth than are dreamt of in your philosophy —*"

"Thank you, I know Shakespeare, too, okay?" I seethed.

The voice came closer. It was different, but the same. "John. The things inside us. They simply want to live."

"And so, what? They saved you?"

"Well, no, I don't think that's entirely true. These things—"

"The damn thorns."

"Thorns? As you like. In any event, they are living creatures. They wish to survive, to reproduce, to avoid the black, endless chasm of death that eventually awaits us all. They will do anything — anything at all in their power — to stay alive."

"Okay, but that still doesn't explain how you're here," I said, eyes shut.

"Do you know what a parasite is, John?" the voice asked. No, not exactly the same voice, but still with that same arrogance.

"Yes, of course. Something that lives off something else."

"Right, yes. Often inside of that something else. And of course when something lives that way, inside another being, it can be said to *infect* its host." The voice paused, waiting. For what?

"So? What's your point?" I asked, back still turned.

Another chuckle. Why this? Why this again? This should be over. Damn it. "My point is simply this, John. If the parasite infects the host, can the host not *infect the parasite*, too? If the parasite finds a way to live, why can't the host..." He searched for the right way to put it. "Perhaps come along for the ride?"

"No."

"Well, you can continue this absurd denial, if you like."

"No." I started to turn, eyes closed.

"Or you can accept the truth of the reality before you."

There was nothing but silence as my body pivoted, but I could feel his bravado. He hadn't just cheated me. He'd cheated death. Facing the place where the voice had been, I slowly opened my eyes and saw him in those same khaki clothes, Jake's clothes. But the man before me no longer looked like Jake Weissman, the man they called Ranger. The strange lumps and oddities of his skin had fallen away, leaving something fresh and new behind. Now, he looked like someone I knew much, much better.

Sol.

THE END OF

AND IT AROSE FROM THE DEEPEST BLACK

but

JOHN BLACK WILL RETURN

in

ON A BLACK WIND BLOWS DOOM

Keith Soares

About the Author

By day, Keith Soares runs an interactive game, web, and app development agency. But by night, his imagination runs wild. A fan of classic authors such as Stephen King, Robert Heinlein, Arthur C. Clarke, and newer writers like Justin Cronin, Hugh Howey, and Andy Weir, Keith writes stories of science fiction, the apocalypse, fantasy, revenge, and horror. He lives in Alexandria, Virginia, with his wife and two daughters, who are all avid readers.

Sign up for email news at KeithSoares.com to get release information and free books, including private giveaways and preview chapters.

Keith Soares

www.ingramcontent.com/pod-product-compliance
Lightning Source LLC
Chambersburg PA
CBHW022206030726
47494CB00021B/1441